She couldn't seem to tear her gaze away from him.

He didn't seem to want to stop looking at her, either. His eyes confronted her with an undeniable sexual energy. Without even trying, he aroused the passionate side of Frani's nature and she felt an irresistible urge to kiss him again. This time for real.

She adjusted her headset. "I'm sorry, Cam. I didn't mean to—"

"Please, don't apologize," he drawled. "Or you'll ruin my whole day."

Mesmerized, she watched as he unsnapped his seat belt, removed his headset and reached toward her. Gently he lifted the earphones from her head. The sound of the engine vibrated through her.

When he leaned closer, her eyelids fluttered closed and she held her breath, anticipating the taste of his lips. His hand, pleasantly roughened with calluses, stroked her cheek.

He whispered in her ear, "Let me show you how we kiss out here in the West."

Dear Reader,

Welcome to the McQuaid family—three brothers who are easy to love and hard to forget. They live their lives the way their father taught them—by "The Cowboy Code."

This month meet Cameron McQuaid, brought to you by Laura Gordon. Laura is the author of eleven novels. Her greatest joy comes in creating characters who face extraordinary challenges and discover that the magic of their once-in-a-lifetime love is worth the risk. When not writing, she hikes the high country trails near her Colorado home.

You'll want to be sure you don't miss any of these sexy cowboy brothers. So be on the lookout next month for Matthew McQuaid's story in Joanna Wayne's *Lone Star Lawman*.

Regards,

Debra Matteucci
Senior Editor & Editorial Coordinator
Harlequin Books
300 East 42nd Street
New York, NY 10017

A Cowboy's Honor
Laura Gordon

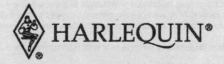

HARLEQUIN®

TORONTO • NEW YORK • LONDON
AMSTERDAM • PARIS • SYDNEY • HAMBURG
STOCKHOLM • ATHENS • TOKYO • MILAN • MADRID
PRAGUE • WARSAW • BUDAPEST • AUCKLAND

Dedicated to the memory of the late
Roy Rogers,
King of the Cowboys,
whose life exemplified
the cowboy code of honor

ISBN 0-373-22501-6

A COWBOY'S HONOR

Copyright © 1999 by Laura Lee DeVries

Printed in U.S.A.

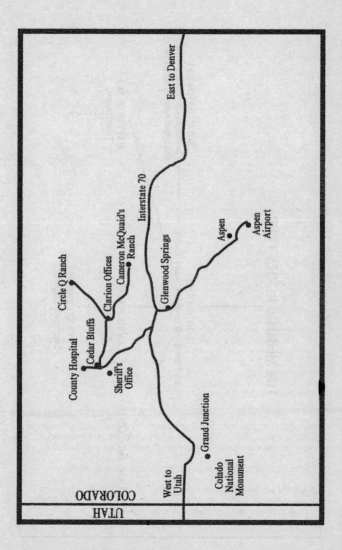

THE McQUAID FAMILY TREE

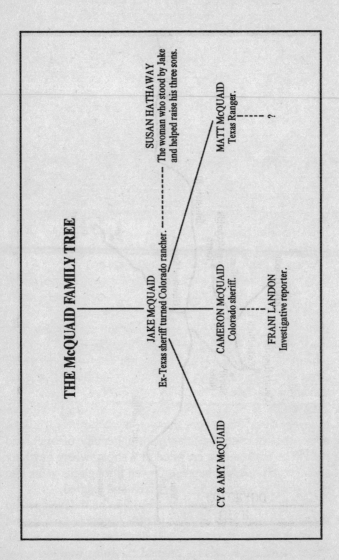

JAKE McQUAID
Ex-Texas sheriff turned Colorado rancher.

SUSAN HATHAWAY
The woman who stood by Jake
and helped raise his three sons.

CY & AMY McQUAID

CAMERON McQUAID
Colorado sheriff.

FRANI LANDON
Investigative reporter.

MATT McQUAID
Texas Ranger.

?

Prologue

For Zach Hollingsworth, Colorado's western slope defined loneliness. Off Interstate 70, he sped in his rental car over two-lane straightaways. Beneath overcast February skies, the landscape seemed tortured and bleak, marked by left-over snow, stunted juniper and sagebrush.

Where the hell was everybody? Except for a ranch house now and then in the distance, vast acres between the small towns that lazed along the banks of the Colorado River seemed largely uninhabited. Rugged thirteen-thousand-foot peaks loomed behind him, and the uneven line of semiarid mountains ringed the valley. Unfortunately, the low cloud cover obscured the view of snowcaps and made Zach feel uncomfortably disoriented and vulnerable. Desolate.

Given the choice, Zach would choose the city over country every time. The bigger the city, the better. He liked the noise, the concrete, the man-made ingenuity of brick and steel. The tension of a crowded city street, where anything and everything could happen, flowed through his veins like neon and kept him sharp, energized and excited.

During fifty-seven years of urban life, he'd developed an appetite for the best a city had to offer—gourmet food, aged whiskey, good jazz and the sexiest ladies in the world. Those sleek, savvy, sharp-tongued creatures who knew not only how to survive but how to prevail in what was still largely a man's world.

Lately, though, there hadn't been many women in his life, not since his breakup with wife number four. His reputation as a world-class journalist could always attract the brightest kind of women, but recently, he seemed to be losing a step, somehow lacking the energy to pretend he cared about anything but the next breaking story. Lonely? Sometimes. Maybe it *was* more than this hostile terrain that made him feel so small inside.

Fence posts whizzed past at the side of the road, and when he caught sight of the exit marker, he signaled to turn off the highway, glad to finally have reached his destination. He hung a right and followed the two-lane, passing a square metal sign that advertised the Sunrise Diner, where you could get the "Best Homemade Pie in the West." The sign was pockmarked with bullet holes—the cowboy version of graffiti. He passed a rusted pickup, a couple of trailer homes, the ruins of a wooden shack.

Another bullet-riddled sign announced the entrance into the city limits of Cedar Bluffs, population 3,550. Zach slowed to the speed limit. He wasn't in the mood to be pulled over and ticketed by some local yokel with a badge looking for a quick way to enhance Cedar Bluffs' revenues.

He squinted at his wristwatch, which was still set to Chicago time, one hour later than Colorado. His meeting was scheduled for two o'clock, thirty-four minutes from now. He needed to get directions quickly. There was no way he was going to be late. The woman who'd called him—her name was Susan—had promised the solution to a twenty-four-year-old mystery about a kidnapped heiress, still missing and declared dead. In fact, she'd claimed to be said heiress, but Zach would wait and see for himself. If it was all true, if this woman was who she said she was, it would be the headline of the year.

The wide main street in Cedar Bluffs looked like an updated movie set for the Old West, with tired clapboard storefronts advertising video movie rentals and computer servicing. Zach eased his rental car to the curb, lowered the passenger-side window and called out to a woman in a down vest with a long silver braid hanging to her waist. "Excuse me, ma'am."

When she turned, he saw that she had her arms full of newspapers. The sign on the storefront behind her read: The Chaparral Clarion, Best Little Newspaper in the West.

Best little newspaper? Best homemade pie? People in these parts seemed long on pride.

"Could you direct me to the Circle Q ranch?" Zach asked.

She dropped most of the newspapers into a metal distribution box and allowed the front to snap closed. "Who wants to know?"

He was tempted to tell her, just to see her reaction. After twenty years with a syndicated column, not to mention three books and a Pulitzer, his name was well-known. Some folks were already calling him a legend. But today, he was chasing a story, and he didn't want or need to draw attention to himself.

"I'm a friend of the family," he said.

"Well, now, isn't that lucky for me. That's exactly the kind of news I print," she said. "Weddings, funerals and visits from old friends."

Her startling blue eyes stared curiously from a weathered face that had probably once been pretty. She was too scrawny for Zach's taste. His past three wives had all been blondes with hourglass figures.

She tossed a copy of her newspaper through the open window of his rental car. "Take a look."

The banner headline read Wedding Bells for Cy Mc-Quaid.

He grinned as he scanned the article. Hard-bitten old newsman that he was, Zach Hollingsworth had a sentimental streak, and he was glad to see that Cy McQuaid, a man he knew as an upright FBI agent, was engaged to Amy Reeves, a woman he'd suspected, chastised and ultimately defended while her father was being investigated for a Supreme Court appointment.

He glanced at the byline, then to the woman. "Addie Lindstrom?"

"That's right, Zach Hollingsworth."

So much for anonymity. "I guess you saw me on the news yesterday."

She nodded. "But I would've known you, anyway. I've read your column for years, and the header has a picture of your mug at the top."

He tapped a cigarette from the pack stashed above the car's visor and lit up. The woman amused him. "Well, Addie, what do you think of my column?"

"Not bad, for the most part, but I could give you a few pointers."

He nearly choked on his smoke. Who the hell did this backwater, gossip-mongering, small-town newspaper-woman think she was?

She continued, "And I'll give you the first tip for free. Stick to the writing end of journalism. You have neither the face nor the style for TV. Old farts like you and me? We don't belong on the tube."

Amused by her unabashed candor, he laughed. "Oh? And just where do you think we belong?"

"In the trenches, the background. Using our instincts.

Digging for the real story. That's what you're good at, Hollingsworth."

He took a second look into those perceptive blue eyes. Addie Lindstrom was a straight-talking woman, probably a damn good reporter. He'd bet that once she got her hooks into a story, she'd never let go. In that way, she reminded him of Frani Landon, his assistant and protégé.

"I'm wondering," she said. "Why a celebrity reporter like Zach Hollingsworth is headed for the Circle Q?"

"Chrissake, woman. All I wanted was directions."

"Here's the deal. I'll give you directions if you give me your word as a journalist that you'll come back to the *Clarion* and join me for dinner afterward and fill me in."

"Maybe." Dinner sounded intriguing, but Zach wasn't about to share his story, not if it was the one he sensed it might be.

"Half a promise is no good at all." When she leaned down to peer through the opened window, the front of her vest gaped open, revealing a heavy turquoise squash-blossom necklace. "You've changed, Zach Hollingsworth. And not for the better. You might be famous now, but I remember when you first got started. You were a fighter, enraged when people bent the law to suit their personal agendas. Back then, you were looking for the truth."

Discomfited, he said nothing, reluctant to admit he might have slipped in recent years.

"Don't you remember, Hollingsworth? The truth. That's what it's *really* all about. Maybe I could help you dig out the story behind the story."

"What is that supposed to mean?"

"Meet me for dinner, and maybe you'll find out."

"Okay, Addie. You win. You've got yourself a date."

She granted him a wry smile and then rattled off a series of landmarks, concluding with, "There's a security gate.

You'll have to get out of your car and talk into the intercom.''

"Thanks."

"If you don't keep your word, I'll track you down like a spavined coyote,'' she promised. "Maybe I'll even send Sheriff McQuaid after you.''

"*Sheriff* McQuaid? How many damn McQuaids are there?''

"Cameron McQuaid is sheriff of Chaparral County. His brother, the man in the headline, is Cyrus McQuaid, FBI. There's another brother, Matt, who's a Texas Ranger. And the Circle Q is owned by Jake McQuaid, a retired lawman.''

Thinking of his source, Zach asked, "What about Susan? Isn't she Mrs. McQuaid?''

"Nope, she's Susan Hathaway. Though I suppose she might as well be Jake's wife. They've lived together for more than twenty years, and she's been like a mother to his sons.''

"She and Jake McQuaid are kind of old to be playing for anything but keeps, aren't they?''

Addie's eyes narrowed. "What's age got to do with love?''

Zach snorted and shook his head. "Damned if I know, lady. When it comes to matters of the heart, you're asking the wrong man.''

She eyed him intently.

"I'll see you later, Addie.''

"Be careful,'' she warned, glancing up at the gray skies. "Looks like we're in for snow.''

Zach cruised east through town and turned south at the heralded Sunrise Diner. Then east again. Overhead, the cloud cover had thickened, and seemed to touch the peaked crest of the pine and spruce trees that lined the highway.

Gloomy weather, but his conversation with Addie Lindstrom had gone a long way toward lifting his spirits. Every once in a while, he needed to remind himself that there were still people like Addie, ready, willing and eager to cut through the crap and tell the plain unvarnished truth. Despite her bluntness, she hadn't seemed bitter. He sensed she was no stranger to the darker side of man's nature, and yet she seemed refreshingly optimistic.

Cynicism was easier. Zach could always fire up another stogie and throw back a shot of blended whiskey and pretend that he didn't give a damn about the treachery he'd come to expect in people. Sometimes, he felt he was no better than they were, choosing a particular slant because of some old personal vendetta. What would Addie say about that? he wondered. Some country saying like: Lie down with dogs, and you'll wake up with fleas, no doubt.

Thinking of dogs reminded him of a certain mangy cur who'd risen to high renown—Senator Phillip Gould. Still driving, Zach pulled his ever-present notebook from his coat pocket, balanced it on the steering wheel and scribbled a reminder to verify Gould's connection to the missing heiress. He'd tell Frani to check it out when he called her tonight.

Addie would approve of Frani's brand of reporting. Frani submerged herself in a story, dug relentlessly for the truth. She could be as fiery as the red in her hair, demanding justice for the downtrodden. As a human being, her righteous outrage was a fine attribute. But as a reporter? He'd told her a million times that too much passion would only break her heart.

Before he hopped a plane in Chicago, he'd telephoned his assistant and told her about the tip from Susan. Naturally, Frani had wanted to come along. But the travel logistics just didn't work. He'd had to catch the very next flight to Denver, grab a flight to Grand Junction this morning, then rent a car to make the ninety-minute drive to Cedar Bluffs. There just hadn't been time for Frani to catch up.

Buried in his thoughts, Zach almost missed the final turn onto a short graded gravel road. Thirty yards away stood the security gates for Circle Q.

He parked and climbed out from behind the steering wheel to approach the intercom. After sitting for so long, his legs were stiff. He stretched, and shivered in the frigid air. God, he hated the cold.

Wrapping his long herringbone wool overcoat more tightly around him, he tried to fasten the buttons over his potbelly, but gave up. He needed to exercise more. A woman like Addie—she *did* seem to linger in his mind—would whip him into shape.

"Hey, you!"

When Zach turned and saw the gun pointed at his chest, the sight was so unexpected that danger didn't register in his brain. "What do you want?"

"Are you Zach Hollingsworth?"

"Yes."

As the first shot echoed across the desolate land, Zach recoiled from the jackhammer blow to his chest. In shock, he felt no pain. Then he looked down and saw his lifeblood staining the mustard wool of his sweater.

The second and third bullets knocked him off his feet, and as he hit the frozen ground, Zach knew he was dying. In that last cold moment, he thought of Frani. What a headline—Legendary Reporter Gunned Down. *Go get 'em, Frani. Don't let the bastards get away with it.*

Chapter One

Be careful, Zach. Please, please, be careful.

Frani Landon had no tangible reason to be so worried about her old friend and mentor. But she had a hunch, a fierce premonition that something wasn't right.

Her fingers clenched white-knuckled on the steering wheel as she stared through the windshield at the rugged land beneath low-hanging storm clouds. Pushing the speed limit, her rental car ate up the miles on the interstate. The next exit was Cedar Bluffs.

Zach would've laughed out loud if she'd told him about her nervous intuition. He always told her to stick to the facts. As a reporter, the facts were all she was supposed to care about. Even so, he gave her plenty to worry about.

Fact: Zach smoked constantly, both cigarettes and foul-smelling cigars.

Fact: His lack of regular exercise, love of rich food and fine whiskey had earned him a potbelly, high blood pressure and constant heartburn.

Fact: When he investigated a story, Zach Hollingsworth took risks.

Without a thought for his own safety, he'd confront venomous people, some more dangerous than pit vipers, with nothing to protect him but his own bravado. The power of the press, he called it. Unfortunately, the threat of newsprint exposure wasn't always a successful shield. Seven years ago, when she first signed on as his assistant and researcher, Zach had his nose broken when a South American ambassador took offense at his "take-no-prisoners" style.

Even then, Zach wouldn't admit he should have used a less direct approach. "A reporter has to be tough, Frani. No room for sentiment."

She'd argued back. "It's not always so black-and-white. Everyone has their own story, their own slant. Extenuating circumstances."

"But there's only one truth."

"But people make mistakes, Zach," she told him. "Sometimes, they deserve a second chance. Isn't there room for compassion?"

"You're too damn soft, Frani." Over time, this argument had become a familiar one, his assessment an oft-repeated refrain.

Still, he'd taken her under his wing and kept her there. Everything she knew about good, aggressive, solid journalism came from Zach's teachings. And she loved the guy like a father.

If anything happened to him...

Trying to relieve her tension, Frani unclenched one hand from the steering wheel and shook it. Then the other. She hunched her shoulders and twisted her head from side to side, causing her jaw-length auburn hair to brush her shoulders. A glance in the rearview mirror showed traces of red in her green eyes. What did she expect? She'd been up since four this morning.

Last night, after Zach called and told her she couldn't possibly make it to Cedar Bluffs in time for the two-o'clock interview, she'd been determined to do exactly that. She'd left her apartment before dawn, caught a flight from Midway to Denver, rented a car and driven like a bat out of hell for the next five grueling hours.

Even if she hadn't been worried about Zach, Frani would have moved heaven and earth to be in on this interview. She'd developed a particular fascination for this story. Though she'd been only a toddler when the major events took place, she'd studied Zach's notes so thoroughly she knew the story like her own history.

She mulled over the facts as she drove. Twenty-four years ago, Pamela Jessup, a California socialite, had been kidnapped. When her wealthy family refused to pay the ransom, Pamela joined the kidnappers in a bank robbery and was caught on film with a Kalashnikov AK-47 automatic rifle in her hand. Apparently, she'd been a willing accomplice. But when the robbers were apprehended, Pamela Jessup had been left behind, locked in a deserted warehouse.

That intriguing contradiction played over and over in Frani's mind. If Pamela had truly been a part of the gang, why had they held her captive? Was she a victim or a criminal?

Subsequent revelations had not been in her favor. The kidnapper turned robber, David Eisman, claimed that Pamela loved him and that she'd suggested the kidnap scheme herself to extort money from her family. When that scheme failed, she'd married Eisman secretly. The marriage license made for a compelling piece of evidence. It appeared Eisman had been telling the truth about the heiress. Also, many of the people from Pamela's past called her a bad seed. And there were suggestions of an intriguing connection with Senator Phillip Gould, now a state senator from California, and Byron Reeves, the former candidate for the Supreme Court. And that's when the waters got murky.

And, then, there was Pamela's family, wealthy California

vintners. Where did their loyalties lie? Even her sister, Candace, had refused to defend Pamela against accusations of wrongdoing.

Still, based on nothing more than pure intuition, Frani thought there was more to this story. When she studied Pamela's photograph, Frani saw a fashionable blonde, obviously pampered, with a four-carat diamond pendant nestled at her slender throat. The firm jaw and the tilt of her head hinted at a stubborn defiance. Yet her cool blue eyes held a reservoir of strength—and sadness—that Frani had never been able to dismiss.

Pamela's determination was evident in the way she'd escaped from the warehouse by literally clawing her way through the locked door. She was on the run for a year. Then, tragically, her body was found facedown in a swimming pool outside a cheap motel.

Her death should have been the final chapter, but Pamela's story was far from over. News of Zach's renewed investigation into the events that had taken place nearly a quarter of a century ago broke like a landslide, and the repercussions had already caused a shake-up in the highest court in the land.

Based on his personal connection to the missing heiress, Judge Byron Reeves had decided to decline his nomination for a seat on the Supreme Court. The fateful decision to give Pamela Jessup the time she'd insisted she needed before turning herself into the authorities had proved to be Reeves's professional undoing.

At the end of his investigation into the judge's background, Zach had determined that Reeves had not broken any laws. He was no criminal, merely a man who'd let his personal life get in the way of his duty. A grave error in judgment, as far as Zach was concerned. By looking the other way, Reeves had allowed a suspected felon to escape justice.

Zach believed Reeves had pulled his nomination hoping to quell interest in the Pamela Jessup story once and for all. The tactic seemed to work. The media, as a whole, quickly lost interest. But not Zach.

When the good judge removed himself from the spotlight in an effort to protect his old friend, Zach's interest in the events surrounding Pamela Jessup's disappearance redoubled. For weeks, he'd been working on the premise that if the judge had had something to hide, chances were good he wasn't the only one. And if there were more skeletons in the Jessup closet, Zach was determined to rattle them until the whole truth came out. In the process, if bigger fish than Judge Byron Reeves found themselves swimming for their political lives, then so be it. As Zach was fond of saying, the truth couldn't hurt an honest man.

Last night, when Zach had called Frani from O'Hare, he'd said there was reason to suspect Pamela Jessup might still be alive. Frani heard the excitement in his voice and imagined the spark in his tired old eyes.

She'd known, even before she'd hung up the phone, that she wouldn't miss this dramatic conclusion for the world. The story of the missing heiress was the kind of scoop reporters lived for. *And died for.*

Pushing the negative thoughts from her brain, she drove past the sign for Cedar Bluffs at twenty-three minutes past two. Surely the interview would be a lengthy one. She could still make it. She was almost there. Zach was all right. It was only exhaustion and nerves that were making her worry.

On Main Street, Frani pulled up to what appeared to be the one and only stoplight in Cedar Bluffs. She repeated the reassurance like a mantra: *Zach is all right.* He had to be.

The scream of an ambulance siren ripped through the homespun atmosphere and Frani's heart convulsed.

Operating on instinct, she punched the accelerator and prepared to follow the emergency vehicle. A police car with red and blue lights flashing slipped in behind the ambulance and in front of Frani. She knew that any sane person would have pulled over but, she thought philosophically, no one ever said reporters were normal.

Where there's an ambulance, there's a story, Zach would say.

She careened around a sharp turn, keeping pace with the cop car in front of her. This could be breaking news. Adrenaline pumped through her veins, fueled by the wailing sirens and the speed. She was still anxious to find Zach, but she told herself she'd stay with the ambulance for ten minutes. If she got too far from Cedar Bluffs, she'd double back and find the Circle Q ranch.

The emergency vehicles sped along mostly deserted roads, and Frani stayed tight on the tail of the cop car. It was easy. A chase in Cedar Bluffs was nothing compared to a chase through the congested streets of Chicago.

Finally, the ambulance swung onto a narrow graded road and halted. The siren went dead. The police car followed, but Frani held back. She parked on the shoulder and got out of her car.

Paramedics in blue jeans and parkas went into action, hustling toward another parked car and a couple of people standing in front of a large iron gate. On either side of the gate were tall columns of mortared stone. Spanning the top was a burnt wood sign. Staring at it, Frani's blood went cold. This was the Circle Q—Zach's destination.

Please, not Zach. Was it a heart attack? Had the high

blood pressure and the cigarettes finally gotten to him? Rising panic churned within Frani, flushing her cheeks with unnatural heat.

She grabbed her shoulder bag, automatically checked the film in her camera and made sure she had fresh tape in her handheld recorder. Then, she headed toward the gates.

A cop blocked her way. In his black Stetson, split leather jacket and Levi's, he looked as though he'd just ridden off the set of "Bonanza." She didn't need a doctorate in psychology to know he was angry. His dark eyes burned like embers. A muscle in his square jaw twitched. "Get the hell back, lady!"

"I'm a reporter." She pulled the tape recorder from her purse and turned it on. "Could I have your name, please?"

"McQuaid," he said. "Sheriff Cameron McQuaid. Now, get back in your car."

She ignored his command. "I'm Francesca Landon." Craning her neck, she tried to see around him and the ambulance. She had to get closer, to make sure it wasn't Zach. "Can you tell me what happened here, Sheriff? An accident?"

"What are you doing here, Ms. Landon?"

"Frani. Call me Frani."

"You don't belong here."

"Ever heard of freedom of the press, Sheriff?"

"We have a local reporter, and you're not her. In fact, I know you're not from anywhere around here."

"Obviously." Frani was dressed in a style she liked to call urban-guerrilla chic. A black wool peacoat, black beret and loose-fitting gray slacks tucked into high-topped Doc Marten boots. Not beautifully attractive, but wonderfully comfortable and warm. "I'm from Chicago."

A flicker of tension tightened the skin across his high cheekbones. "Do you know Zach Hollingsworth?"

Frani swallowed hard. "I'm his assistant."

Other sirens screeched and cut to silence as two more cop cars pulled up and parked behind Frani's rental car.

McQuaid lightly grasped her upper arm and directed her away from the ambulance. "You should leave now, Frani. I'll be in touch later. Right now, I'll have one of my deputies escort you back to town."

"What happened to Zach?" she demanded. When she yanked at her arm, she found his grip as effective as handcuffs. "Tell me, Sheriff. I have a right to know."

"I can't tell you anything right now."

Her pulse hammered. Every muscle in her body tensed. She was certain that Zach had been hurt, and she was not about to be hustled out of the picture by this cowboy. Zach needed her. She needed him.

She inhaled a deep breath. Putting on an air of reasonableness, she confronted McQuaid. "Please release my arm, Sheriff. I understand your position."

Warily, he studied her.

"Please, Sheriff McQuaid." She even managed a tentative smile. "I'll be good."

The instant he let go of her arm, she took off. With McQuaid on her tail, Frani sprinted down the narrow graded road to where the paramedics hunkered beside a body. Zach! He lay motionless, his chest covered in blood. She knew by the ashen pallor of his face that he was dead. He'd been shot. Murdered.

"No!" The single word tore from her throat. He couldn't be dead. Not here. Alone in the cold. Zach hated the cold.

Her gaze lifted to the other two civilians on the scene. They stood together, holding hands. The old man wore a cowboy hat and a stiff aura of pride. The woman who stood beside him had blond hair fading into gray. Her blue eyes stared back at Frani with a familiar, direct gaze, touched by deep unshakable sadness. Frani knew those eyes, knew that face. It was her. Pamela Jessup!

"You!" Frani shouted. "It's you! Pamela Jessup! Why? Why did you kill him?"

Choking on a sob, she turned her back on the missing heiress. How could she have done this? And how could Frani have been so very wrong? All this time, she'd thought Pamela Jessup was a victim. She'd actually felt sympathy for the woman everyone else condemned as a criminal. But she'd been wrong, clearly. It was all true. Pamela Jessup was a deadly criminal. A bank robber. And now, a murderess.

"Oh, Zach." Blindly, Frani shoved past the paramedics and fell to her knees beside Zach's body.

Zach's lively eyes would never again search out the truth behind the story. His lips would never snap out hard questions.

She grasped his cold hand and held it to her cheek. These nicotine-stained fingers would never again tap out a story on his ancient typewriter. *Don't leave me, Zach.*

She could almost hear his gruff voice, scolding her show of emotion. *Back up, Frani. Find the facts.*

But she didn't care about facts, couldn't think of the story when all she wanted to do was weep over the loss of a man who'd been more than a father to her. He'd believed in her and tried to give her the confidence to believe in herself.

Gently, she leaned over and rested her head against the shoulder of his scratchy wool herringbone overcoat. Inside his coat pocket, she felt the hard edges of the little leatherbound notebook he carried everywhere. All at once, she knew what she must do. What Zach would expect her to do.

Deftly, her hand slipped inside his coat, closed around

the notebook and pulled. In one subtle movement, she hid the notebook inside her own coat.

Taking the notebook was wrong. This was evidence. She was tampering with a crime scene. But Frani didn't give a damn. She would dig out the truth, find the facts. If it was the last thing she did, she'd see Zach's murderer punished.

When she felt the sheriff's hand on her shoulder, she rose unsteadily to her feet. Her legs trembled, and she had the surreal sense that she was somehow disconnected from her body, floating through a desolate, lonely nightmare.

Sheriff McQuaid directed her away from Zach's body. In spite of her earlier trickery, his touch on her arm felt gentle and forgiving. She leaned against him, breathing hard. "It's the altitude," she said.

"Sure it is."

"And the snow." Light flakes had begun to fall.

Suddenly light-headed, she thought she might swoon into his strong, cowboy arms. It would've been nice to have someone comfort her. With Zach gone, she felt utterly alone.

Painful tears burned her eyes and she angrily dashed them away. Zach would have wanted her to be tough.

"I'm sorry for your loss," the Sheriff said.

"Sorry doesn't cut it." She broke away from him, standing as steady as she could manage on her own two feet. "I want you to keep me apprised of every step of this investigation. No ducking, no dodging. Understand?"

"Listen, Frani. I don't think you—"

"That's good," she interrupted. "We're on a first name basis. What was yours again? Cameron?"

"Cam," he said.

To look at him, all rugged angles and tanned strength, she assumed he was more of an expert in herding cattle than in criminal forensics, Frani decided. "Tell me, Sheriff Cam. Have you ever investigated a murder before?"

"This isn't Chicago," he said, the words edged in steel.

She nodded. "Right. I should have known you have no experience in this kind of thing. I mean, look at this crime scene! People are walking all over. You need to be more concerned about footprints and tire tracks. You need evidence to get a conviction, Cam. You need..." Her voice trailed off as she watched the paramedics load Zach's body into the ambulance. "Where are they taking him?"

"Chaparral County Hospital, Third and E Street."

"The morgue." A fresh wave of sorrow washed over her. "Oh God, I don't know what I'm going to do without him," she murmured, nearly unaware that she'd spoken aloud.

"It's hard to lose someone you care about." He put a hand on her shoulder. "You'll be okay, Frani. It'll just take time."

That was exactly what Zach would've said. But when she gazed up at Cam's rough-hewn features, she saw a very different man from Zach Hollingsworth.

Frani had always prided herself on her ability to sum up a person quickly, to see through to their heart at a glance. And one look at Cameron McQuaid told her he was a man to reckon with. Cam McQuaid's midnight-black eyes shone with bold strength. He seemed willing and able to protect her, to shield her from the bad things in the world. But it was his apparent sincerity that most impressed her. In her line of work, it was a rare thing to come face-to-face with an honest man. Did such an animal really exist?

Or was she leading with her emotions again? Losing objectivity? She shook her head and lowered her gaze to the rounded toes of his leather boots. Fighting for a cynical attitude to blunt her pain, she told herself this was all just his persona. Chivalry was part of his M.O., and fairly easy for a small-town sheriff whose most difficult job amounted to arresting the town drunk on Saturday night.

He asked, "Were you related to him?"

She shook her head. "I started as his intern when I was in grad school, seven years ago."

"Who's the next of kin?"

She shrugged. "Four ex-wives. No children." She swallowed hard. "I'm the closest thing to family he had."

Pulling herself together, she said, "Sheriff, I have information that will lead to an arrest. Zach Hollingsworth came to this godforsaken place on a tip from the woman who's standing at that gate. She's a fugitive. She's been in hiding for twenty-four years. Her name is Pamela Jessup."

"Her name is Susan Hathaway," he corrected.

"An alias," she said impatiently. "I suggest you take her into custody now, before she runs again."

"Not likely," he said tersely.

"Why not?"

"Susan Hathaway is the only mother I've ever known."

IN THE LARGE FRONT ROOM at the Circle Q, Cam McQuaid paced back and forth across the polished hardwood floor. Behind him was a moss-rock fireplace that rose two stories, past the open rafters that crisscrossed the ceiling. This warm, pine-paneled room was his boyhood home, the place where he'd grown to manhood. His backside knew the feel of every blue and gray patterned chair and the sofa. He'd read every book on the shelf. The photographs on the wall, lovingly framed and hung by Susan, revealed the history of Cam and his two brothers.

Standing at the front window, he gazed out at the gathering dusk and the high country snow. The front security gate was a half a mile away, separated from the house by a stand of ponderosa pine. Cam had left four deputies out there, searching for evidence. The snow, however, would make the job difficult. For himself, he claimed the job of questioning the two prime suspects in the murder of Zach Hollingsworth: His father and Susan.

"Why?" Cam asked as he turned toward them. "Why was Zach Hollingsworth here?"

"I called him," Susan said quietly. She wore her favorite denim skirt and a denim vest over a pretty white blouse with lace at the collar. All dressed up for the meeting with Zach Hollingsworth that never took place. "I wanted a chance to set things straight. I wanted to tell my side of the story, so everyone—especially you boys—would know the truth, at last. I never meant for it to turn out this way... For a man to die."

"Cam knows that," Jake said. "He knows you're not a suspect in this murder."

His father planted himself directly in front of Cam. Half a head shorter than his son and skinny as a stretch of barbed wire, the old man was still intimidating. Six days ago, he'd suffered a stroke that had landed him in the hospital. Any other human being would still be flat on his back, recuperating. But not Jake McQuaid. Even now, at near seventy years old, he acted like the toughest son of a bitch west of the Platte.

His unspoken message to Cam was clear: *If you intend to accuse my woman, you'll have to go through me.*

"Why the hell didn't you talk to me first, Dad? Why didn't you tell me? I could have tried to help her."

"You didn't need to know."

"That's bull!"

"You're a lawman, Cam. Just like me. Like your brothers." Jake's dark eyes were hard and unflinching. "If I'd told you Susan was a fugitive from the law, you'd have been obliged to take her into custody."

How could Cam tell the old man Cy had already given him all the facts, that the news had been digging at his gut ever since? "You really think I could take her in?"

"I'd expect it." Jake raised a gnarled finger and pointed in Cam's face. "It's your sworn duty to uphold the law."

"You don't have to tell me how to do my job."

"Boys!" Susan interrupted. She glided across the floor, soft and sweet as an angel, especially compared to his flinty-eyed father. Gently, she took Jake's arm and tugged. "Come and sit by the fire. We're all still edgy over what's happened. Jake, all this excitement isn't good for you."

"Stop that, Susan. I won't have you treating me like an invalid."

"I'm doing this for myself as much as you," she said. "I never want to see you in the hospital again. It scared me so badly when I thought you were going to die. Please let me care for you, Jake."

The hard, straight line of Jake's mouth relaxed. For as long as Cam could remember, Susan had had a gentling effect on his father. Whenever one of the boys broke the strict rules of the house, Jake would bluster and fume and lay down the law, then Susan would come along and lighten the punishment. She'd make hot chocolate and soothe tempers. This time, however, it was going to take more than a cup of cocoa to make things right.

A man had been murdered at their front gate. Both Susan and his father had reasons to want him dead. Zach Hollingsworth had reopened the investigation into the kidnapping, disappearance and death of a California heiress, Pamela Jessup. Who was also known as Susan Hathaway.

As she directed Jake to his beat-up La-Z-Boy recliner and fussed around him with afghans and pillows, Cam thought back twenty-four years. He was eight years old then, the middle son. They'd been living in Dry Creek, Texas, where Jake divided his duties as sheriff with ranching, heaping a mountain of chores on his three motherless boys. Even then, Jake McQuaid had been a hard, cold man who'd had to bury his first wife, the mother of Cy and Cam. His second wife hadn't been able to stand the miserable loneliness of a ranch wife whose husband was busy upholding the law when he wasn't working the cattle. After giving birth to Matt, she took off and was never seen again.

"It was February fifteenth," Cam said, "twenty-four years ago."

"My birthday," Susan said. "The day after Valentine's Day."

She always made a big deal about family birthdays. There were cakes and parties and thoughtful gifts. Nothing unhappy was allowed to touch the birthday boy on his special day. Cam hated to remember the bleak time before Susan had come into their lives. "That's not your real birthday."

She lifted her chin proudly. "It's the day I chose. The day I became Susan Hathaway. The day you boys found me."

The three McQuaid boys had played hooky from their chores that day and gone into town for a movie. Afterward, they were walking home at dusk, making up excuses to tell Jake about why their work wasn't done. They'd only been about a mile from the ranch, which was located precisely in the middle of nowhere, when Cam had heard a low, groaning noise from the side of the road.

He'd thought it was a wounded critter and ran to look. Instead, he'd found Susan. Battered and beaten to within an inch of her life, she was lying in the drainage ditch beside the road.

"On February fifteenth," Susan said, "you saved my life. I remember, Cam. Yours was the first face I saw. You were scared."

"I thought you were going to die."

"But I couldn't," she said simply. "You boys were the answer to my dying prayer. I asked for one more chance to start over and live a good life. And there you were."

"We broke so many rules that day."

Cy, the oldest and therefore the leader, left Cam and Matt with Susan and ran the last mile back to the ranch house. Then, though he was only ten years old, Cy drove the pickup truck back to where they were waiting.

Together, they loaded her onto an improvised stretcher, lifted her into the back, drove home and put her into bed. When Jake came home from work, he found the three boys tending to a strange woman who was seriously injured.

"I still remember when Jake walked through the door," Cam said. "Little Matt, who was only five, marched right up to him. 'We found a mommy,' he said. 'She's ours, and you can't make us give her back.' That boy needed a woman's influence."

"Broke my heart," Jake said. "Little Matty had never stood up to me before. He was always so quiet, like a timid little mouse. That day was the very first time he ever said he wanted anything."

"He's stood up for himself plenty since then," Cam said. Matt had gone back to Texas to become a Ranger, and he harbored a serious grudge against Jake, still blaming him because his real mother had abandoned the family.

But it wasn't only Matt who'd had reason to resent their taciturn father. None of the three boys could understand why Jake had never married Susan, who'd regained her health and stuck with him.

Though Jake had raised them to believe there was a code

of honor among the McQuaid men, he'd never made Susan an honest woman. It didn't make sense, but his lessons took root anyway. Jake made sure his boys knew right from wrong. No matter how hard it was, they always did the right thing. It wasn't coincidence that all three of them had gone into law enforcement.

"Dad. Susan. I have something to tell you," Cam said, knowing the time had come. "Call it a confession."

His father stared. "What's that, boy?"

"Cy told me everything, just after his investigation of Byron Reeves. I've known Susan's true identity for some time."

Susan's lovely face crumpled in distress. "Oh, Cam. I'm so sorry. I know how that information must have been eating away at your conscience."

"Not much," he admitted.

"But it's your job to take me into custody."

"On a piece of flimsy hearsay from my brother?" Both he and Cy had decided to let sleeping dogs lie. He offered her a thin smile. "It's a federal matter, and if Cy can live with the situation, so can I. As far as the rest of the world is concerned, Pamela Jessup died a long time ago. I can't imagine that any purpose would be served by dragging you through the system now."

"I raised you better than that," Jake said.

"Don't give me that crap, old man," Cam drawled.

"Cameron McQuaid! You think you can backtalk me? Hell, boy, I might be seventy years old but I can still whup your sorry butt."

Cam shook his head. "Now you listen to me, you old codger. Before any whupping takes place, let me tell you a couple of things. You raised Cy, Matt and me to follow a code, you drilled it in our heads from the time we were old enough to listen. We've walked the line, all three of us, under pressure you can't even begin to imagine. I respect you, Dad. You raised me and you taught me respect for the law. You kept a roof over our heads, turned us into men. But it was Susan who made our house a home." Who'd taught Cam about mercy and compassion. "If she hadn't come into our lives and treated us with love and respect, you would've had three hell-raising heathens on your hands, and you know it."

Jake's jaw was tight. The old man was unaccustomed to backing down. When it came to Susan, however, to the truth of what she'd done for all of them, what choice did he have? "You're not telling me anything I don't know, son. Damn it, I know I was hard. But I did what I thought was right by the three of you boys."

Cam strode across the room and stood over him. "Granted. But all three of us were always on the edge. Every time you told us we couldn't break the rules, we were bound and determined to find a way to get into trouble. How do you think Cyrus knew how to drive a truck when he was only ten years old?"

"I guess I never gave it much thought."

"Well, you should have. He had been sneaking out for a year, taking me and Matt for joyrides when you weren't home."

"Why, that little—"

"When Susan came into our lives, we knew we had to straighten up. We wanted to make her proud. We defied you, but we wanted to please her. Wanted to make her proud of us."

Susan's blue eyes glistened with unshed tears as she touched Cam's arm. "And I am proud," she said. "You're the finest sons anyone could have. I love you, Cam. Cy and Matty, too."

"We love you, too." He squinted hard to keep the tears from falling.

She took a lace hanky from the pocket of her denim skirt—always the lady, without being the least bit prissy or pretentious—and dabbed at her eyes. "At least now, you understand why your father and I never married."

Cam nodded. His brother had told him the history of Pamela Jessup. "Because, technically, you were still married to that bank robber, David Eisman."

"I made a lot of mistakes," she said gravely. "But your father backed me up. One hundred percent. Always."

"Always?"

"Right from the start," she assured him. "As soon as I was well enough to move, I told him everything."

"I'll be damned." Until this moment, Cam had never realized the sacrifices Jake had made for his woman. "You knew from the first. You *knew* Susan was Pamela Jessup."

Jake only nodded.

"That's why you resigned as sheriff and moved us from Texas to Colorado."

"I couldn't very well continue as a lawman, now could I? Not when I was breaking the law every day."

"I have only one thing to say about that, Dad."

"Yeah?" Jake asked defensively. "What's that?"

"Thank you."

Jake blinked, obviously taken aback by Cam's response. It had been too long, Cam thought, since Jake's sons had felt compelled to thank their father for anything.

When Jake spoke again, his voice was gruff with uncharacteristic emotion. "I love her, son. She's the best thing that ever happened to me, to all of us. What else could I do but protect her?" He cleared his throat before he added, "And it means a lot, knowing you finally understand."

Cam could only nod; his own emotions had risen dangerously close to the surface.

For a long moment, neither of them spoke. In the silence, each in his own way savored the rare moment of closeness they'd just shared.

Now Cam was faced with the same dilemma his father had wrestled all those years ago. He was a lawman, the Sheriff of Chaparral County. He didn't have a problem letting Cy make the call as far as Susan was concerned, but this crime, Zach Hollingsworth's murder, had happened in *his* county. And the logical suspects stood within arm's length at this very moment. Susan and his father. Murderers? Unlikely. But the circumstantial evidence seemed to point to no one else. Jake, especially, had a motive. The old man had said it often enough; he would do anything for Susan.

Cam sat down next to Jake. It was time to do his duty. "Tell me what happened here this afternoon, Dad."

"Susan made an appointment with Zach Hollingsworth for two o'clock. We got ourselves all ready. We were going to tell him the whole truth, everything."

"Why?"

Susan answered, "After Byron Reeves withdrew from his Supreme Court nomination, I felt terrible. Byron is one of the only people I remember kindly from when I was Pamela Jessup. I felt in light of what he'd been through, I had to come forward. It was time to tell the truth, Cam. I felt I couldn't take the chance that somebody else would be hurt."

Cam turned back to his father. "Give me the sequence of events. What happened today at two o'clock?"

"We waited for Hollingsworth. At ten past two, I figured something had gone wrong. I didn't figure Hollingsworth would be even a minute late. It's a helluva story, and I know he wanted it real bad.''

"All right, you started wondering, so what did you do then?"

"We'd been having some trouble with the intercom on the security gates, so I decided to drive down there to make sure it was working."

"Alone?"

"That's right. Susan stayed here. I took the pickup. When I got to the gate, I found him. Dead."

Cam rubbed his forehead, trying to erase the beginnings of a headache. "I don't suppose you saw anything. A car driving away? A man with a gun?"

"Not a thing. I came back here, called the ambulance and then you. Then, Susan and I drove back to the gate to wait for you." He glanced at Susan and said, "Some of your hot chocolate would taste real good about now."

"All right, but I'm making the non-dairy, sugar-free kind," she said. "You know what the doctor told you about too much sugar."

"That's fine," Jake said. "You're all the sweetness I need."

She gave them a weak smile before leaving the room, and Cam forced himself to smile back, even though there wasn't one damned thing to feel happy about.

Jake McQuaid had gone alone to meet Zach Hollingsworth. Jake who had already proven himself to be a man who would quit his job and move to another state to protect his woman. For twenty-four years, he'd kept her secrets. Inevitably, some would say he'd even kill to keep them hidden.

Cam stretched his arms across the back of the sofa. Slowly, he lifted his gaze to confront his father. "Did you kill him, Jake?"

"No."

Silence spread between them. They both knew Cam had had no choice but to ask. He was the law and there had been a murder. He would have to investigate this crime like any other. If he stayed on the case, he couldn't offer his protection to his father or to Susan. Ironically, at this moment, when he regarded Jake as a potential suspect in a capital crime, Cam had never felt closer to the man.

Like his brothers, Cam had spent more years than he could count resenting Jake for dishonoring the woman they'd come to regard as their mother. Susan had warmed Jake's bed for twenty-odd years, raised his sons, and made his house a home, and yet the old man hadn't seen fit to marry her. As his respect for his father eroded, so had their relationship. Too often their conversations, even about the most mundane subjects, ended in shouting matches. The resentment on both sides simmered. Finally, for Susan's sake, Cam made the conscious decision to avoid confrontation with the old man as much as possible. As a result, their relationship had become pathetically superficial. With the exception of this terrible night, Cam couldn't remember the last time he and his father had engaged in more than obligatory small talk. The thought of all those wasted years caused a tightening in his chest. If only he'd known the truth, known just how deeply the old man cared, what he'd sacrificed for the woman he loved. What a difference it would have made...

Susan bustled back into the room. "I set the water to boil. What did I miss?"

Cam leaned forward again. "Let's assume that neither of you murdered Zach Hollingsworth."

Jake snorted. "Good assumption."

"All right, so why would someone else?"

"Information?" Susan suggested. "Hollingsworth had

been digging into the past, rattling skeletons in some very dark closets. That's why Byron Reeves had to back out of his nomination. I'm betting Zach found something else, something someone didn't want hitting the newspapers.''

"Any idea what it could be?"

She shook her head.

Cam considered her theory. It was as good a place as any to start. Zach Hollingsworth, a reporter, had been killed because he knew too much. If the information that had resulted in his death died with him, there wasn't much basis for an investigation. Chances were good the reporter had left a paper trail. But where to start?

The answer flashed through his mind like neon. As bright as a pair of very green eyes. Zach's assistant. Frani Landon. She had been more than Zach's assistant, she'd been like family. She knew what he knew, and if she didn't, she'd know where to find out.

Cam rose quickly from the sofa and grabbed his hat. "Gotta go," he said over his shoulder on the way to the door. "I'll be in touch. Don't talk to anyone without consulting your lawyer."

If his hunch was right, one very gutsy little redhead was wandering around Cedar Bluffs with a head full of dangerous information. And it wouldn't take long for a murderer who had already killed once to find his next target.

Chapter Two

With only four motels in town, it was pretty easy for Cam to track down Frani Landon. Her rental car was parked outside room number 12 at the Hacienda House. When Cam checked with the motel manager, he confirmed that she had checked in with a credit card.

The manager combed his fingers through his bushy gray beard. "Hey, Sheriff. Is it true that the guy who got himself killed over at the Circle Q is famous?"

News traveled fast as a brushfire in Cedar Bluffs. "He was a newspaper reporter. How'd you hear?"

"Everybody's talking. And this redhead who's staying in room 12? She's a suspect, right?"

"Can't say. I haven't had much chance to investigate yet."

"When she checked in, she said she might be staying a week."

"A week?" Inwardly, Cam groaned. He might be stuck with her for a whole week? Life would be a hell of a lot easier if Frani would give him the information he needed, then pack up and go home to Chicago.

"She didn't much look like a killer to me," the manager commented. "Pretty little thing."

Cam had to agree. Frani was easy on the eye. Not only

that, but she was spunky and smart. In different circumstances, he might have been attracted to her. As soon as that idea formed, Cam shoved it out of his head. Frani Landon was the wrong redhead at the wrong place and the wrong time.

His only concern for Frani Landon was making sure she didn't turn out to be the second murder victim in Chaparral County. He stepped outside into light, blowing snow. Nightfall came early in winter. Soon it would be dark, an easy time for a murderer to catch an unarmed woman alone.

Cam walked to the far end of the plain two-story structure of white stucco with a red tile roof. One thing was for damn sure, he thought. He couldn't let Frani stay here at the Hacienda. Though this was the best motel in town, there wasn't anything resembling decent security. All the rooms had windows that could easily be broken. And the locks on these doors would be a cinch to pick.

The best solution was to talk her into packing up and hightailing it out of town. Under the light outside her room, Cam checked his wristwatch. With half a dozen phone calls to return and a murder investigation to organize, he didn't have time to waste.

Bare-knuckled, he rapped at her door.

The drapes rustled, then the door opened a crack and Frani peeked around the chain. "What do you want?"

"May I come in?"

The door slammed and he heard the rattle of the flimsy security chain before she opened wide and the light from within silhouetted her like a perfect target. Cam hustled her inside and locked up tight.

She still wore those clumsy steel-toed boots and the baggy slacks that looked as if she did her clothes shopping at an army surplus store, but her snug-fitting forest-green sweater showed off delicate shoulders and high breasts. The

soft, expensive-looking material barely covered the waistband of her pants, and when she bent to remove her laptop
computer from the table beside the window, he caught a
glimpse of firm, well-toned midriff.

Physically, she was in fine condition. But then, he'd already seen that when she'd broken away from him and
sprinted to the ambulance, moving faster than any woman
he'd ever seen, and taking him completely off guard. He
had the impression Frani was chock-full of surprises.

She flung herself into one of the chairs next to the table.
Her green eyes gleamed like hostile jade in an otherwise
pretty, heart-shaped face. "Congratulations, Cam. I assume
you've already finished interrogating the obvious suspects.
Or, should I say, having a chat with Mom and Pop?"

"I'm concerned about your safety." Ignoring her sarcasm, he jumped right in with both feet. "I believe Zach
Hollingsworth was murdered because he had damaging information in his possession. This means you're also in danger. As his assistant, you'd have access to that same information."

"So that's your murder theory? Zach was killed because
he knew too much." She gave a disbelieving snort. "Not
very original."

"Most murders aren't."

"And it's such a handy premise for you. It gets your
father and Pamela Jessup off the hook, doesn't it?"

"I'm keeping an open mind," he said.

She leaned across to a manila file folder on the bed and
pulled out an eight-by-ten glossy print, which she handed
to him. "Here's what Pamela looked like twenty-four years
ago."

There was no mistaking Susan's physical resemblance to
the attractive blond woman in the photograph, but Cam
found it difficult to reconcile the pampered, privileged lady

in the photo with the careworn expression of the woman who'd reared him. The Susan he knew never wore diamonds. She never looked down her nose at anybody. During all her life with the McQuaids, she'd worked as hard as any other ranch wife.

"It's her," Frani said. "Isn't it?"

"I'm not disputing the fact," Cam said. "The woman I've always known as Susan Hathaway is Pamela Jessup."

Frani tossed out another picture. The grainy texture indicated that it had been reproduced from a video camera image.

"The bank robbery," Frani said.

Unfortunately, the blurred image was still identifiable as Susan with an automatic rifle in her hands. Behind her, a hostage cowered on the floor.

The picture seemed to tremble in his hand. Instead of the stern resolve Cam usually experienced when confronting a criminal, excuses ran through his mind. *She must have been drugged. Must have been coerced or threatened.*

She would never do a thing like this. Not Susan Hathaway, not the woman who comforted the McQuaid men with hot chocolate and endless nurturing. Damn it, she wasn't a lawbreaker. She was too...good.

"Is there some reason," Frani demanded, "why you haven't arrested this woman?"

Because he'd rather cut off his own right arm than take Susan to jail. "It's not my jurisdiction," Cam said. "I've got my hands full with one murder."

"Does that mean that while you're investigating Zach's murder, other crime doesn't exist?"

"I have priorities," he said. "Number one is to make sure you're safe and secure."

"I can take care of myself."

"Is that so?" It'd serve her right if he took her at her

word and walked out the door, leaving her to face whatever threats came her way. But he didn't work like that. Cam was responsible for the people in Chaparral County, citizens and visitors alike. "Well, Frani, I can't take the risk that you might be wrong."

"Fine," she said. "Go ahead and assign one of your ace deputies to keep an eye on me."

A good idea, but Cam didn't have an extra deputy to watch over Frani. His entire department amounted to fourteen full-time employees, including the dispatcher and the indispensable office secretary. Right now, he had three deputies out at the Circle Q, searching for evidence before the snow got too heavy. "I was hoping you might see fit to go somewhere where you'd be safe."

"Like back to Chicago?"

He nodded.

"Not a chance," she said. "I'm sitting right here in Cedar Bluffs until this murder is solved."

"If you stay here, you'll only be an obstacle. I'd have to take a man off the investigation to watch out for you."

"If I leave," she countered, "how will I know you're doing the job?"

"Because I'm the sheriff," he said simply.

She planted her fists at the flare of her hips and stared up at him. "I don't trust you, Cameron McQuaid. Your personal connection to Pamela Jessup is too strong."

Anger twisted inside him. Being a lawman was his whole life. Who the hell did she think she was? Francesca Landon had no right to come here and accuse him of not being able to handle an investigation. "You're wrong about Susan."

"Pamela. Her name is Pamela Jessup."

"Either way, you're dead wrong." He matched her determination with his own. "Think about it. If Susan intended to kill Zach, why would she invite him to come here and listen to her story?''

"I'm sure she had a reason."

But Cam noticed a shadow of doubt in Frani's eyes. "Doesn't make sense. Why would she kill him on her own doorstep?"

"You might be right," she admitted. She dropped her guard, slowly shaking her head. "I hadn't thought of that. But Pamela Jessup is an intelligent woman, smart enough to stay in hiding for twenty-four years. Nobody even knew she was alive."

Actually, someone else had known. Cam's brother, Cyrus, had figured out Susan's hidden identity during his FBI investigation, but Cam was certain the secret had gone no further than him and his brother.

Seemingly lost in thought, Frani moved away from him. She pushed aside the manila folders and absently sat on the bed with one leg curled under her. The other leg dangled, not even touching the floor, and he realized how petite she was. Small and slim, her head barely grazed his shoulders and her tiny waist couldn't have been larger than the span of his hands.

"If not Pamela," she said, "then who else would have had a motive to kill Zach?"

His gaze lingered on the manila file folders. This was the opening he'd hoped for. "You could help me find out. Let me take a look at Zach's files."

"I don't think so." She stacked one on top of the other. "I need to protect my sources."

"I thought you wanted to catch the murderer."

"It's all I want."

"Then, help me. Let me—"

"Forget about it, Cam. Maybe I was wrong about Pamela killing Zach. But you're wrong, too."

"How so?"

"In your heart, you must realize that you're too close to the case. You should recuse yourself from this investigation."

More likely, he'd be forcibly removed. One of the calls he needed to return was to the Chaparral County district attorney. The murder of Zach Hollingsworth represented the most high-profile crime in this county since Cam had been appointed sheriff, and he figured there were a lot of people who'd want to stick their fingers in this pie. The Criminal Investigation Department for Colorado. State patrol. Maybe even the feds.

But Cam didn't trust anybody else. "It's because of my personal involvement that I want to stay on the case."

"To protect Susan? Or your father?"

Cam had been a lawman all his adult life. When he was a kid, Jake had instilled a firm, almost rigid set of values in his sons. "If I find evidence to arrest Jake or Susan, I'll do it. You have my word, Frani."

When he heard a knock at the door, Cam drew his gun and pointed Frani toward the bathroom. "In there. Close the door and lock it."

She rolled her eyes and called out, "Who is it?"

"Addie Lindstrom."

"Never do that again," he said coldly. "When I tell you to do something, do it. Ask questions later."

"Oh, please!"

When she started toward the door, he blocked her way. "I'll answer."

"Why?"

Instead of explaining that she could very well be a killer's next target, he opened the door and pulled Addie inside. The gray-haired publisher of the *Chaparral Clarion* looked pleased to see him. The fine wrinkles around her blue eyes crinkled in a smile. "Hey, Cam. I've got some questions for you."

"Not now, Addie."

"I can't wait long," she said. "The phones in my newspaper office are going crazy with reporters asking questions about Zach Hollingsworth's death. It's best if I give them a response."

Frani approached her with hand outstretched. "Thank you for coming here. I'm Frani Landon."

"Pleased to meet you." Addie offered a sad smile. "I'm truly sorry about Zach. I might have been one of the last people to speak to him."

"Excuse me, Addie." Cam stepped forward. "When did you talk to Zach?"

"When he came through town. He stopped and asked me for directions to the Circle Q, and we hit it off. He even asked me out to dinner." She exhaled a short sigh. "First date I've had in eight weeks and he ends up dead. Sorry, Frani."

"Was he alone?" Cam asked.

"Yes," she said.

"Did he say any—"

"Sorry, Cam. Our conversation wasn't anything significant. Just me being my nosy self." She turned to Frani. "We talked about truth in journalism. Thought I might write it up as a memorial, but I'd very much like if you'd do the obit on Zach. We can release it nationwide on the wire."

"I hoped you'd say that. You have a fax?"

"The *Clarion* may be a tiny newspaper, but my equipment is up-to-date." Addie glanced down at her gloved hands. "I have a touch of rheumatism, and I need everything to be as easy as possible."

Frani grabbed her shoulder bag, tossing in several items.

With her other hand, she scooped up her laptop. "Let's go."

Cam stepped in front of the door, creating a physical barrier. "You're in danger, Frani. Whoever killed Zach might come after you."

"The danger will have to wait. This is a breaking story, and I owe it to Zach to make sure it's handled right."

"She's right," Addie said. "We have to get on top of this, Cam. Would you please step aside?"

Reporters! They didn't have the common sense of quartz rocks in a driveway. Cam had seen this phenomenon before at political events when he pitied the lawmen trying to control reporters. In this case, with Frani and Addie, haste seemed particularly odd. Zach was dead and not going anywhere.

On the other hand, Addie might be a solution to Cam's problem: how to keep Frani safe. Last year, a break-in at the newspaper office had resulted in two computers being stolen. She'd taken steps to make sure it didn't happen again. "Addie, I want you to tell me about your security system."

"The *Clarion* locks up like a vault. The windows are that unbreakable glass and I have shutters on the inside I lock up tight in the evening."

"And there's an apartment on the second floor, right?"

"Nothing fancy. Just somewhere for me to sleep and have dinner when I'm working late." She turned to Frani. "You know how it is when you're on deadline."

"I do."

Cam interrupted before they could get into a story swap. "Addie, until we apprehend the murderer, I'm concerned about Frani's safety. Can she stay at the *Clarion*?"

"I'd be honored," Addie said.

"Agreed," Frani said with a quick nod. "Thank you so much, Addie."

After she'd gathered her things from the motel room, Cam instructed Frani to ride with Addie and leave the rental car as a decoy. Outside, the gathering snow created a thick darkness permeated by patterns of swirling flakes, but it was still early enough that there were people out and about.

Driving through town, Cam followed Addie's ancient Jeep Wagoneer to the rear parking area behind the newspaper office. Having Frani here with Addie was a perfect solution. Not only was she protected by the best security system in Cedar Bluffs, but his office was less than a mile away.

He hustled her inside with one last warning. "Don't let anybody in unless you identify them first. Understand?"

"Sure." Standing just inside the door, she looked up at him. The expression in her unbelievably green eyes was gentler than before. "Thanks, Cam. For your concern."

A lightning bolt shot through him. For an instant, he was paralyzed by a sudden vision of the real woman beneath the cynical armor. The warmth buried deep inside her showed itself in a flash. "Take care, Frani."

"I will."

She closed the door, and Cam shook himself, trying to erase the aftereffects of the storm that had raced through him. If the circumstances had been different, he might have fallen hard for this supposedly tough city gal with a gentle heart.

CAM DROVE to the square brown brick building that housed the Chaparral County sheriff's office and jail. Next door was the most impressive structure in town, the county courthouse. Lights were still burning in several of the windows.

One of the first phone calls Cam needed to make was the county district attorney. Now that Frani was safe, he had a new priority. He couldn't let this case get away from him. Though Frani had been one hundred percent correct when she'd said he ought to pull himself off the investigation because of his obvious personal involvement, Cam was determined to keep the investigation within his control, if not his jurisdiction. It would be too easy for someone with a grudge against Cam to go after his father and Susan.

Inside the sheriff's office, he spoke briefly with the dispatcher before Rachel Beck, the department secretary, popped up beside him. She was a sweet-faced, plump woman who'd raised four children. She treated the officers like her own personal brood, but at the same time, she was ferociously efficient.

"Are you all right, Cam?" Rachel asked.

"I've been better."

"You'd better settle down quick. We've got a lot of work to do."

Rachel was in such a rush that she practically carried him into his office and dumped him behind his desk.

"Hold on a sec," Cam said.

He needed to clear his mind before he took on one more thing. His usual ritual was simple. When he handled county business, he changed hats. Dealing with the paperwork was his least favorite aspect of the job. When he attended to it, Cam felt more like a clerk than a lawman. If he was going to work like a clerk, he figured he ought to look like one. Standing at the coat rack inside his office, he removed his split leather jacket and hung up his Stetson. Returning to his desk, he opened the bottom drawer and stashed his automatic pistol, a state-of-the-art gun that was lightweight and more accurate than the old revolver his father used to carry.

He sat behind the usual clutter on his wide oak desktop and looked up at Rachel. "Shoot."

She handed him a stack of messages.

"First, call Harold." Harold T. Cisneros was the county district attorney. "These others are messages from the state patrol, the CID in Grand Junction, the FBI and the coroner."

"Thanks, Rachel."

"And there's more of the usual stuff. A prisoner at the jail has a tummyache and wants to see a doctor. There's a reported break-in over at Conifer Junction. And you still haven't called back the woman whose truck was stolen earlier today."

Cam sighed. The routine business of being sheriff wasn't going to stop just because he had a murder investigation. "Leave the messages and call Joe Bradley. I'm going to need him to come in right away."

"Consider it done." Rachel nodded. "I'll bring you some coffee."

"Rachel, things are fixing to get real crazy around here. Expect some major overtime. And I want you to know, if I don't have time to tell you later, I don't know what this office would do without you."

She gave him a wink and zipped out the door.

Cam punched in the phone number for the D.A., who had promised he'd still be in his office no matter how late Cam called. Harold T. was an ambitious man for such a small county, and his voice betrayed his excitement over this high-profile investigation.

"We've got a problem, Cam."

"I know." His gaze wandered to a framed photograph of Susan and his two brothers, taken six years ago when Cy received yet another promotion with the Bureau.

"I've already had phone calls from high places," Harold said.

Cam sighed. "They want me off the case."

"They say you're too close. Your father is a suspect, Cam."

"On the other hand," Cam said, "if we step aside and let the state officers handle the—"

"No way," Harold interrupted. "The primary responsibility for the murder investigation is going to stay right here in Chaparral County. This could be my big opportunity to prove to everyone we're more than a bunch of hicks."

Cam knew exactly what Harold meant. As a small county, Chaparral didn't count for much statewide. About twenty years ago, it came into some prominence when oil companies proposed strip mining and ran afoul of the environmentalists, but that had been before Harold's time.

The murder of Zach Hollingsworth and the discovery of the missing heiress—when the story broke—would promise nationwide publicity. If Harold played his cards right, his face would be all over the newspapers, not to mention the six-o'clock news.

"What's your plan, Harold?"

"We keep it here. Do it our way. This is our chance to prove to the big boys that we can handle a major crime. We've got the *cojones—Comprende, mi amigo?*"

"Okay." Harold's lapse into Spanish indicated how much the case had rattled him. Although three generations removed from his ancestral roots, Harold had never forsaken his proud Hispanic heritage. Whenever he wanted to make a point, he fell back on the language of his grandfathers, the language still spoken in the homes of many of his constituents. "But how are we going to convince everybody else that I can supervise a case where my father is the prime suspect?"

"I only have one question," Harold said. "Did Jake shoot that man?"

"Hell, no," Cam answered without hesitation. There was no question in his mind. His father might have skirted the edges of the law by not turning Susan over to the proper authorities when he'd found out her true identity, but Jake McQuaid was no murderer.

"I'll back you up, Cam. Here's how we do it. We name someone acting sheriff, at least until we make an arrest."

"Are you telling me to take a leave of absence?"

"That's right," Harold said. "Starting tomorrow morning."

"I don't like it." Cam had never run from any fight and he wasn't about to start now. Especially now.

"You don't get it," Harold said. "We tell everybody you're on leave, but you still run the investigation. Our acting sheriff will be—for all intents—a front man. He'll talk to the press and handle communications."

"You're telling me to go undercover."

"Exactly."

Cam thought for a moment. Harold might have hit on the perfect solution. If Cam didn't have to worry about the day-to-day operations of the department, he could concentrate fully on solving Zach Hollingsworth's murder. "You've got yourself a deal, Harold. I've already put in a call to Joe Bradley. He's my best deputy."

"*Bueno*. As far as anyone will know, Bradley is acting sheriff of Chaparral County, effective immediately."

"I like it," Cam said. "We'll still have to deal with the feds. They'll want to talk to Susan."

"The FBI." Harold groaned. "We've got to cooperate with them. Those *hombres* can be serious trouble."

"Not all of them." Cam picked up the framed photo on his desk and studied the face of his older brother, Cy. Everybody said they looked alike with their thick black hair and dark eyes. More important, he and Cy thought alike. They would both go to any lengths to protect Susan. "Harold, I think I've got a solution to our FBI problem."

"I DON'T NEED any help," Frani said firmly.

She resisted an urge to bang the telephone receiver on the desktop. This hadn't been a call she'd wanted to make, but there hadn't been a choice. She had to discuss Zach's death with Lloyd Rogers, the managing editor at the *Chicago Daily Herald* where both she and Zach were employees, even though neither of them spent more than a couple of hours a month in the offices.

"Fran, sweetheart," Lloyd said, "this is too big for you to handle by yourself. The Jessup heiress? And Zach's murder? We're talking headline."

"And bylines," she added. "*My* byline. I'll have the story on your desk in three hours. I'm already here. I can handle the on-scene coverage."

"Two hours," he said. "Nine o'clock in Colorado."

"I'll fax it," she promised.

"We'll do the obit here," he said. "We've got all Zach's history on file in the library."

The facts, she thought. They had all the facts about where Zach was born, where he'd grown up, which schools he'd attended. But nobody knew Zach Hollingsworth the way she did. "I want to do a memorial piece," she said.

"I don't know…"

"I worked closely with him, Lloyd."

"Zach was my friend for twenty years," Lloyd said. "I thought I'd do the memorial."

Frani doubted that Lloyd knew anything personal about Zach. All they'd done was get together over a couple of beers and talk about the Bears and the Bulls. She knew

Zach well enough to write about the man behind his legendary, Pulitzer-prize-winning stature. "Go ahead and write your piece, Lloyd. And I'll do mine. There are other papers, you know."

"The *Daily Herald* happens to be the name at the top of your paycheck, Francesca. Don't threaten me."

"No threat," Frani said coldly. "But you should know I fully intend to write a memorial for Zach, if not for the *Herald,* then for someone else. As my employer, you have the right of first refusal, of course. But after that, I have every right to send it out to the wire services."

"You have until nine o'clock to get that lead story in," he snapped. "We'll discuss the memorial later."

"You'll have your headline," she promised.

When she hung up the phone, her heart was beating triple time. She had two hours to write a front-page headline piece about the breaking murder investigation. Later, she would go another round with Lloyd over the right to compose Zach's memorial. It would be so good, he wouldn't risk losing it to the wire services.

And what about the other story behind the headline—the story of Pamela Jessup? If Cam was correct in assuming Zach had information worth killing for, that was the bigger story.

Frani's only real source was the ratty old notebook she'd lifted from Zach's body. The pages inside were covered with chicken scratchings, Zach's own peculiar shorthand. If anyone could decipher this mess, it was Frani. But she just wasn't sure.

She looked up when Addie placed a fresh cup of coffee on the desk in front of her. "I've got two hours to write a story covering the murder and the investigation, so far."

"How can I help?" Addie asked, her clear blue eyes shining with savvy intelligence.

"You're a godsend, Addie," Frani told her gratefully.

"Just a journalist," the older woman said with a casual shrug. "But I warn you, I might be a little rusty when it comes to hard-edged reporting. After all, I've spent the past fifteen years in a place where my biggest stories have to do with the county fair and the latest social event at the Elks Lodge."

Somehow, Frani didn't doubt Addie's competence for a millisecond. "It's like riding a bicycle," she quipped.

Addie grinned.

"Okay, get me everything you can on the local angle. Check with the D.A. and sheriff's office. See what you can pry out of Cam's deputies. Who can you talk to over there?"

"Rachel Beck," Addie said. "She's the department secretary, and short of the good sheriff himself, she knows more about what goes on over there than anyone."

"Great. See what she knows." Frani breathed a sigh of elation. She could do this, she told herself. With Addie working on the investigative side, Frani could focus her attention on the Jessup story.

While Addie returned to her own desk, Frani stretched her arms over her head and flexed her fingers. The *Clarion* offices, though stuck out here in the middle of nowhere, offered miniaturized versions of the latest in print technology. Clean and modern with a counter facing the front door, there was space for four desks and a layout table. A constant flow of news spewed over the AP wire.

Though the presses were in the basement, the scent of newsprint and ink permeated the air like fine perfume. Frani felt right at home.

She opened Zach's notebook on the desktop in front of her and stared down. *I won't disappoint you, Zach.* When she realized the stain at the leather-bound edges was Zach's own blood, her stomach clenched and sadness washed over her. It took an effort, but she pushed her sorrow aside. Zach would have told her to gut it out, to be the reporter she'd been trained to be. To deal with the facts.

In less than half an hour, she'd typed a summary of the Jessup case, carefully avoiding the connection to Byron Reeves, which had not as yet been fully proved. It was obvious she needed to talk to Pamela Jessup. "Addie, I need the phone number for the Circle Q."

It came as no surprise that her call was picked up by an answering machine. The ranch phone was no doubt ringing off the hook. But Frani had another source—Cameron McQuaid. If he cooperated, he could fill in the blanks. *He could give her everything she needed.*

When she thought of the Stetson-wearing sheriff, she felt the corners of her mouth lifting in a thoroughly inappropriate grin. The man really was larger than life. Tall and ruggedly handsome from the top of that sexy hat to the tips of his well-worn cowhide boots. The quintessential cowboy. The kind of man women spun fantasies around. A man who stood head and shoulders above a world of office politics, pinstripes and stuffed shirts.

With a sigh, Frani yanked herself out of her fantasy and called to Addie again, "Do you think Cam McQuaid would talk to me about Susan?"

"Ask him yourself. He's on his way over here right now."

Fighting an impulse to run to the bathroom and put on fresh lipstick, Frani asked, "Why?"

"Not sure," Addie said. "He just called to let us know he was coming."

And there was his knock, right on cue.

Quickly, Frani slid Zach's notebook into the top desk drawer and closed it. She had less than eighty minutes to file her story with the *Daily Herald,* but the only thought in her mind right now was seeing Cam again.

He strode into the newspaper offices, immediately taking command with his strong, masculine presence. The snow must have picked up outside because his black Stetson was lightly dusted with white, lacy flakes.

"Frani, I need you to come with me."

A dangerously wanton voice in the back of her head whispered, *I'd follow you anywhere, cowboy.* She ignored it and went for a more characteristic response. "Why?"

"I hate to ask you to do this," he said. His voice held a solemn note, and his gaze expressed deep compassion.

Her energy level dropped. When she worked on a deadline, Frani generally operated on a whirlwind of enthusiasm. Suddenly, the adrenaline vanished. "What is it, Cam?"

"The county coroner requires an official identification for the deceased before he signs the death certificate," he said. "I'm afraid I have to take you to the morgue."

Chapter Three

The morgue. Frani sank into the chair behind the desk. With the nine-o'clock deadline pushing her, she'd had the perfect avenue to escape her grief. Working, she could almost pretend Zach's murder was just another story. Absorbed in her writing, concentrating on accuracy and the approaching deadline, there was no time to grieve. No time to think, or remember.

But now, Cam was forcing her to stop, to confront the truth of Zach's death without the protection of a byline. The irony of her situation struck her. Zach had always accused her of letting emotion get in the way of her story. Tonight, however, just the opposite had occurred. She was leading with the facts, instead of her heart, clinging to the details for dear life.

"Why do you need me?" she asked Cam. "Wasn't Zach carrying identification?"

"Yes, of course he was," he replied. "But this was murder, Frani. The coroner isn't willing to release the body without identification from the next of kin. If there is someone else…"

She shook her head. "No. There's no one."

"What about funeral arrangements?"

"He wanted to be cremated," Frani said. "He hated the cold."

It seemed a cruel twist that Zach should have died on a cold February afternoon, in the snow. Despite his urban sophistication, his whirlwind pace, his celebrity, Zach Hollingsworth had died alone in the country, without even a traffic-stopping ride in an ambulance. How ironic life could be. Suddenly, Frani knew exactly how Zach's memorial story would begin. She turned to the computer and began to type.

"Excuse me, Frani," Cam interrupted. "But I need you to come with me to the morgue. Now."

"Can't," she said distractedly over her shoulder. "I need an hour with this. I'm on deadline here."

She barely noticed him standing behind her as the words poured out of her heart and mind and onto the page. At that moment, there was nothing in Frani's world but the story. Every detail had to be right. For Zach's sake, only the most accurate accounting would suffice.

"Cam," she said, turning around in her chair to face him. "May I ask you a few questions?"

He wore a strange expression, as if he had never seen a woman working before. "That depends. I can't let you print something that might compromise the investigation."

"I understand completely. That's the last thing I want to do. I just need some background."

"Shoot."

"All right, when you first got the call that a man had been shot, where were you? What did you do? Did you follow normal procedure? Was anything about this call unusual?"

When he didn't answer immediately, she pushed. "Well?"

He shook his head. "I can't believe you."

Frani blinked.

"What the hell kind of woman are you, anyway? You claim to have cared about this man, said the two of you were like family."

Frani's defenses sprang to life. "We were!"

"Yeah, some family." He sneered. "You won't stop chasing your precious story long enough even to identify his body."

"I'm a reporter," she said flatly. "It's my job."

She could almost feel Zach's spirit standing behind her, egging her on. *Give 'em hell, Frani.* The sensation was so strong, she could nearly feel his hand on her shoulder.

"I'll come back when it's more convenient," Cam said.

His cold disapproval felt like a slap. Frani glanced past Cam and saw Addie shake her head. "Leave her alone, Cam. Can't you see this is what she has to do?" Addie pushed back from her desk and crossed to hand Frani her notes. "Here's the statement from the paramedic."

Frani nodded her appreciation, and Addie turned to Cam. "Sit down, Sheriff, and give her what she wants. Please, Cam. Just do this."

Cam hesitated, his jaw set as his gaze shifted to Frani. The tension stretched between them until he finally lowered himself onto the chair beside her desk. "What do you want to know?"

Quickly, Frani scanned what she'd already written. "Zach died at approximately two o'clock in the afternoon. The probable cause was three bullet wounds to the chest." She swallowed hard and went on. "His body was discovered by Jake McQuaid, owner of the Circle Q ranch." She looked at Cam.

"Jake and Susan had been expecting him. When he didn't show, Jake drove down to the gate." Cam went on to explain how they'd been having problems with the security system. "He called the ambulance and then me. I was in my office. I got the call at approximately two-twenty. You know the rest. You were on my tail all the way out of town."

"Thank you," she said. She had to fight to keep her voice from shaking.

He removed his hat and shrugged off his split leather jacket. "I can get you a copy of the police log if you need the exact time the call came in, along with the name of the dispatcher."

He stretched his long, jeans-clad legs out in front of him.

"That won't be necessary, but I could use a quote from Jake."

"Don't hold your breath. I'm sure his lawyer won't allow it."

And even if the attorney would allow his client to make a statement, you'd be there to stop me, wouldn't you, cowboy?

"How about a little background on Jake?" she said. "Where's he from? What's his background? And the Circle Q. Is it a working ranch? How many employees?"

"Jake's a former lawman, a county sheriff in Texas for most of his life."

"Where exactly in Texas?"

"Dry Creek."

Startled, she looked up. Dry Creek was where the body of Pamela Jessup had supposedly been discovered, face-down in a swimming pool. "Let me guess. Jake resigned as sheriff about twenty-four years ago, right after the woman you call Susan came to live with your family."

"That's right." His dark brown eyes narrowed.

"What can you tell me about Susan? Specifically, about her life as Pamela Jessup? How did she manage to avoid—"

Cam held up a hand, cutting off her barrage of questions. "Look, Frani. Susan's situation is a federal matter."

Frani opened her mouth to ask if the FBI had been notified, but before she could pose the question, Cam went on. "I can't give you particulars, now. Suffice it to say, someone in the bureau has been apprised of her whereabouts."

"So you won't give me anything about Susan?"

"Can't. Not yet. And I'd count it a personal favor if you'd hold off the Pamela Jessup story until we nail down Zach's murderer."

Frani was immediately rankled. "No way, Cam. This is news. The public has a right to know."

"What if I told you that if you print a story about Susan now, you might be damaging the investigation into Zach's death?"

She leaned forward, eager to know more. "Naturally, I'd want to know why."

Cam looked around to see that Addie had gone to make coffee before he explained. "It's logical, isn't it? If Zach's death was somehow tied to Susan's past, revealing that now could drive our suspect even deeper into hiding. Whoever it was will be covering his tracks, erasing the trail even faster if he knows that's the direction we're heading."

She glanced at her wristwatch. Only fifty-five minutes to make her deadline. She would have to save the revelations about Pamela Jessup for a longer, better researched piece anyway. It was the story of the decade and she didn't intend to break it until she could do it justice. "All right, let's focus on your current investigation."

"Does that mean you won't break the Pamela Jessup story?"

Frani sighed. "I guess it does, at least for the time being. But rumors spread fast. The paramedics, your own deputies, any number of people heard me call her by name yesterday. You can't keep something this big a secret for long, Cam. If I don't break this story, believe me, someone else will.''

He acknowledged her wisdom with a stiff nod.

"Let's get back to the investigation,'' she said.

Cam seemed relieved. "First, you should know I'm not officially in charge of the case, anymore. Matter of fact, I'm on a leave of absence from the department.''

From behind Frani's shoulder, Addie gasped. "Oh, Cam. I'm sorry.''

"Thanks. But it was the only thing that made sense.''

Warily, Frani studied him. Though she would have raised a whirlwind of objections if Cam had been allowed to remain on the case, she hadn't expected such quick action. "Who's in charge of the murder investigation?''

"Deputy Joe Bradley. You can talk to Harold T. Cisneros, the Chaparral County district attorney, if you need an official statement.''

The political pieces fell together quickly in Frani's well-trained mind. "Cisneros pulled you off the case before there could be any accusation of impropriety.'' It wasn't a question and Cam wasn't confirming or denying her statement.

Addie said, "Harold T. is a smart politician. Should I get a quote from him?''

"Absolutely.''

Frani turned back to the computer screen. She now had less than an hour to do a front-page story for the *Daily Herald*. A story that would no doubt be picked up by a dozen news services. It wasn't every day a man of Zach's standing was gunned down. Her fingers felt stiff and unwieldy on the keys. *Concentrate. Get it right the first time.* She wiped all distractions from her mind and began to write in earnest. Occasionally, she called out a question to Addie or to Cam, but her concentration never wavered from her task.

Whenever she consulted Zach's notebook, Frani took care to conceal her movement from Cam. Addie brought them coffee. From time to time, Cam rose to pace to the window and gaze out at the storm.

With six minutes to go, Frani hit the print command and leaned back in her chair. "Okay, Addie. Now all I need is for you to fax it to Lloyd Rogers at the *Daily Herald*."

"You did it," Addie said. "I'll bet Zach is up there somewhere cheering."

It was hard to imagine crusty old Zach Hollingsworth in paradise, an angel with feathery wings and a long white robe. Frani preferred to think that in Heaven—as on Earth—he'd be racing around trying to get the real story, a cigarette dangling from the corner of his mouth and his eyes squinted against the rising smoke.

Cam reached for his jacket. "Ready?"

She could only nod.

While he settled his hat, Frani slid Zach's notebook into her shoulder bag. Once she had a chance to fully translate his scribblings, she'd have a better handle on the case. Until then, she didn't intend to let the notebook out of her sight.

Outside the snow was now falling with a vengeance. Frani ducked her head against the buffeting wind as she followed Cam in to the Land Rover with police lights on top and a five-pointed sheriff's-star emblem on the doors.

The windows were covered with a layer of ice and snow, enclosing them both in a dark cocoon.

Frani's breath came in moist, visible puffs through lips that were already beginning to chap. She dug into her purse for moisturizing lipstick.

Cam glanced at what Frani called her "war bag." "What

all have you got in there?'' he asked as he turned the key in the ignition.

She shrugged. "You know, just girl stuff."

The Rover snarled before it purred to life, and Cam sat back, allowing the engine to warm up. "I saw you put a book in your bag before we left. What was it?"

Panic shot through her. "Just a book I've been reading," she said evasively.

"It must be a fascinating story to keep your attention while you're racing a deadline. What's the title?"

She waved her hand in a dismissive gesture, glad for the dim light that made it difficult for him to see the guilt she felt etched on her face. "You wouldn't recognize it if I told you. Not your kind of reading, I'm sure."

"The title, Frani."

She gazed at the outline of his profile, shadowed against the white snow on the windows. "It's about a cowboy...in fact, that's the title. *The Cowboy and the Lady.*"

Cam flipped on the dashboard lights, and the glow illuminated his high cheekbones and firm chin. "Is the lady in your story a redhead?"

"As a matter of fact, she is."

He reached up to adjust the brim of his Stetson, then turned to look directly into her eyes. "So what happens? Is there a romance?"

Had she imagined it, or had there been a hopeful note in his question? Her breath caught and she swallowed. "I don't know. I haven't gotten that far."

"You'll have to let me know how it turns out."

"Sure."

His expression grew doubtful and he reached for the door. "I'll clear the snow from the windshield and we'll be on our way." Having said this, he hesitated. "If you expect to get information from me about the investigation, you're going to have play it straight. I might be just a country cop to you, but I'm no one's fool, Frani.'' With the scraper in hand, he slammed out of the vehicle, leaving Frani behind feeling shaken and exposed.

She glanced at the lipstick in her hand. Could she trust him? Could she risk sharing the information in Zach's notebook? After all, her ultimate aim was to solve Zach's murder, and who better than Cam McQuaid to help her achieve that goal?

On the other hand, how could they work together when all Cam wanted to do was protect his father and the woman who'd been like a mother to him? At this point, all the evidence pointed to Jake McQuaid as Zach's murderer. Jake, the lawman who'd rescued Pamela Jessup, a fugitive from the law, who had hidden out in Cedar Bluffs for more than twenty years. Obviously, Jake would do anything for this woman. By his own admission, Jake had been alone with Zach at the gate at the approximate time of the murder. The facts spoke for themselves. Jake McQuaid had motive *and* opportunity. Two strikes…

When Cam returned to the Rover, Frani busied herself by applying her lipstick. He slipped the Rover in gear and drove through the snow-clogged streets toward the hospital. Due to the storm, the streets of Cedar Bluff were empty of traffic. Sensible people were indoors, keeping warm in front of their fireplaces. Only those who dealt with the extraordinary aspects of society would be out; lawmen, rescue personnel, reporters.

Frani leaned back against the seat, massaging her temples. The hours of stress and the tight rein she was holding on her emotions had conspired to give her a whopping tension headache. Her nerves felt ragged and her grief had swelled again to knot in her throat.

And to top it all off, Cam presented a whole catalogue of problems. How was she going to deal with him?

Although she wanted the kind of information that only he could give, concerning Pamela Jessup, she knew Cam's vested interests were keenly aimed at protecting his family.

If she wanted the unvarnished truth about Pamela Jessup and Jake McQuaid, she could ill afford to alienate the man. But could she trust him? Logic told her to tread lightly, say little and keep her own counsel.

But there was something about Cam that made her think she could trust him. Something that seemed decent and honorable. Zach would have scoffed at that emotional assessment. *Stick to the facts, Frani,* he would have said.

Fact: No one could muddy a murder investigation better than the good sheriff.

Fact: No one could initiate a cover-up as easily or effectively.

Although intuition told her to trust, she had no real basis in logic to support that emotion. No corroboration. No substantiation. Not yet, anyway.

Frani glanced toward those broad shoulders and the hard outline of his thigh encased in tight, soft denim and realized Cam wasn't the only one she couldn't afford to trust tonight. With his clean citrus-and-leather scent teasing her nose and his overwhelmingly masculine presence invading her senses, she had to wonder—how long she could trust herself?

ONCE INSIDE the three-story county hospital, Cam led the way through clean, white corridors. The hallways were quiet, unnaturally so. The snowfall outside seemed to muffle the normal day-to-day activity within the hospital walls, resulting in a thudding stillness.

As sheriff, Cam had never minded a winter storm. Crime

slowed to nothing and his office switched to rescue mode, digging through to people who had lost power, supplying transportation and assistance to those who required medical attention, and aiding travelers who found themselves stranded on the road.

Of course, he wasn't the sheriff at the moment. Joe Bradley had that job. The heavy snow would be a mixed blessing for his official replacement, as well.

On the plus side, bad weather kept visitors away from town. For a few more hours, Joe wouldn't be bothered by interference from other law-enforcement officials or the flock of reporters who would no doubt be descending on the town. Unfortunately, the snowfall created an obstacle to the investigation at the Circle Q. Physical traces of the perpetrator would be obliterated. So far, the search for the murder weapon had proved futile and this storm wouldn't help.

"Nice hospital," Frani commented.

Cam pulled himself out of his thoughts to reply. "Yes, ma'am," he drawled. "No coal-oil lamps and poker-playing docs with Bowie knives."

When she smiled he chuckled softly.

"Actually, we have reason to be proud of this facility. It's the best hospital in three counties. Our flight-for-life chopper covers a lot of territory."

"What about forensics?" she asked.

"More than adequate. If there was a question, we'd ship Zach's body to Grand Junction or Denver. But in this case, the cause of death is straightforward. Nothing our coroner can't handle."

"An autopsy," she said. Her voice had taken on a slightly breathy quality, as though she couldn't quite get enough oxygen. "I hadn't even considered that, but, of course, there will have to be one."

"After you make the positive identification."

Her eyelids flickered nervously, and her gaze slid from wall to wall. For a minute, he thought she might take off running again.

What was going on with her? She looked scared and shaken. This had to be hard for her. Having seen her throw herself on Zach's body at the crime scene, Cam knew just how deeply she could hurt. What a contradiction to the driven dynamo he'd witnessed at the *Clarion* offices. Working toward her precious deadline, she'd seemed as tough as rawhide, proud to be part of a profession that Cam considered frivolous at best. In his opinion, the state of justice in this country would be a helluva lot better off if reporters stuck to the written word, and left fact-finding to the authorities.

And that's why he had to get shed of her soon. He needed the freedom and latitude to conduct his own unofficial investigation. He could just imagine her reporter's mind having a field day with that bit of information.

But he still felt responsible for her safety. Sharing that concern with Joe, he'd received little reassurance of the department's ability to protect her. There was a murder investigation under way, after all, and their small department would be stretched to capacity handling the weight of that. Keeping tabs on the independent, defiant redhead would not be easy, even under normal circumstances.

For the time being, the task of protecting Frani Landon fell to him, almost by default. The job, however, was not without some benefit, he thought. In order to get a handle on the murder, he needed to know everything Zach knew. And what better place to start gathering that information than from Zach's assistant? He needed information. And that was *all* he needed, he reminded himself. That he felt himself strongly attracted to the maddening redhead was nothing but a purely physical response. The tug he felt pulling him toward her, just when he should have been backing away, was something he didn't want, or need. *She's the wrong woman, McQuaid,* he reminded himself, *in the wrong place at the wrong time.*

Jake's future and the future happiness of his family depended on his ability to keep that indisputable fact firmly in mind. As evidenced by her steely determination this afternoon, Francesca Landon was out to get a story. And that story, if and when she broke, could destroy the people he cared most for in the world.

Within a few minutes, Cam located the coroner in the basement lab, and accompanied the doctor and Frani to the single-room morgue at the far end of a basement corridor.

Outside the closed door, the coroner turned to Frani. "Are you ready to do this, miss?"

She nodded and the doctor looked to Cam for confirmation.

"She'll be fine," Cam said. This wasn't the first time he'd accompanied a next of kin for an identification. He'd seen a myriad of reactions, from numbed silence to hysteria. Whatever her reaction, Cam could take care of Frani.

"He's over there," the doctor said when they entered the room.

Frani drew in a deep breath and straightened her shoulders. In the fluorescent overhead lights, her complexion paled to ashen. "Let's get this over with."

Cam followed them across the chilly room. There was only enough room for three stainless steel tables. Only one of them was occupied.

The coroner took a position beside the body that had been covered with a white sheet. He looked to Frani.

Stiffly, she nodded, and the coroner peeled back the edge of the cover to reveal Zach Hollingsworth's face.

Cam thought the reporter looked cynical even in death. Beneath sunken cheeks, his full lips twisted in what seemed to be an eternal smirk.

Frani nodded. "It's Zach," she said and then she stumbled back a few steps before she spun away from the body, bumping into the table behind her, causing it to crash against the wall. Reacting to the loud noise, she whirled again.

Her eyes were wild and glassy. She clung to the edge of the table for support, and for a moment Cam thought she might faint.

"I—I can't breathe," she stammered as he moved up beside her. "Get me out of here. Please!"

Her slender body slumped against his as he ushered her out of the room and into the hallway. She gasped, as though she'd been holding her breath and suddenly remembered to breathe. Her face had lost all color.

"Frani?"

"I—I just need to…sit down," she said.

Still supporting her, he eased her down onto a plastic chair beside the door.

Her breath was coming in short gasps and her whole body was shaking.

"Bend over," Cam ordered. "Put your head between your knees."

She shook her head. "I—I'm fine."

"Do it, Frani. You're hyperventilating."

When she hesitated, he put his hand on the back of her head and eased her gently but firmly forward.

Bent over at the waist, with her hair obscuring her face, she muttered to herself. "He's gone. He's really gone."

"Breathe, Frani. Come on, now, I don't want you to pass out on me."

She obeyed and took long, slow, ragged breaths. When

she straightened, she was still shaking, but at least she was breathing normally.

The coroner joined them and handed Cam a paper cup filled with water. He pressed it into Fran's hands. "Drink."

Though her fingers trembled, she managed to slug back the water. Then she doubled over on the chair again and rested her head on her knees. Her shoulders quaked with silent sobs.

The coroner looked over her head at Cam. "I need a signature. Before I release the body, I'll need authorization from his attorney."

"I'll take care of that," Cam said.

The doctor motioned Cam to move a few steps away from Frani before he said in a low voice, "I'll perform the autopsy tonight. If there are no objections from the sheriff's office, the body can be released tomorrow."

Cam nodded. "I'll let her know."

The coroner left them alone, and Cam sat beside Frani, watching helplessly as the grief poured out of her without a sound.

Less than an hour ago, she'd stalled making this identification, claiming her deadline took precedence. Now, she was completely undone by grief.

For the life of him, Cam couldn't get a handle on this woman. Tough one minute, wrenchingly vulnerable the next. The contradiction moved him. Clearly there was much more to Frani Landon than met the eye.

Wanting, almost needing to console her, he rested his hand on her back and lightly massaged. She sat up, leaned back against the wall and stared straight ahead with bloodshot eyes. Cam moved his hand to her nape and continued massaging and soothing. Her auburn hair brushed against his hand. Even in the harsh hospital light, the strands shimmered with rich, vibrant life.

"I'm sorry," she said finally. "Zach always accused me of being too emotional."

"Nothing wrong with emotions."

"There is if you're a reporter." She exhaled a long, shuddery sigh. "A reporter needs to maintain distance, to achieve objectivity. Somehow I have to keep myself separated from the story."

"And you have," he said. At least she'd given it one monumental try. "Despite everything, you met your deadline."

She snorted lightly. "Yeah. My deadline. So why don't I feel better?" Her gaze drifted toward the morgue. "Damn it, I'm really going to miss that old man."

He slipped the paperwork onto her lap. "The coroner needs your signature. And he said—"

"I heard him." She took the pen Cam held and scribbled her name. "I'll make arrangements for his body to be flown back to Chicago."

Though her strength seemed to be returning, she allowed the pen to slide out of her hand as she leaned back against the wall, and closed her eyes. When she spoke, her voice was a whisper. "I started working for Zach when I was twenty-two, just an intern fresh out of school. I was in awe. Meeting him the first time, I couldn't even speak. When I tried, my voice came out a pathetic squeak." She opened her eyes and for the first time turned to look at Cam. "He just looked at me for a moment, took a deep drag off his ever-present cigarette, and then he asked me if I was a reporter or Minnie Mouse."

A shadow of a smile crossed her lips, but the humor didn't reach her eyes.

"And you became a reporter," Cam said. "And a good one, I'll bet."

She sighed. "I hope so. Zach always said I had promise. He taught me everything."

"I'm sorry, Frani."

She rose slowly. "Not as sorry as you're going to be if it turns out your father killed him."

OUTSIDE, STINGING ice crystals hit Frani's cheeks like painful tears. Without Zach, she felt so completely alone, not the first time she'd experienced that kind of aching loneliness, but for some reason this time the hurt seemed much deeper.

She climbed into the passenger side of Cam's police Rover and stared out at the snow as he brushed and scraped the windows again.

All her thoughts were fixed on Zach, on her own personal loss. She'd told the truth when she said they'd been like family to each other. Together, they'd shared not only a working relationship but a friendship, one that went deeper than either of them could have ever imagined. Zach, with his string of broken relationships and no children, had operated strictly solo until Frani had come along. She'd never known why he'd decided to give her a chance to work with him, but deep down, she suspected he'd glimpsed some aspects of himself in her.

During those first months, working together, they'd slipped easily into a mentor/protégé relationship. Gradually, that relationship changed, and for the past three or four years, Zach had treated Frani more like a daughter than an assistant or a protégé, or even a friend.

Delighted and gratified by the respect and admiration Zach offered, Frani had thrived under his guidance and what she could only call—though he showed it in his own prickly way—his devotion.

She'd never known that kind of love, having grown up feeling distanced from her own father. It had been a distance she'd never understood until one night she discovered the truth.

When she stopped to think about it, she realized her own family history had been her very first scoop.

Her mother's revelation that the man she called daddy was not really her father made for startling headlines in Frani's adolescent brain.

The deep, dark family secret came out in answer to the innocent question: *Why am I the only redhead in the family?* Both of her parents and her two older sisters had dark, almost black hair. Frani looked different. She felt different. She *was* different. And that night, she'd found out why.

"Your father and I decided there was no sense ruining everyone's life over one little lapse in judgment," her mother had said. "Just remember, Frani, he's a good man. He's given you his name and security. He stood by me and gave me a second chance and agreed to raise you like his own. Not every man would have acted so honorably. We owe him a great debt."

Devastated by the truth, Frani felt disconnected from the family. But at the same time, she remembered feeling a measure of relief finally understanding why her father had never been able to show her the kind of love he gave so freely to her sisters. Even then, it seemed the truth was something she craved.

James Landon had done the right thing, he'd lived up to his familial obligations, given her a name, put a roof over her head, paid for her braces and sent her to college. He'd done his duty.

But to Frani, duty without love was the worst kind of

hypocrisy. Maybe that's what she'd admired most about Zach Hollingsworth. The old man had been a lot of things—cynical, impatient, demanding—but he was real. The genuine article. Not a single hypocritical bone in his body. He had his own code. Black and white. Simple, straightforward, unyielding: Uncover the truth and damn the consequences. At times his view of the world had seemed too harsh, especially to a young woman who continued to be fascinated by endless shades of gray.

When Cam climbed back into the car, Frani pulled herself out of her somber reverie.

"You're staying with Addie tonight."

She nodded. "Yes. In the room above the newspaper office."

"Tired?"

"To the bone."

"Is there anything I can do for you, someone I can call?"

"There's no one," she said, then added quickly, "I'll be fine, thanks."

"Don't ask and don't expect anything from anyone. Is that how it is with you, Frani Landon?"

She turned to face him directly, shocked by his dead-on accurate description of the way she'd learned to cope with life. "I find it cuts down on the time I spend disappointed."

"I'm sorry," he said, and something in his eyes told her he meant it.

She sighed. "Don't be. I usually get what I want and make my life work."

He slipped the key into the ignition, but didn't turn it. "What do you want, Frani?" he asked.

"The truth. Information. Zach's killer to be brought to justice."

"And you're wondering if I want the same thing."

The man was nothing if not direct. Unsettled as she was, Frani found herself admiring his candor. "Frankly, yes."

"Well, you can stop wondering." He turned the key and gunned the engine to life. "The truth is exactly what I'm after."

"Then maybe we can help each other and both get what we want."

"Sounds sensible," he said. "You were close to Zach. If anyone would know what he was working on before his death, it would be you."

"And you have the inside track on the investigation," Frani reminded him.

"Yes," he admitted. "I guess I do."

"When do we start?" she asked.

"Tonight. The snow is letting up. Come tomorrow morning, there will be reporters as thick as fleas all over town, asking questions. And there are going to be all kinds of law enforcement types, everyone with a badge, from the FBI on down to the highway patrol."

"You're right," Frani said and then remembered Zach's notebook. She'd planned to spend the rest of the night alone poring over it. "But I don't know if I can handle anything else tonight."

"Addie can help. She could take notes."

"Tomorrow morning," Frani insisted. "First thing."

"I'll swing by my office and then come over to the *Clarion* office around seven."

Though her thought processes were sluggish, Frani realized that something was wrong with this picture. "Wait a minute, I thought you said you were on a leave of absence."

"I am," he replied. "But I'm still my father's son. I know he didn't kill Zach, and I intend to find out who did."

She wasn't too exhausted to remind him what he was up

against. "Fact: Jake McQuaid had opportunity. He was at the crime scene at the approximate time of the murder. Fact: He had a motive. He was protecting the woman you call Susan."

"Fact," Cam countered. "Jake McQuaid's no fool. If he was going to commit murder, he would choose a better place than his own doorstep. Fact: My father is no murderer. He's lived his whole life by a code of honor."

"That code," she said, remembering the father who had fulfilled his responsibilities but withheld his love, "can mean different things to different people."

"Granted," he allowed. "But to my father it's all black and white. He knows right from wrong." He pulled the Rover in behind the newspaper offices. "I'll see you in," he said.

"I'll be all right. It isn't that I don't appreciate the offer—" whatever else he was, Cam McQuaid was a gentleman, "—it's just that—oh, never mind. Men! I get so sick and tired of them thinking I need to be protected." Her declaration had come out of nowhere, with far more emotion than she'd intended. In the darkness, she could feel Cam studying her face.

"Why do I get the feeling we're not talking about me walking you to the door?"

Frustrated, exhausted and close to tears, Frani pushed the passenger door open with an angry shove. "He could have waited for me," she declared. "He could have insisted I bust my tail to get here. If he had agreed to let me be a part of this, maybe he wouldn't have gone and gotten himself killed."

In the glow of the dome light, Frani saw Cam's eyes grow dark and unreadable. "Or maybe you would have died beside him."

Chapter Four

At four-thirty-five that morning, Frani lay wide-awake in an unfamiliar bed, staring up at the acoustic-tile ceiling in the makeshift apartment above the offices of the *Clarion.* Her slumber had been restless, a segue from one nightmare to the next, with each fearful image leading to the same inescapable conclusion: Zach was dead, and Frani was on her own. Again.

When she exhaled a sigh, Addie shifted on the double bed beside her. Frani held herself rigid, hoping she hadn't wakened her bedmate. Addie had insisted on staying with her, determined to be up early to assist Frani should she need help for the stories she'd be faxing to the *Daily Herald.*

Frani appreciated Addie's support and valued the older woman's journalistic skills. It was a shame that Addie and Zach hadn't gotten together, she thought sadly; they'd have been a formidable couple.

When Addie's regular peaceful breathing resumed, Frani slipped out of bed. The long, open room stretched the full length of the building. There were no walls except those that enclosed the tiny bathroom. The bed, a bureau and a rag rug defined the bedroom area, near the stairs. In the carcerated in the federal penitentiary near Salt Lake City, the getaway driver had been paroled four years ago. The ex-con's name was Bud Coleman. According to Zach's notes, Coleman lived in a remote town in the Utah desert. From what she could gather, Zach had been planning to visit Coleman next.

Frani mentally shuffled the bits of data as she sipped black coffee. How did each fact relate to the others? Was there anyone, besides Pamela Jessup herself, who would have been hurt by Zach's story? Frani's level of concentration was so intense she was surprised by the knock at the back door. Could it be Cam already? If she remembered correctly, he'd said he'd swing by at seven. It was barely six-thirty.

After hiding Zach's notebook in the desk drawer, she went to the door. "Who is it?"

The response was mumbled.

"Cam?"

The reply sounded like an affirmative, but she couldn't be sure. How annoying! Cam was carrying his image as the strong, silent type a bit too far.

She disarmed Addie's alarm system and unfastened the locks, prepared to lecture Cam about the value of speaking up. It would serve him right if she'd kept him waiting in the cold for another minute or two.

Keeping the chain fastened, Frani opened the door a crack. In a teasing voice, she called out, "I didn't hear you, sir. Could you please identify yourself more clearly?"

An icy chill blew through the open inches. Outside, the night had faded to a blue-edged dawn. "Cam?"

She peeked. Standing on the concrete stoop was a stocky man in a ski mask. He was holding a gun.

Frani jumped back as the stranger threw his weight against the door. The chain strained, but held.

Heart pounding, Frani raced to Addie's desk where she'd seen a pistol in the bottom drawer. Locked! The drawer was locked and she didn't have a clue where to find the key.

With hard, methodical thuds, the man pummeled the door. The slender chain twisted on its hinge.

Desperately, Frani searched through the clutter on the desk. She yelled, "Stay back! I have a gun!"

Her warning was answered with a muffled pop, a sound so utterly benign she almost didn't realize it had come from a gun. The splintered wood paneling behind her, however, left no doubt.

In horror, she saw the tip of a gun poking through the crack in the door. She ducked behind the desk, seconds before the next shot shattered the lamp on Addie's desk.

Now more desperate than ever to defend herself, Frani crept around the corner of Addie's desk and pulled open the center drawer. To her utter relief, her fingers closed around the set of keys buried beneath a pile of paper clips. Frantically, she flipped through the keys to find one small enough to fit the desk.

The wood frame of the door screeched as bolts tore loose. The chain was clinging by a single screw. She found what she hoped was the right key and shoved it into the lock. It turned, and the next thing she knew she held the gun in her hand.

Just as the door took another powerful hit, Frani slipped the safety off and fired blindly at the door. She heard a muffled curse, and then silence.

The realization that her bullet might have hit its mark crashed into her consciousness. She'd never shot a gun in her life, much less at another human being.

"Frani?" she heard Addie call from upstairs. "What's going on down there? Are you all right?"

"Call the police!" Frani shouted. "Hurry, Addie."

Still holding the gun in one trembling hand, she stood straining to hear the slightest sound. Frigid air seeped through the door that was still clinging to the nearly ruined safety chain. Moving on shaking legs across the room, Frani stood to one side of the door and listened. The only sound was the drumming of her own heart, Addie's muffled voice on the telephone upstairs, and the whisper of the forced-air heater as it clicked on across the room. Her would-be attacker was either dead or gone.

With a quick, sure movement, she slammed the door closed and slid the dead bolt in place.

Upstairs, a door opened. "They're on their way," Addie said. "What in blue blazes is going on down here?" she asked as she descended the stairs.

It took a full ten seconds for Frani to find her voice.

"I think someone just tried to kill me."

CAM'S EIGHT-MILE DRIVE from his ranch to Cedar Bluffs was accompanied by George Strait on the CD player instead of the usual squawks from the police radio. Technically, he wasn't on duty. For the time being, Joe Bradley was sheriff, and Cam didn't feel compelled to listen in on the county's business this morning.

Besides, he had his own concerns to consider. Late last night, he'd learned that his father and Susan had pulled up stakes and fled the Circle Q to stay with friends in nearby Glenwood Springs. They'd made the move on the advice of their attorney. Although Jake had raised holy hell, and said it looked like he was running scared, his attorney had finally convinced the old man the move would make everyone's life easier, at least until the expected media frenzy died down.

Cam was still having a hard time believing his small

county could be the focus of so much attention. But as Frani had pointed out, it wasn't every day an internationally known, prize-winning journalist was gunned down. Reporters from all venues took that kind of story personally. She likened it to the reaction of every cop when a fellow officer went down. And the fact that the prime suspect was related to the sheriff made this the kind of story that sold newspapers and increased ratings.

The only person, other than Cam and Cy, who knew where Jake and Susan were staying was Harold T. Cisneros. Harold T. had warned Jake not to leave the state, but he'd agreed getting the two of them away from Cedar Bluffs was probably a good idea.

Cam was relieved to have his father and Susan out of the line of fire. According to Susan, the telephone at the Circle Q had rung without ceasing yesterday. Today, it would only be worse. The weather had cleared enough for travel, which meant there would be a horde of reporters descending on Cedar Bluffs, camping outside the gates of the Circle Q, waiting like vultures for the smallest scrap of information.

Jake didn't need that kind of excitement. Whether the old man liked to admit it or not, he was still recuperating from a stroke. And then there was the risk of someone snapping a photo of Susan. Thinking about what that kind of publicity could lead to made Cam shudder. For the time being, he had convinced Frani to hold off on Susan's story. There was no way he'd have that kind of persuasive power over any other reporter.

In the murky light of predawn, Cam arrived in town. On an impulse, he drove past the sheriff's office, deciding to check in at the *Clarion* offices first. If there had been any late-night developments or leaks from any source to the press, Frani would know. If there was a story breaking, he could at least give Susan a head's up.

When he pulled in behind the *Clarion* offices, he found Joe Bradley's Rover parked in his spot. It wasn't even seven. Was it possible Frani had gotten herself into trouble already?

As he approached the door, he spotted the scarlet dots in the snow. Cam knew what he was seeing. He'd been a lawman long enough to recognize fresh blood.

His heart lurched against his chest as a single word exploded in his mind: *Frani!*

If anything had happened to her, he'd never forgive himself. He charged up to the door and grabbed the knob, but it didn't turn. Pounding on it with his fist, he shouted, "Open up, Addie! It's Cam."

He heard a shuffling sound on the other side of the door and Addie's voice telling him to hang on. The moment she opened the door, Cam brushed past her into the room. "Where is she? Where's Frani? Is she all right?"

"She's fine," Addie assured him. "Now, don't go getting yourself all worked up."

"I saw Joe's car outside. And the blood... Addie, what's going on?"

"It was Frani."

His heart froze.

"She shot someone."

The breath went out of Cam in a gasp.

Addie's blue eyes squinted in a tense grin. Still wearing her long flannel nightgown under a plaid wool bathrobe, she looked as though she'd been pulled too soon from her bed. "Go out and knock the snow off your boots and then I'll tell you what happened."

Cam did as he was told. Standing at the door cleaning his boots, he noticed the mangled metal safety chain hanging by a single screw. There was a bullet hole at shoulder height in the wall beside him.

He heard the sound of footsteps on the stairs and looked up to see Frani and Joe coming down. Although Addie had already told him Frani was all right, seeing her gave him an unexpected rush of relief.

As she descended the stairs and Joe followed, her mouth moved nonstop. Clearly, she was reading Joe Bradley the riot act. As she talked, her head bobbed for all the world like an angry, redheaded woodpecker.

"Roadblocks," she said, pecking at Joe. "I don't see why not!"

Cam turned to Addie. "Bring me up to speed."

"Frani heard a knock at the door, thought it was you and unlocked the dead bolt. Luckily, she didn't remove the chain. There was a man outside with a gun. He tried to bash the door down, and even took a couple of potshots. Frani found my gun and shot him before he could break in. She said she doesn't know for sure if she hit him, but judging by that blood outside, I think it's safe to say she did. I heard all the commotion and called Joe. By the time I got down here, it was all over and the guy, whoever he was, was gone."

He touched Addie's arm. "How about you? Are you doing okay, Addie?"

She rocked back on her heels. "Don't worry about me, Cam. My only problem is a couple of holes in the wall, nothing a bit of spackle won't fix," she said. "I'm just glad Frani wasn't hurt. You brought her here so she'd be safe, but we know now this is the last place she should be staying."

Cam scowled. "We'll have to think of something else."

"Good luck. She won't admit she needs looking after, but she does."

Cam glanced at the bullet holes in the wall and thought they made for a compelling argument.

"You've got to take care of her, Cam. Believe me, you're the only one who can."

"What makes you think that?" Cam didn't know how he felt playing bodyguard for the contentious green-eyed reporter, but he knew how he'd felt a few minutes ago when he'd feared that something might have happened to her.

"Women just know about these things," Addie told him. "Besides, who else can control her? Just look at her! There's Joe, just trying to do his job, and she's bulldozing right over the top of him."

What Addie said was true. Joe Bradley was over six feet tall, well-muscled and strong enough to wrestle a four-hundred-pound steer to the ground in the rodeo ring. Facing Frani's onslaught of words, however, he seemed shriveled to the size of nervous adolescent.

Joe looked up, saw them both staring and signaled for Cam to rescue him.

"Like it or not," Addie said as they crossed the room together, "she's your problem, Cam."

"Do you suppose we could convince her to go back to Chicago?"

Addie shook her head. "Not a chance. Not until she knows Zach's murderer has been caught."

Cam moved up in front of Frani. The acting sheriff seemed shaken, but Cam wasn't fazed by either her rapid-fire rhetoric or her criticism of the sheriff's department. He knew Frani was mostly bluster. Fussing and fuming were her coping skills, the bravado she used to hide her real emotions. Last night, he'd glimpsed her vulnerability, the tenderness she tried so hard to override with logic and reason.

He nodded a greeting and allowed his amused gaze to slide down her body, taking in the baggy sweater and droopy wool socks. "Frani. Joe."

The acting sheriff nodded gratefully at Cam.

"You know, for a city gal, you're not much of a fashion plate this morning," Cam quipped.

"I haven't had time to look in a mirror," she informed him. "I've been too busy fighting off a gunman. One heck of a town you run here, Sheriff."

Cam let her sarcasm slide off him. "Can you describe him?"

"He had on a bulky parka and a ski mask over his face," she said.

Her description fit half the men in the county, especially on a cold wintry morning like this one. "How tall was he?"

"I don't know. He was trying to beat down the door with one hand and shooting his gun at me with the other. There wasn't time to snap a Polaroid."

"What about the gun?"

She shook her head.

"I don't suppose you saw what kind of vehicle he left in," Cam said. "Or the license plate number."

Again she shook her head. "He could have been riding a wild stallion or driving a tank, for all I know."

Cam glanced at Joe. "Doesn't sound like you have much to go on, Sheriff."

"He's got plenty!" Frani snapped. "And instead of standing around here, he should be getting his deputies out on the street. They should be going door to door looking for eyewitnesses. Apparently, the man was shot. That should help narrow the field of suspects. Check the local motels and see if there are any strangers in town," she told Joe. "And it might be a good idea to talk to the people at the Circle Q."

"If you're referring to Jake and Susan, they're gone," Cam said in a voice strained by the anger Frani's thinly veiled accusation had inspired. "They can't be blamed for this."

"Excuse me?" Joe interrupted. "Where'd Jake take off to?"

"On the advice of their attorney, Jake and Susan have left the Circle Q, but they haven't gone far, if that's what's worrying you. Harold T. gave the move his approval and he knows where and how to reach them."

"I'm going to need access to the grounds and the house," Joe said. "It's a crime scene, Cam."

"The ranch manager and a couple of hired hands are still around. They'll cooperate."

"So Jake and Susan's employees are still in town?"

A muscle in Cam's jaw twitched. The woman was downright insulting. It took some effort, but he squelched his irritation before it took root. To be drawn into anger would weaken his position with Frani, cut him off from the information he needed and lead to a useless argument. He couldn't, however, let her continue making baseless allegations.

"Neither Jake nor Susan killed Zach and they sure as hell did not engineer an attack on you this morning. Now, if Joe thinks it's warranted, he'll question the hands at the Circle Q. But until you have some facts to back up your allegations, I suggest you keep an open mind."

With a tilt of her head, she fixed him with a steady, green-eyed stare. "Good advice," she said. "I suggest we *all* delay judgment until the evidence is in."

The tension between them seemed to ease a bit, and Cam felt he'd made his point.

"We'll check all the hospitals and clinics within a hundred-mile radius,'' Joe said as he moved to the door to see if there were any fingerprints worth lifting.

Addie excused herself and went back upstairs to get dressed.

Frani dropped down onto a chair, at last seeming to run out of steam. "I blew it, didn't I?" She stared down at her hands. "I should have gone outside and looked instead of locking the door."

In Cam's mind, she had reacted perfectly logically. "You did the right thing."

"Maybe, but now the murderer has slipped away again," she said morosely.

"What makes you so sure the man who tried to break in here was the same man who killed Zach?"

"I'm not sure," she said. "But it does make sense. The two incidents have to be connected." She sighed, running a hand through her sleek red hair. "Besides, I haven't been in town long enough to get anybody that ticked off at me."

Despite himself, Cam had to smile, but he kept his comments to himself.

"I just have to believe that whoever wanted to silence Zach has now turned his sights on me. It's well known I worked with him. Whoever killed him must think I know what Zach knew, whatever secrets made him too dangerous to live."

Cam restrained himself once more. It would have been so easy to say, "I told you so." Instead, he merely said, "Go get dressed, Frani. I've got a lot to do today, and you're coming with me."

Her jaw dropped, and she stared up at him in disbelief. "Excuse me, but that sounded suspiciously like an order."

"It was," Cam said. "You need protecting, Frani, and it appears that duty has fallen to me." Despite his own personal reservations, there was no way around the obvious. He couldn't leave her to fend for herself. She'd come out shooting this time, but next time the outcome could be vastly different. "Go on, Frani," he said again. "We have a lot to talk about and a lot of ground to cover."

Without another word, she rose and crossed to the stairs. Though she held her head high, it was hard to reconcile the princess-like attitude of superiority with baggy wool socks drooping around her ankles.

Cam expected her to spin around and shoot off one last remark before she made her exit. Instead, when she looked over her shoulder, she said, "I won't be a minute," in such a small voice, he almost didn't hear. She was shaken, obviously, by the harrowing events of the morning. Her vulnerability struck Cam more powerfully than any show of bravado. Whether he was ready to admit it or not, Cam cared about the lady, despite the fact she seemed ready, willing and more than able to make his life as difficult as possible.

After she'd gone, he crossed to where Joe was examining the door. "You need to alert the state patrol, let them know we have an assailant on the run. Tell them to keep their eyes peeled on the interstate. Warn them not to take any chances. He's wounded, yes, but still armed."

"I'll make the call from my car," Joe said. "Look, Cam, any fool can see I'm not up to this job. Everything's happening too fast. I need you to come back."

Cam shook his head. "Sorry, Joe. I can't do that right now. It wouldn't look right. Not while Jake's still a suspect." Cam clapped Joe on the shoulder. "You're doing just fine, Joe. I'll be around and if you have questions about procedure, contact Harold. He's dying to shine in this spotlight."

"Well, that makes one of us," Joe said miserably, removing his hat to rub his forehead. "The sooner you get back to being sheriff, the better for me."

"I'm mighty pleased you feel that way," Cam said. "On account of I plan to stay sheriff for a long time after this is over."

At the door, he said goodbye to Joe, grateful he had an honest man to serve as his replacement during this difficult time.

Addie came back downstairs and stood leaning against one of the desks with her arms folded below her breasts. Her sharp blue eyes regarded him steadily. "You like her, don't you?"

"Like isn't the word I'd have chosen." He poured a stream of dark liquid into a foam cup. "But, yeah, I guess I do. I know I admire her. She's interesting. Different."

"Interesting," Addie said. "And that would make you interested, wouldn't it?"

Cam merely smiled. He knew better than to engage in a verbal battle with Addie. "Whatever you say, Addie."

"Just be careful not to get *too* interested, Cam. Until this thing is resolved, the two of you are going to be spending a lot of time together and I don't want to see that little gal hurt."

Cam put on an injured expression. "And what about me?" he asked. "Aren't you the least bit worried about your old friend taking on this one-woman army?"

Addie chucked him playfully on the arm. "You know darn well what I mean, Cam McQuaid."

"I'd never take advantage of her, Addie, if that's what's worrying you. You know I'm a gentleman."

She smiled. "Ah, yes. The famous McQuaid code of honor. Just like Jake."

"What exactly are you trying to say, Addie?"

"Well, just look at Jake and Susan. The man would walk

through hell and high water for the woman, even slay a dragon or two, if he had to.''

"The way you talk, one would think Jake was a romantic.''

She took his cup and refilled it. "He is. If there were ever two people more in love than Jake and Susan, I haven't met them. If that isn't romance, what is?''

Cam sipped his coffee and considered. Instead of betraying Susan, Jake had retired as sheriff and moved the family to Colorado. He'd skirted the edges of the code that meant everything to him. "Jake loves the lady, there's never been any doubt about that.''

"Which is exactly why I'm worried about you and Frani. There's something very romantic about a man protecting a woman. One thing leads to another, and before you know it somebody's lost their heart.''

He exhaled with a snort. "You're forgetting something. Frani and I barely tolerate each other.''

At that moment, Frani charged down the stairs with her steel-toed boots clunking heavily with each step. A pair of black leggings defined her well-shaped calves and thighs. On top, she wore a tunic-style sweater in a pastel blue. Her first stop was the fax machine.

"Where's your suitcase?'' Cam asked.

She blinked.

"Turn yourself around,'' Cam said. "Go back upstairs and get packed. I told you you were coming with me.''

"I took that to mean for the day.''

"For a smart woman, you're acting mighty dense,'' he said. "The guy who tried to bust down the door knows you're here. You're moving, Frani. If I can't talk you into leaving Cedar Bluffs and going back to Chicago, then I've got no choice but to do the next best thing for safety's sake.''

"And what exactly would that be, given this town's rapidly rising crime rate?"

"She can stay at my house," Addie said. "I've got double locks on all the doors and a German shepherd who will adore sleeping at the foot of her bed."

"Thanks, Addie," Cam said. "I think that might be a good solution, at least for the next couple of nights."

Frani added her thanks.

"But you're spending the day with me," he said simply. "And if anyone does any more shooting, that someone will be me."

FRANI DESPISED anyone giving her orders, but she had to acknowledge the validity of what Cam had suggested. There was no point in taking unnecessary risks, and she certainly didn't want Addie at risk on her account. Still shaken from this morning's episode, she had to admit staying somewhere else tonight would make her feel less spooked. If her would-be attacker was still in the area—if he was still alive—at least she could make it a little more difficult for him should he decide to come after her again. Besides, the more time she spent with Cam, the better access she'd have to breaking news regarding the investigation.

"I'll get my things," she told Cam, but before she could reach the stairs, the fax machine sounded.

Addie crossed the room and peeled off the message.

"What is it?" Frani asked.

"It's for you. From your editor at the *Daily Herald*."

Frani crossed to accept the message Addie held out to her. She skimmed the words and smiled. "My managing editor sends his congratulations on a well-done front-page article."

"Wonderful!" Addie exclaimed.

"But he's sending two more experienced reporters to handle the continuing coverage of the murder investigation. They're coming in on a charter flight and should be here before noon. I am instructed to turn over all of my notes and give them the key to Zach's filing cabinet in Chicago."

Cam's expression was sympathetic.

"They can't do that to you!" Addie declared.

"Oh, yes they can. And they have," Frani said. "It's a tough business and I have to live with it." Despite these accepting words, her mind was racing through alternatives. Or did she?

There was no way she could accept Lloyd's decision. Although her first concern was finding the murderer, she was still a reporter, and, damn it, this was her story. She'd worked with Zach for years. By rights, the story of his death belonged to her. She was the only one capable of decoding the information in his notebook, the only one who really realized its importance. She was not prepared to hand that power over to anyone.

But how could she ignore a direct order from her editor? Technically, Zach's research, whether in the form of his files or his notebook, was the property of the newspaper that issued his paycheck. There had to be some way around this complication. She'd have to give it some thought. In the meantime, she meant to get the jump on every other reporter.

She crossed to the desk where she'd tucked Zach's little notebook for safekeeping this morning. The next person Zach had intended to interview was a member of the gang that had robbed the Salt Lake City bank, the driver of the getaway car, Bud Coleman. He seemed like a logical place to start.

Turning to Cam, she said, "I have an idea."

"As long as it doesn't involve endangering yourself or anybody else—especially me—I'm listening."

"You want to get me out of town, right?"

His expression mirrored a wealth of suspicion. "I can only hope that means you want me to drive you to the airport so you can go back to Chicago and give your editor a piece of your mind."

Frani smiled. "Appealing as that sounds, I can't afford to waste the time. But what would you say to a trip to Utah? That's where I need to go. Want to tag along, cowboy?"

Chapter Five

Within two hours, Frani had her wish. They were on their way to Utah, near Zion National Park. In a plane!

Like a hawk on the wing, the two-seater Piper Cub soared through the startlingly blue Western skies. Below them, the landscape unfolded like a topographical map. Ribbons of highway wound across fields lightly dusted with snow. Ravines carved dark serrated shadows. The flattop mesas and vast valleys alternated like swelling waves, while jagged ridges reached toward them, giant natural monuments.

"It's breathtaking," Frani said into the microphone attached to the headset. "It must come in pretty handy for your department having a sheriff who's also a pilot."

"It's the best way to cover a lot of distance quickly," he said. "What Chaparral County lacks in population, it makes up for in acreage."

Low population was an understatement. Few settled areas interrupted the natural panorama. "It's a fascinating area. Why don't more people live out here?"

"Water," he said simply. "You're looking at what they call the high desert. It's obvious when you see it from up here. Most towns are located near rivers and creeks."

Unaccustomed to thinking in terms of nature and development, Frani appreciated his authoritative insight. And she could tell from the warm tone in his voice that Cam felt truly connected to this rugged country. "Tell me more."

"The area we're headed toward is part of the Great Basin that goes from Salt Lake to Death Valley in California. It's arid land, not much good for farming or ranching." Disdainfully, he added, "Except for sheep."

"Spoken like a true cattle man. You mentioned a ranch. Do you have cattle?"

"I run a few head."

"In addition to being sheriff? Well, you're a regular cowboy Renaissance man, aren't you?" she teased. "You dabble in a little bit of everything. Law enforcement, ranching, flying...where do you find the time?"

"It doesn't seem like much," he said. "It's how I was brought up."

"Is this your plane?" She couldn't imagine how he afforded an airplane and a ranch on a sheriff's salary. "Isn't it expensive?"

"I manage."

She waited, but he didn't elaborate. When the subject turned to his personal life, Cam wasn't an easy interview. But Frani's specialty was ferreting out information, and it was important to try to pry open his memories. By the end of this trip to Utah, she planned to have garnered enough details to write the Pamela Jessup story, when the time came.

"How long will this flight take?" she asked.

"Three, maybe three and a half hours."

"That long?"

"We're not flying in a jet, Frani. A single-engine prop doesn't go much faster than a car. The difference is we go in a straight line."

"As the crow flies, as you cowboys would put it."

He chuckled softly and Frani craned her neck for a view of the high Rockies receding behind them, then, facing forward, she gazed through the windscreen past the whirring nose propeller. The incredible grandeur of this wide, open countryside seemed foreign, like an alien landscape—and yet oddly compelling.

"I like it," she said. Sweeping across the sky exhilarated her senses, making her feel as if anything was possible. In fact, the mood of the West seemed to inspire her to stretch her capabilities, to expand and reach higher.

She reached across the small space in the cockpit to touch the sleeve of his split leather jacket. "Thank you, Cam. I appreciate you hauling me all the way out here."

When he smiled, she realized this was the first time she'd seen him completely relaxed. The tension lines across his forehead smoothed. Without his ever-present Stetson, she could appreciate the thickness of his dark, wavy hair.

His well-shaped lips curved lazily. Perfect lips, she thought. Eminently kissable.

"I figured you for the type who'd like flying," he said. His voice through the headset sounded like an echo, resonating over the noise of the small engine. "Some folks get nervous traveling in a plane this size, but you didn't strike me as someone with a fear of flying. Or a fear of anything, for that matter."

"Some things scare me," she admitted. Her gaze drifted to the side window beyond the gleaming white wing. "I'm terrified of public speaking."

"You?"

"I freeze like an ice pop. My father used to get so frustrated with me. He's a history professor at University of Chicago. He routinely lectures to auditorium classes of more than two hundred. I used to sit in the back of the room watching him, thinking I could learn from him how to overcome my fear.''

"Did it work?"

"Not really."

Her father had been so easy and comfortable in his classroom. His enthusiasm for history, especially the military strategies of World Wars I and II, flowed from him and inspired his students. When she went to his classes, Frani pretended he was talking only to her, sharing his knowledge with her, taking care that she understood. From a distance, it was even possible to imagine he might actually love her.

"Then you didn't inherit your father's ability," Cam said.

Usually, she didn't talk about her family. The memories were too painful, but up here, alone with Cam, her defenses seemed to have disappeared. "He isn't my real father."

"You're adopted?"

"That would have been easier," she said. "My mother had an affair, and I was the unhappy result."

Soaring through impossibly boundless skies, hiding her secret pain seemed unnecessary. "I didn't figure it out until I was old enough to realize that my red hair and green eyes didn't fit the family pattern."

"But your father—your mother's husband—stuck with the family. He raised you?"

"Yes. He even gave me his name. He did the right thing," she said, unable to hide the bitterness in her voice. "He stayed and did the honorable thing, but he could never quite bring himself to accept me."

Even as a little girl, she remembered throwing her arms around him and feeling him draw away from her. "Sometimes I think duty and honor are highly overrated qualities."

"Is that why you formed such a strong attachment to Zach Hollingsworth? Looking for a replacement father?"

"Partly," she admitted. "Zach liked me. He encouraged me."

And he was gone. The realization intruded like a storm cloud on the otherwise perfect sky, and Frani recalled her true purpose in flying to Utah. "Maybe we should use this time to discuss the case."

"Good idea," he said. "Let's start with the assumption that I was right, and you were wrong."

When she swiveled her head to stare at his profile, she noticed the playful quirk at the corner of his mouth. Apparently, this was Cam's idea of teasing. "Not necessarily."

"Admit it, Frani. I was right. I suspected somebody might come after you, and somebody did."

She swallowed hard, remembering. Only a few hours ago, she'd struggled with an armed man intent on harming her. A sudden rush of fear trembled through her. If she hadn't kept the chain fastened, he would have burst inside the offices. She couldn't have stopped him. "I could have been killed." The strangled whisper was almost unrecognizable to her own ears.

"But you weren't." He reached over and rested his hand on her forearm. "You did a good job of defending yourself."

"If it had been a good job, I would have killed him." The screaming outrage she'd felt during the horrific minutes of the attack and immediately afterward had faded, leaving behind an echo of terror, a terrible awareness of her own vulnerability. "Why would someone want to kill me?"

"Just as you said—for the same reason they thought they had to eliminate Zach," he said. "You know too much. Or at least someone thinks you do. Zach's investigation was leading him to information that your attacker must assume you now possess."

"But that doesn't make sense. If I knew something worth dying for, don't you think I'd know what it was?"

"Let's start with what you do know," he said.

This conversation wasn't going according to her plans. Frani had intended to extract nuggets of information from him. Not vice versa.

"Okay," she said with a sigh. "I know Zach was looking into two general areas. One was the bank robbery. Which is why we're on our way to Utah. To interview the guy who drove the getaway car, Bud Coleman."

"And what are we hoping to find out from him?"

"I honestly don't know."

"Is it possible," Cam supposed, "that the money from the bank robbery is hidden somewhere and Zach was about to locate it?"

"No. Most of the money from the robbery was recovered at the time of the arrest."

In Zach's notebook, he'd written a dollar sign and a question mark beside the names of the bank robbers. But the cash wasn't the motive. In fact, as bank robberies went, the Eisman gang—which consisted of Eisman, Pamela and Bud—had been spectacularly unsuccessful.

Without betraying the source of her information, Frani said, "I think Zach's desire to talk to Coleman had something to do with money, but it couldn't have been the money stolen from the bank."

Wryly, he said, "Money is at the root of most crimes. Maybe we'll find a cash trail, yet."

As they retreated into their private thoughts, they flew in relative silence, accompanied by the endless whir of the plane's engines. When five minutes stretched to ten, Frani realized how different this inquiry was.

When she and Zach worked together on an investigation, they'd talked it to death, running one scenario after another until her head spun.

Obviously, quiet contemplation came naturally to Cam. He didn't need to fill the empty air with words. A confident man, she thought, content with himself and his abilities. Independent, smart, savvy.

"Here's a thought," he said finally. "*Somebody* had to finance this crime."

"What do you mean?"

"They used automatic weapons, which aren't cheap. And they had a getaway car. The money for those things had to come from somewhere."

She liked his thinking. "So there might have been somebody else involved in the planning of the robbery, or at least in financing it."

"Maybe," Cam said. "Maybe there was someone else, someone who wasn't named, or ever arrested and prosecuted."

Excitedly, she completed the rationale. "And that person would definitely have something to hide. He wouldn't want Zach digging into the past, especially if Susan could identify him."

"Staying out of federal prison is a powerful motive for murder," Cam said.

She'd stared at Zach's notes for hours without making that deduction. "Hey, cowboy. I think you might just have hit on something. Good job!"

Impulsively, she unfastened her safety belt, flung her arms around his neck and kissed his cheek.

She hadn't really meant anything by the impulsive gesture. In the past, she'd often hugged Zach as a friendly gesture, like a daughter and father.

But this nearness to Cam felt completely different. Instantly, she was aware of the warmth and clean scent of his skin. Slowly, she pulled away from him and sank back into the copilot's seat. Her lips were still tingling with the taste of him, an electric jolt that seemed to reverberate through her nerve endings. Oh, Lord! What had she done?

She couldn't seem to tear her gaze away from him and he didn't seem to want to stop looking at her, either. His eyes confronted her with an undeniably sexual energy. He aroused the passionate side of her nature, and she felt an irresistible urge to kiss him again. This time, for real.

She adjusted her headset. "I'm sorry, Cam. I didn't mean to—"

"Please, don't apologize," he drawled. "Or you'll ruin my whole day."

Mesmerized, she watched as he unsnapped his seat belt, removed his headset and reached toward her. Gently, he lifted the earphones from her head. The sound of the engine vibrated through her.

When he leaned closer, her eyelids fluttered closed and she held her breath, anticipating the taste of his lips. His hand, pleasantly roughened with calluses, stroked her cheek.

He whispered in her ear. "Let me show you how we kiss out here in the West."

His mouth slanted across hers. Slowly, he savored her lips. His tongue slipped inside her mouth, quite simply taking her breath away. Her heart soared with the wind through the blue skies around them. He ended the kiss by tugging her lower lip gently with his teeth.

Eyelids still closed, she leaned back in the copilot's seat and sighed. Blissful contentment warred with an aching desire for more. More kissing, more caresses, more passion. Her vaguely considered plan to romance information out of him seemed to have backfired. At that moment, Frani would have told him all the secret longings of her heart.

She consoled herself knowing Cam, this cowboy with his own special code, was far too much of a gentleman to ask.

THE MINUTE HE'D stopped kissing Frani, Cam started questioning his sanity. He sure as hell hadn't planned this. He wasn't a man who started something he couldn't finish. And there was no way he could take this situation to the conclusion his body demanded. What point was there in forming a personal relationship with Francesca Landon?

Such a pretty name... His thoughts drifted back to her again. *Francesca*. If he made love to her, he would repeat that name over and over and...

With as much self-control as he could muster, Cam forced his thoughts away from her and concentrated on landing the plane.

Twenty minutes later, the Jeep he'd rented after they'd touched down in Springdale plowed over a bump and he told himself again that there wasn't going to be any lovemaking between them. She was just plain Frani, not Francesca. A woman who had stumbled into his life at exactly the wrong moment. The wrong woman, at the wrong time. His attraction to her could only spell trouble.

"It's warm out here," she remarked, tugging him away from his thoughts of her.

"Come nightfall, it'll be plenty cold."

She pushed up the sleeves of her light blue sweater. Her forearms were slender, but toned. Her wrists tapered to delicate fingers that she raked through her thick russet hair.

Bending over in her seat, she fought with the laces on her boots. "I'm going to change into a pair of sneakers."

From the first moment he'd laid eyes on her, he'd been wanting to tear off those steel-toed clodhoppers. Now, as she removed the boots and heavy socks, the sight of her naked foot was downright erotic. When she massaged her high arch, he had to stifle a groan of longing.

"What's wrong, Cam?"

"Nothing."

Except maybe he was losing his mind. He'd never before been turned on by the sight of ten pale toes and two slim ankles. What was it about this woman? Every inch of her body seemed to entice him. The sound of her voice did funny things to his heart, and the essence of her clean, slightly floral perfume seemed to have permeated the deepest part of his senses.

"We're going to a lot of trouble tracking this guy down," she said. "I hope Bud Coleman has information we can use. Some worthwhile clue."

Dragging his wandering mind back to the logic of the situation, Cam reasoned, "Except for Eisman, Coleman is the only person who can tell us anything about the bank robbery, how it was financed and engineered. Coleman could be a suspect, but Eisman couldn't have been involved in either Zach's murder or the attack on you, at least not personally, since he's still behind bars."

"There is one more person," she said. "Someone who knows the inside information about the bank job. Pamela herself."

"Susan?"

"I know you don't like considering the link, Cam, but you have to admit, everything about Zach's murder revolves around her. Won't you let me at least talk to her?

When we get back to Cedar Bluffs, won't you let me at least have an interview?''

"I don't control Susan, Frani. You'll have to convince her attorney. He doesn't think she or Jake should talk to anybody.''

"I'd be willing to have the attorney present,'' Frani said. "Please, Cam. Help me get close to her.''

Looking at her eager face, something in Cam clenched and froze. The possible threat Frani posed to Susan cooled him faster than a headfirst plunge into a glacial lake. How the hell could he have been interested in Frani? They were still on opposite sides of the fence, even though at the moment they seemed to be working together.

Although she'd been willing to believe there might be someone else who financed the bank robbery, and therefore had reason to murder Zach, her number one suspect was still his father. And after Jake, Susan. He could only imagine the story she was composing in her mind, a story that would destroy the lives of those he held most dear.

Frani pointed out, "*She* contacted Zach. She wanted to talk to him. There's no reason if she was ready to tell her story once, she wouldn't be willing to talk again. Frankly, I'm the next best thing.''

"When we get back to Cedar Bluffs, I'll talk to Susan about your interview.'' The hardness in his voice registered on her face.

"I'd appreciate it,'' she said. "Even a phone call would be better than nothing. If she'll talk to me, I know I can convince her to trust me.''

It seemed to Cam she was implying he wouldn't really approach Susan even though he'd said he would. "You don't trust me much, do you?''

"Not when it comes to your family,'' she said without hesitation.

Well, that makes us even, he thought. Staring through the windshield at the wide flat desert terrain that stretched to tiered cliffs and eroded rock formations, he fumed. Damn her! She didn't have any trouble trusting him when it came to doing her favors, like getting her out of town or flying out into the desert.

"I'm a lawman, Frani," he said tersely. "Whether you believe it or not, I'll do the right thing." *No matter who it hurts.*

She surprised him with a touch. Her slender fingers rested on his shirt sleeve. "What happens if it comes down to a choice between honor and love?"

"I'd choose honor," he said without thinking twice. A man couldn't live without honor.

She sighed and drew her hand away. "How much longer will it take to get there?"

"Hard to say."

There were no street markers in the high desert, and Bud Coleman's address was simply General Delivery, Springdale, Utah. He didn't have a telephone, so they couldn't call and tell him they were coming. The directions to his cabin had come from his parole officer.

Cam glanced at the mileage counter below the speedometer. "We've gone twelve miles on this road, which means we're just about there. Then we turn west and drive toward the Devil's Fist."

She pointed her toes and stretched. "The Devil's Fist?"

"According to Coleman's parole officer, we can't miss it. There's a hogback of rocks that look like a man lying flat on his back, raising his arm and making a fist to curse the sky."

"A terrifically inefficient method of locating somebody," she said. "I would think a few well-placed road markers would do the trick."

"You've been in the city too long, Frani. It takes more than a couple of signposts to tame the wilderness."

She stared curiously at him. "Very poetic, Cameron."

"Thank you, Francesca."

When he spoke her full name, the taste lingered on his lips like good Kentucky bourbon. Cam cursed the comparison. He couldn't afford the intoxicating effects of this particular lady.

"I've heard it said all cowboys are poets at heart."

He scoffed. "People back east tend to romanticize the Old West. I'll tell you, Frani, there's nothing poetic about slapping a brand on a steer's butt."

She laughed. "I'm sure the cow feels exactly the same way."

The Jeep rounded a jagged outcropping of adobe-colored rock, and another desert vista opened before them.

Frani pointed. "That must be it. The Devil's Fist."

He turned the Jeep onto an even more rutted dirt road that led toward a tower of red rock. It was almost five o'clock, and the sun had dipped low in the sky, creating dramatic shadows across the land textured with clumps of sage and yucca. They hadn't seen another car or any sign of human life for miles. Why would a man choose to live out here with only snakes for company? Bud Coleman might have some powerful secrets, Cam thought. So powerful they kept him isolated from the rest of the world.

Cam brought the Jeep to a halt in the middle of the dirt road. Even with four-wheel drive, he didn't want to risk being stuck out here in loose, sandy soil.

"Why are we stopping?"

A sense of danger grew within him. They were searching for an ex-con who might have been involved in Zach's murder and the attack on Frani. "I think we'd best proceed with caution."

Though he expected her to protest, she nodded. "What do you want me to do?"

"First, put on your shoes."

As she reached behind her for her bag, he flipped open the glove compartment, and removed his pistol. The magazine held fifteen bullets and he took an extra clip.

"Here's what we're going to do, Frani. We'll make a lot of noise on our approach. Since we couldn't telephone Coleman, he doesn't know we're coming, and he might be one of those guys prone to shoot on sight and ask questions later."

"Do you have a lot of homicidal hermits out here?"

"More than you'd think. A man's got a right to protect his land. At the moment, we're trespassing." He addressed the heavy sarcasm in her question. "And this isn't a joke, Frani. We suspect this man of being involved in a murder. We know he's an ex-con. And anyone who lives this far from civilization is bound to be a little nervous about unexpected visitors."

"What should I do?"

"If he shows a gun, get out of the way fast." He started up the Jeep. "I hope I'm overreacting."

The shack, nestled at the base of a cliff, was about the size of a Winnebago. The weathered boards had been neatly framed, and the roof was constructed of corrugated tin. A painted green door marked the middle, and there was a single window. As a sheriff, experienced in investigations, Cam knew they had to go inside, and he wasn't looking forward to it.

She gestured toward the aging gray pickup truck parked in front. "It looks like somebody's home."

Coleman had to be watching them. In the deep desert silence, he must have heard them approaching.

"Stay in the Jeep, Frani."

Warily, Cam opened the door. As he stepped out of the Jeep, he gripped the automatic in his right hand, concealing it from view.

Scanning the area, he figured if Coleman was outside the shack, preparing to ambush them, he would be hidden behind a spire of rock that was behind them to the left. Other than that spot, there wasn't much cover unless Coleman climbed the cliff.

"Hello in there. Coleman," Cam shouted. "We're here to ask you a few questions."

His voice echoed across miles of desolate country.

"Hey, Coleman."

He was answered by a bullet.

Chapter Six

Frani heard the shot and saw the spray of fine gravel that kicked up onto Cam's boot. He caught her eye and inclined his head toward a pile of terra cotta rocks about twenty yards away. "Get down," he whispered.

She slid onto the floorboards of the Jeep and ducked behind the seat. Adrenaline spurted through her veins. Her heart pumped like mad, and she realized she was as frightened for Cam as for herself. Why hadn't he returned fire?

His movements were slow and nonthreatening as he slowly faced the rocks and called out in a loud clear voice, "I'm a sheriff, Mr. Coleman. But you aren't in any trouble. I just want to ask some questions."

Cam took one step, then another.

Again, a shot rang out.

Glancing back at her, he instructed in a low voice, "If I'm hit, you take the Jeep and drive like hell into town. Get help."

"I won't abandon you."

"Don't argue. We could both end up dead."

But if she left him here to die, she wouldn't be able to bear the guilt. It would be far better to be shot right here and now. Frani couldn't live with the knowledge that she'd caused the death of a good, honest man.

Again, Cam yelled, "Did you hear me, Mr. Coleman?"

"I hear just fine." The voice creaked like an old door hinge that hadn't been opened in a long while.

"We just want to talk."

"You toss down your weapon, and I might talk to you."

She saw Cam's hesitation to face Coleman unarmed. *Don't do it, Cam.* Mere words couldn't protect them. But when he held out his gun and dropped it to the sandy earth, she thought it was the bravest act she'd ever seen. Dealing with this bizarre hermit was like facing a cornered rattlesnake, avoiding fast moves and hoping the creature wouldn't strike.

The scratchy voice hollered, "Tell the girl to get out of the Jeep and stand beside you."

"Can't do it," Cam said. "She's too scared to move, Coleman."

"Hell's bells, I'd never hurt a woman."

"Why don't you come down here and talk to us? Show this little lady you don't mean her any harm. Come on, Mr. Coleman, you can trust us."

"Why?"

In that single syllable, Frani heard a rising note of panic. He sounded spooked.

Still, Cam stayed calm and reasonable. "Pamela Jessup sent us. You remember Pamela, don't you?"

"You bet I do. I'll never forget Pamela. I heard she was dead."

"You heard wrong," Cam said. "Pamela Jessup is my mother."

Frani heard a scuffling from the direction of the rocks. When she peeked out, she saw a scraggly man with a sandy gray beard. He wore baggy jeans with wide, red suspenders over a dirty white undershirt. His battered gray hat was sweat-stained.

Coleman kept his rifle aimed at Cam as he approached. When he was standing about ten feet away, he demanded, "Show me a picture. I want to see what Pamela looks like now."

Slowly, Cam reached into his hip pocket and pulled out his wallet. He removed a photograph and held it out. "This was taken about five years ago."

Coleman darted forward to snatch the picture, then scampered backward. He squinted at the photo and gasped. His rifle lowered. When he looked up again, he appeared to be trying to smile. "She was so dang pretty."

Cam nodded. "Still is."

Coleman's laugh was even rougher than his voice. "You come inside and sit a spell. Tell me about Pamela."

When Frani climbed out of the Jeep, the old hermit greeted her politely, "Sorry, miss. I don't get many visitors, and I've clean forgot my manners."

The weird twinkle in his eye was almost charming. Likewise, the interior of his shack was spotlessly clean with a wood stove, a table, a bed and stacks of well-thumbed books. He offered a glass of bottled water from a dispenser, and she accepted.

"Do you have the water delivered?"

"I pick up in town once a week when I drop off my trash and buy groceries." He shrugged. "Gives me something to do."

The details of his solitary existence were fascinating. When he showed them a collection of carved white bone jewelry, as delicate as scrimshaw, Frani's reporter's mind was musing that Bud Coleman might be worth at least a sidebar to the Pamela Jessup story.

But that wasn't why they were here. "Could we ask you some questions about the bank robbery?"

"It's not very interesting," he said. "David Eisman

talked me into the whole thing. Back then, I did some work as a car mechanic.''

Frani remembered from Zach's notes that Coleman's ''mechanic'' work was mostly grand theft auto. ''You were driving the getaway car,'' she said.

''That's right. Eisman gave me a thousand dollars to put my hands on a car that couldn't be identified.''

Frani exchanged a meaningful glance with Cam. ''Where do you suppose Eisman got that kind of money?''

''He had rich friends,'' Coleman said. His eyes narrowed. ''I didn't trust none of them.''

''Do you remember any of their names?''

''I'd know them if I saw them,'' he said. ''Living up here, under the Devil's Fist, I can see anybody coming for miles and miles.''

His behavior was seriously paranoid, but Frani could have deduced that from his gunshot greeting. ''Have any of those people visited you?''

''No, and they'd better not try.'' He glanced around as if he was suspecting a stranger to pop out of the woodwork. ''They were Eisman's friends. He was a damn good con man. David Eisman could charm the birds right out of the trees and get rich people to open up their bank accounts.''

''Do you remember anyone in particular?''

Coleman's face took on a faraway expression. ''Eisman was always talking about the big score. A cool million dollars. He said someday he was going to be rich, and he'd do anything to get there.''

Cam dragged him back to the subject. ''Pamela is in danger, Coleman. Somebody from a long time ago is trying to get her, and we need to find out who it is. We need names or descriptions.''

''All those cheap bastards in her family. If they'd paid

Eisman the million dollars in ransom money, the bank robbery wouldn't ever have happened."

Frani asked the question that haunted her from the first time she laid eyes on Zach's files. "Was the kidnapping Pamela's idea? Was she the mastermind or the victim?"

"She was no criminal." He lifted his chin. "Pamela Jessup was a kind woman. Not much of a cook or housekeeper, but she tried. She was always nice to me. When I heard she was dead, I almost cried."

"But did she plan the kidnapping?"

"Don't know. But I can tell you that she didn't want to go along on the bank robbery. Eisman forced her every step of the way."

As he rambled on with vague reminiscences, Frani decided that Bud Coleman was an unreliable source. Nineteen years in prison and four years in the desert had dried up his ability to reason and left him a wary paranoid. His talent resided in his hands, his ability to create pretty designs from scraps of old bone he'd scavenged from the land around him.

Before they left, Frani gave him every penny of the cash she had on her for a pair of carved earrings.

When they stepped out of Coleman's shack, night had overtaken the land. In the moonlight, the Devil's Fist took on a surreal appearance. The skies lit up with a sparkling canopy of stars, and a strange blue-tinted glow outlined the sprawling panorama. Frani had never seen anything like it in her life.

"This is an amazing view," she said. "Simply breathtaking."

"These are my riches," Coleman said. "All the time I was in prison, I thought about this openness. I carried it inside me."

Cam shook his hand. "If you'll allow me, I'll tell my mother your address."

"That's fine with me. I'd like to hear from Pamela."

"Before we go," he said, "I'd like to mention a couple of names. If you remember anything about them, anything at all, tell me."

Coleman nodded. "I'll try."

Cam said, "Candace Jessup."

"I guess she must be one of Pamela's relations."

"Byron Reeves."

"Nope," Coleman said. "He don't sound familiar to me."

"Phillip Gould." Cam dropped the names slowly, like pebbles into a bucket of water, allowing each to resonate and sink before adding another. "Jake McQuaid. Zach Hollingsworth."

Slowly, the old man shook his head from side to side. "Should I know these people? Are they famous or something?"

"Not so's you'd notice," Cam said. "Thanks for your hospitality, Coleman."

"Come back anytime." He flashed a smile at Frani. "You, too."

She waved goodbye as they returned down the rutted dirt road. When they were out of sight, she turned toward Cam, regarding him with a mixture of respect and suspicion.

During the few hours they'd spent with Bud Coleman, Cam had not only handled himself with courage but also his inquiries showed a keen intelligence. Frani had no doubt he was one of the finest investigative lawmen she'd ever seen in action, including the FBI and homicide detectives in Chicago. He was also smart enough to conceal information from her.

"Sorry, Frani," he said. "Looks to me like Coleman is

a dead end. Whatever he knew about the bank robbery has been erased over the years. And he surely wasn't part of a conspiracy to murder Zach."

"You're right," she said. "I'm sure he was telling the truth."

"This trip was a waste of time."

Not necessarily. Though Coleman hadn't offered any clue to solve Zach's murder, Frani was more convinced than ever that the key to this investigation was Pamela. Certainly, they needed to talk with her sister, Candace. And possibly even pay a visit to Eisman in jail, but Pamela/Susan stood at the center.

Also, Frani had fastened on a piece of information that Cam mentioned in a casual way. "Why did you ask about Senator Phillip Gould?"

"He was an early associate of the Jessup family." As soon as he spoke, Cam knew he'd betrayed too much. "At least, that's what I've heard."

"I thought you didn't know anything about Pamela."

CAM CONCENTRATED on the road that lay before them. His instincts as a sheriff warned him against full disclosure to Frani. She was, after all, a reporter. When she refused to come with him to the morgue, he'd seen how her journalistic priorities took precedence over everything else.

But there was another side to this coin. He wanted Zach's files, and he needed to deal with Frani to get them.

Frani rephrased her question. "Did you know from the start that the woman you call Susan Hathaway was really Pamela Jessup? Or was that a recent revelation?"

"I haven't lied to you," he said.

"But you haven't told me everything." Her green eyes flashed in the darkness. "I thought we were in this together."

"We're not partners," he said.

"But we share the same goal—finding Zach's murderer."

He couldn't argue with that. Tentatively, he decided to take the first step toward trusting her. "It's no secret my brother, Cy, was the FBI agent in charge of investigating Byron Reeves."

"Another conveniently positioned McQuaid lawman," she said with hostile cynicism. "I was aware of that connection *and* the potential for a cover-up."

"Cover-up?" he exploded. "When are you going to get it through your head that I'm one of the good guys?"

"When you level with me," she snapped. "I know Phillip Gould is important to this investigation. Gould's name was one of the last entries Zach made in his notebook."

"*What* notebook?"

A stunned silence filled the interior of the Jeep, and Cam knew he'd hit upon a vital chunk of information. Zach Hollingsworth had a special notebook, something more current than his files.

"Journalistic privilege," she said. "I don't have to reveal my sources to you or anybody else."

"You're concealing evidence, Frani."

"So are you."

A powerful anger built up inside him, and he fought to control the intense emotion. An outburst never solved anything. Patience was a necessary virtue in his line of work. As sheriff, he'd dealt with drunks, crooks and violent people hell-bent on bloody assault and mayhem. But none of them—no one he could recall—infuriated him as much as this stubborn little red-haired female.

"Tell you what, Frani. I don't care what you know. You follow your investigation, and I'll take care of mine."

"That doesn't make any sense. We both have—"

"Not another word," he said, keying his voice to a low, dangerous level. "I'll stay with you as a bodyguard because I promised I wouldn't let anything happen to you. But that's *all*. I'm through negotiating."

"All right," she said with forced brightness. "What should we talk about? The weather?"

"Anything but the case." The lights of Springdale shimmered in the distance like a diamond bracelet. "We're going to spend the night here. Tomorrow morning, we'll get a fresh start."

"And where will be we going?" she asked. "I have a terrific inside source for Candace Jessup in northern California. Would it be faster to take a commercial flight to Sacramento?"

Purposely, he looked away from her, gazing out his side window. "I'd say the temperature has dropped twenty degrees since the sun went down."

"You can't avoid talking about this, Cam."

"The hell I can't."

He would not be drawn into a discussion of the case. Cam needed some time and space to calm down before he wrestled with her again.

THOUGH THE POSSIBILITY of Frani being attacked while they were in Springdale seemed fairly remote, Cam arranged for them to have adjoining rooms on the second floor at the Zion View Motel. He hauled her soft-sided travel bag to her room and dropped it on the bed before unlocking the door that connected the two rooms.

"We'll leave this open," he said. "If anything disturbs you during the night, call out."

"Do you think it's necessary to be so vigilant?"

Now she was telling him how to do his job. Francesca Landon was a burr under his blanket. He explained, "I filed a flight plan at the Cedar Bluffs airport. Though I didn't give the exact destination, it's not hard to monitor the progress of a small plane.''

"I hadn't thought of that," she said.

"Guess not.'' There were a lot of things she hadn't thought about. If Frani Landon had one glaring flaw, it was the tendency to leap without looking. He turned on his heel to leave her room.

"Cam, wait!"

Halting without turning around, he asked, "What is it?"

"I really appreciate that you're taking the threat against me seriously. I know I can be...difficult. Anyway, thanks.''

When he turned and saw her sitting in the middle of the double bed with her legs curled under her, he recognized the sweetly feminine side she kept hidden behind a barricade of tough questions.

Cam wasn't about to let himself be enticed by either aspect. "You're welcome," he said tersely.

She unzipped the suitcase on the bed beside her, dug inside and produced a zippered plastic file holder. She held it out toward him. "These are Zach's files on Pamela Jessup. I've transferred some of the details onto the computer, but most everything should be there.''

Still wary, he accepted her offering. "Why are you doing this?"

"A show of good faith. I want to figure this out together.'' Her wide green eyes sent out a strong appeal to him. "I'm not accustomed to working alone. Zach was always there to bounce ideas back and forth.''

Frani didn't strike him as a woman lacking in confidence, but he remembered what she'd told him about the father she could never please. Cam hoped she wasn't trying to make him into some kind of replacement father figure. "I'm not Zach.''

"My God, Cam. Don't you think I know that? I never felt about Zach the way I feel about..."

When her tongue darted out to moisten her lips, he wondered if she was remembering, as he was, their kiss in the airplane. Suddenly, he could hardly look at her without tasting that sweetness. But what the hell kind of relationship could they have? Cam wasn't old enough or wise enough to be her mentor. Her talent for getting him all riled up meant they didn't have a future as comfortable, easygoing buddies. Lovers?

He sank into a chair, stretched out his legs and stared at the toes of his boots. Making love to her had occurred to him more than once, but he'd dismissed the desire. He wouldn't take advantage of her loneliness and her sorrow. He didn't believe in one-night stands.

"*Quid pro quo*," she said, businesslike again. "I scratch your back, and you scratch mine. Let's trade information."

"Like partners," he said. That would be their relationship. An uneasy partnership where neither could completely trust the other.

She bounced off the bed and stuck out her hand. "It's a deal."

When he enveloped her dainty fingers inside his own callused grip, Cam managed to ignore the sensual stirrings evoked by even this minimal physical contact. "Deal."

Immediately, she put distance between them, returning to the bed. "Tell me about Phillip Gould, senior U.S. senator from the great state of California."

"When my brother, Cy, was investigating Byron Reeves, he got close to the family. In fact, I'm pretty sure he's going to marry Amy Reeves."

Frani nodded avidly. "Zach covered the story in detail. Gould was the first person who suggested that Zach look into Reeves's background and his connection to Pamela Jessup.''

"I'm sure he didn't mention this to Zach." He hesitated, realizing that he was talking to a reporter. His words could be headlines tomorrow. "This is all hearsay, Frani. Secondhand gossip.''

"I double-source everything I print," she assured him. "It's far more detrimental to me than you if I write a story that's not true.''

"According to Byron Reeves, Pamela Jessup's reputation as a free spirit got her into trouble before the kidnapping. She was raped by Phillip Gould.''

"My God," she whispered. Her immediate reaction was shock. "That poor woman went through hell.''

"But she turned out okay.''

"You think of Pamela as your mother," Frani said. "You must despise Gould. Why didn't you and your brother make this allegation public?''

"We didn't want to force Susan to relive the horror.'' He swallowed the pain and rage that churned within him. As far as he was concerned, Gould was truly one of the lowest creatures on earth. "Besides, it's a case of her word against his. He's a senator. She's a fugitive. Who do you think is going to be believed?''

"But it's a motive," Frani said. "Gould might have killed Zach to keep the story from being made public.''

Sadly, Cam shook his head. "My brother used his FBI contacts to check that possibility. At the time Zach was murdered, the Senator was in San Francisco addressing a conference hall filled with over two hundred computer executives. It's an ironclad alibi.''

"He could have hired it done," she said. "That would be more in character. He's a wealthy man and wouldn't want to get his hands dirty.''

"Murdering Zach would only bring more attention to the accusation of rape."

"Well, we're not going to let him get away with this," Frani said. "I don't know how we get around the he-said, she-said aspect. If we talk to Pamela's sister, she might be able to corroborate the story."

She climbed off the bed and began pacing. "Maybe a sexual assault isn't as shocking nowadays as it was twenty-four years ago, but rape is still a crime. One of the most disgusting, lowdown kinds of assault."

Her outrage pleased him. Cam was finally beginning to understand Frani. She was passionately emotional—so much that it probably got in the way of her journalistic objectivity.

"Of course," she said, "I'll back off if that's appropriate. I would respect Susan's wishes about the rape."

He grinned. "You called her Susan. That's the first time you've called her Susan."

She blinked. "I guess it is."

She returned his smile, and for the first time he noticed a small dimple in her left cheek. Fiery hair and a temperament to match, she was pretty damned cute when she got excited.

"I'll call my contact in northern California and set up a meeting with Candace Jessup."

He watched her as she finessed a conversation on the motel telephone with a mixture of sweetness and hard, direct questions. Cam didn't even need to hear words to know that Frani was getting the information she wanted. When she hung up the phone, she beamed at him. "Candace Jessup, her mother and two nephews aren't in California."

"And?"

"They're on a ski vacation with friends in Aspen," she said delightedly. "How far is Aspen from Cedar Bluffs?"

"About a two-hour drive."

"Don't look now, Cam. But I think we just found our-selves some suspects."

He had to agree. Members of the Jessup family had an old grudge to settle. They were wealthy, powerful people who might commit murder to hide dangerous secrets. This bit of information could break the case wide open and get his father off the hook. "Damn good work, Frani."

"I know." She twinkled delightedly as she came toward him. "Let's map out our strategy for interviewing them. Come on, cowboy. Take off your hat and stay a while."

When she made a grab for his black Stetson, Cam caught her wrist in midair. "Never touch a man's hat without ask-ing."

Still holding her wrist with one hand, he removed the Stetson with the other and stood. He placed her hand on his shoulder and glided his arms around her.

He lowered his head and tasted her mouth for the second time. It tasted even sweeter than the first.

Her slender body pressed against him. He caressed the curve of her waist and the flare of her buttocks.

Though Cam knew he should stop before he passed the point of no return, he had to touch her skin. He eased the pale blue tunic sweater higher and higher, bunching the soft wool. Finally, his hand reached underneath and he stroked her torso along her ribcage. Her flesh was softer than the finest silk.

When she leaned back in his arms and gazed up at him, her emerald eyes invited him to go farther, to taste fully of her charms.

Abruptly, he stepped back. "I apologize."

"Don't," she said in a soft, husky voice.

He grabbed his hat and Zach's files from the table. "Good night, Frani."

SHOWERED AND DRESSED in her nightshirt, Frani stretched out under the clean, rough sheets of the motel bed. When she turned out the light, she saw that the lamp in Cameron's room was still lit.

What would happen if she cried wolf and he came running in here to protect her? Could she say that she was scared and ask him to lie down with her?

She couldn't lie. Tricking him into her bed would be cheating, and Frani wanted the first time they made love to be special. How could it be anything else? The cowboy's kisses were like none she'd ever experienced.

Flipping over on the bed, she tried to get comfortable. But it was impossible. At least, she had to say good night.

She tiptoed to the door connecting their rooms and peeked around the corner.

Propped up on pillows, Cam was reading through Zach's files. The white sheets were pulled up to his waist. His chest was bare. A mat of black hair covered his olive skin. Sharp muscle defined his broad shoulders and arms.

Frani had never before seen a more magnificent man. Not pumped up like somebody who earned his muscles at a gym, Cam's muscular body came from natural hard work.

Her fingers gripped the edge of the door, holding on tight so she wouldn't run across the room and throw herself into his bed. She cleared her throat. "Good night, partner."

When he looked up, the shock of their eyes meeting was too much for her to bear. She fled to the lonely safety of her own bed.

SHE VANISHED like a mirage before Cam's eyes. And like a mirage, she'd seemed too enticing to be real. Her full lips parted. The light shining from her eyes bright with desire.

Her flimsy nightshirt revealed the taut peaks of her breasts. Her bared legs were beautifully shaped.

With a groan, he reached up and turned off the bedside lamp, knowing he might need another cold shower before he could finally fall asleep.

Chapter Seven

The next morning, Cam could hardly look Frani in the eye. He'd spent most of the night dreaming about her in various stages of undress, showing cleavage or a length of firm thigh or a fine-boned shoulder lightly brushed with flame-red hair when she cocked her head to one side. Sitting across from her at a café booth, he ordered breakfast and stared deeply into his coffee cup.

"I can't believe it," Frani said as she rattled the edges of the Salt Lake City newspaper. "Zach's murder is page one, but there's so little substance to it."

"What's it say?"

"There's a bit about his career, but then it says, 'No progress reported in the ongoing investigation.' The only quote is from Harold T. Cisneros, the Chaparral County district attorney." She folded the paper. "I guess I ought to talk with him. What's he like?"

Cam lifted his head to confront the woman of last night's dreams. In the back of his mind, he hoped she would disappoint him, but no such luck. Francesca Landon was as pretty as a sunrise, rosy-cheeked and refreshed. Today she wore a blouse Cam might have described as puke green, but somehow, on Frani, it looked great. The V at the throat directed his gaze lower, toward her breasts.

"Yoohoo, Cam! Hey, you're not awake yet, are you?"

On the contrary, his entire body was ready to pounce. "I was just looking at your necklace."

She lifted the white-gold pendant shaped in a five-pointed star and stroked her thumb across the surface. "Zach gave it to me. He said I reminded him of Brenda Starr, the red-haired reporter in the comics."

"Are you like her?"

"If I remember correctly, Brenda Starr was always yearning, waiting for her mystery man to bring her black orchids. And that's not like me, at all. I'm impatient. When I see something I want, I go after it." She glanced back at the newspaper. "And I'm a born skeptic. For example, I just don't believe there's been *no* progress in the investigation."

"You could be right. Joe hates talking to the press and Harold T. will tread lightly. He's a political animal and he'll be taking care to make sure all his comments are dead-on accurate."

Cam had telephoned Joe before leaving the motel room, but he was reluctant to share every detail with Frani. Even though he wasn't officially wearing his badge, his loyalty remained with the sheriff's office, and their official comment was: No comment.

"What's up, Cam?" she questioned. The natural glow in her eyes sharpened to a laser edge. "Don't try to hide anything from me. Did you talk to your office this morning?"

"Frani, you can't print anything I tell you without my permission."

"I won't. I swear." She placed her hand atop her heart. "Now, spill it."

"Joe checked the hospitals and doctors, trying to get a

lead on the guy you shot outside the *Clarion* office. He came up empty. No clues. No suspects.''

She sighed. "Anything else?"

"The autopsy showed that Zach was killed by a .38. A handgun.''

"So the killer was standing fairly close," she said. "I wonder why Zach didn't hear him creeping up."

"He didn't have to sneak," Cam said. "The guy could've left his car on the road and walked right up to the gate where Zach was standing. Pointed the gun and fired point-blank.''

"In broad daylight? That seems risky."

"The road leading to Circle Q isn't well-traveled," he said. "So far, they haven't found a single witness."

As Cam's mental energies returned to consider the case mounting against his father, his desire for Frani abated. Maybe he could adjust to thinking of her as a partner, he told himself.

"What about the search for evidence at the crime scene?'' she asked.

"The killer lucked out on that front. Getting useful tire tracks or footprints on the gravel-based driveway would've been hard enough, but the snow made it impossible. Joe Bradley said they haven't found a single clue.''

"Except for the .38 caliber slugs in Zach's chest."

"Right.''

She settled back on the booth opposite him and sipped her coffee. "Tell me about Harold T. Cisneros."

"He's in his mid-thirties, young for a district attorney. Married and has three kids. He's a fair man and a good prosecutor.''

"Has he ever handled a case of this magnitude before?"

"He'll do just fine. Harold T. is ambitious, and he wants to make his mark in Colorado politics. He knows that if he messes up on a nationally reported investigation like this one, his chances for advancement will go down in flames.''

The waitress brought their breakfast to the table. Eggs, sunny side up, for Cam. A Denver omelet for Frani.

He was pleased to see Frani attack her food with a healthy appetite. Cam never trusted a woman who picked at her food.

"When we get back to Cedar Bluffs," she said between bites, "you won't believe what's going on. It'll be a media circus. Those twenty-four-seven cable news channels are starved for new material."

He noted the disgust in her voice. "Sounds like you don't approve."

"No disrespect to my colleagues in TV, but I don't consider what they do journalism. Anyone can stick a camera in someone's face, demand a quote and then edit their words down to a sound bite."

She took a swallow of coffee. "I liked the work I did with Zach. He had a column three times a week, and the rest of the time we could really dig into a story and find out what people were thinking and feeling. That's what I love, trying to get inside someone else's skin, feel what it feels like to be them. Figure out their emotions."

"I thought reporters were supposed to avoid emotionalism and stick to the facts."

"You sound like Zach. He was always on my case about how I needed to be more objective." She scooped up another forkful of omelet. "Sometimes, I think people like Addie have the right idea. If I owned a newspaper like the *Chaparral Clarion,* I wouldn't have to answer to a managing editor. I could do in-depth profiles."

"Would that make a difference in how you covered this case?"

"My first concern would still be to help bring the murderer to justice." The fork paused in front of her mouth, and her eyes took on a dreamy quality. "After that, I'd concentrate on the people. Like Bud Coleman. How does a man like him become a hermit? What does he think about during those long, vacant days in the desert?"

"What else?"

"Susan."

Frani chewed quickly, anxious to be talking and eating at the same time. "She intrigues me, Cam. She's so... Oh, I don't know. There's just this quality of sadness about her. I noticed it the first time I saw her photograph in Zach's files. Everyone tried to paint her as a wild, irresponsible young thing who had turned to a life of crime on a whim. But I always felt she was a victim, caught up in circumstances way beyond her control."

He preferred Frani's analysis to the facts he'd read last night in the files. As a lawman, he inclined toward believing that Pamela Jessup was guilty as sin. As her son, he trusted Susan Hathaway more than any person on earth, and he couldn't believe she'd willing engaged in criminal activity.

"Anyway," Frani said, "her story is remarkable. Will you tell me more about her? What was she like as your surrogate mom?"

"Sure, it'll give us something to do on the flight to Aspen."

He'd been thinking about that flight since he got out of bed this morning, and he wasn't looking forward to the long ride in the small cockpit. Sitting so close to Frani would be a severe test of his willpower.

AT THE SPRINGDALE airport, Cam went through his pre-flight checklist and filed his flight plan. All the time, his brain was preoccupied. How *was* he going to cope with being so close to Frani?

He wanted to kiss her again, but this attraction could not be indulged. Deep down, he knew if he made love to Frani, he'd never be able to let her walk away. And she would leave, of that much he was certain. She was as out of place in the west as a kitten in a cactus patch. Except this kitten knew how to use her claws, a skill that was no doubt useful in her line of work, but didn't exactly lend itself to the kind of loving relationship Cam had always thought he'd someday enjoy.

Shortly after they took off into clear Western skies, Cam again brought up the subject they'd discussed at breakfast. "What do you want to know about Susan?"

Frani unfastened her seat belt to grab her shoulder bag from behind the copilot's seat and pulled out a small tape recorder. "I don't suppose there's any way to use this."

"Not over the hum of the engine," he said.

She plopped it back into her purse and took out a small spiral notebook and a pen. "I guess I'll have to do it Zach's way. He always took notes."

Cam had deduced as much from his study of the files. Along with the relevant clippings and typed-up transcripts were leaves from a small notebook, covered with indecipherable scribbling. Some pages were dated. Others weren't. But he hadn't seen anything making reference to the Circle Q.

Though Frani claimed to have turned over *all* the files, he wouldn't be surprised if she'd held something back. *Quid pro quo, my eye.* "So, Zach always carried a notebook."

"Usually," she said lightly. "Okay, let's start at the beginning. How did Susan come to join the McQuaid family?"

THREE AND A HALF hours into their four-and-a-half-hour flight, Frani had almost filled her notebook with quotes from Cam about his early life with Susan Hathaway.

After the dramatic discovery when the three McQuaid boys rescued a woman near death from a ditch beside the road in Texas, they'd been protective of her.

"We wanted a mother," Cam had said.

And Susan filled the bill. Not only had she cooked and cleaned and worked hard on the ranch, but she'd nurtured the boys, each in a different way. Cyrus, the oldest brother, had always been the biggest, brashest and most adventurous until he was seriously injured in the line of duty a few years ago and forced to take time off for contemplation. The youngest brother, Matt, channeled his aggression into rodeo sports when he was growing up. Not even Susan's influence could prevent a split between Matt and his father. Now, he was estranged from the family.

Cam was less forthcoming about himself. "I guess I was the family peacemaker," he said. "That's why I never felt the need to stray too far from home."

Frani gazed through the Piper Cub windscreen at the majestic Rocky Mountains looming before them. The weather was clear, and sunlight glinted off snowcapped peaks. "How did you learn to fly?"

"Air Force," he said.

So he wasn't the total homebody, after all. "How long were you in the Air Force?"

"I got out after Desert Storm." Deftly, he deflected the story from himself. "Susan had a big celebration the day I returned home. She was always big on birthdays and holiday celebrations, which was kind of strange, I guess."

"Why?"

"She claimed her birthday was February fifteenth, the

day we found her. But that's not the date on her birth certificate.''

"How do you know that?''

"I asked her. She said she was reborn as Susan Hathaway on that day. Everything before that happened to another person.''

"Pamela Jessup.''

The idea of a changed birthday touched Frani's heart. She'd always believed people deserved a second chance. Even when she and Zach had investigated hardened criminals, Frani often glimpsed potential for goodness and redemption.

"I like your Susan,'' she said, closing her notebook.

"So do I.''

They'd flown into the mountains and Frani was delighted to see yet another aspect of Western terrain. From the rugged ranching terrain near Cedar Bluffs to the Great Basin desert to the spectacular snow-covered peaks, world renowned for skiing, Colorado was a vastly diverse and fascinating place.

While Cam was busy on the headset, communicating with the airport in Aspen, she quietly absorbed the wonder of soaring jagged rocks mantled in the purest, whitest snow she'd ever seen.

These vast and varied panoramas appealed greatly to her. Each terrain inspired her in a different way. It would be easy to fall in love with the West. She was already experiencing a level of infatuation.

"We're cleared for landing,'' Cam said.

"I've never been to Aspen. It really is a beautiful setting. We're only an hour and a half from Cedar Bluffs, but it seems like a different world.''

"In a way, it is. Half the winter population is out-of-towners, and those snowbirds are some of the wealthiest tourists in the world. We don't get many tourists in Cedar Bluffs.''

Further conversation ended as Cam concentrated on making a safe landing at the relatively busy airport.

It occurred to Frani that if she'd chartered a plane or found a flight into Aspen, she might have been able to catch Zach in time to join him at the Circle Q the day he'd died. But maybe not. The weather hadn't been good, and small planes wouldn't be flying in heavy cloud cover. In Colorado, fate was dictated by the vagaries of the Rockies.

But the Jessups had no such transportation problems. According to Frani's source, Candace and her mother and two college-aged Jessup nephews were staying at the home of a friend for two weeks on a ski vacation. They must have flown in before the storm.

Their plans appeared to be innocent, but Frani was suspicious. There had been no indication that the Jessups knew that Pamela a.k.a. Susan was still alive...but did they? Had Candace known that her sister was less than a two-hour drive away? If she had known, would Candace have tried to stop her sister from telling her story? What embarrassing details might Pamela have revealed? Were there skeletons in the Jessup closet worth killing for?

As Cam swooped the Piper Cub in for a featherlight landing, every instinct told Frani the trail to Zach's murderer was getting warmer.

SINCE FRANI HADN'T called ahead to make an appointment, she and Cam were greeted with strained civility at the door of the gracious home in the exclusive Starwood area of Aspen. A good-looking young man, whose darkly tanned complexion showed his dedication to skiing, blocked their entrance.

"Sorry, but we never talk to the press," he said. "I don't know how you managed to track us down."

"I was a close associate of Zach Hollingsworth," Frani said as if that was a sufficient explanation. "Is Candace available?

"Not to you," he said petulantly. "Now, why don't you stop wasting your time and just go away?"

Not a chance, kiddo. "Right now, I'm the only reporter who happens to know the Jessup family is in Colorado. If I leak this information the paparazzi will swarm over this place like locusts. I'm sure you wouldn't want that, now would you?"

"No, but—"

Cam didn't bother with persuasive tactics. He flashed his badge. "Sheriff Cameron McQuaid. I'm here to question Candace and other members of the Jessup family."

"Sheriff?"

"Either you cooperate or I can come back here with a warrant."

The young man turned his head and bleated, "Candace! There's a cop out here who says he wants to see you."

In moments, a blond woman appeared in the doorway. She was thin, almost emaciated, and pretty in a brittle way. Her features closely resembled Susan's, but this woman seemed to lack the depth that Frani had come to associate with the missing heiress.

"I'm Candace Jessup." She looked to Cam. "Should I have an attorney present?"

"That's your choice, Miss Jessup."

"Please call me Ms. I've been married twice and have only recently returned to using my maiden name." She looked down her nose at Frani. "Who is this person?"

"My name is Francesca Landon. I worked with Zach Hollingsworth."

"A reporter," she said with a sneer. "Of course, you're aware Zach Hollingsworth practically destroyed the career of our distant relation, Judge Byron Reeves."

Frani nodded. There was no way she'd apologize for the good work Zach had done on his last story.

A cruel smile twisted the corner of Candace's lips. "I never had a chance to personally thank Mr. Hollingsworth for what he did to dear, dear Byron. Only wish I'd had the chance to make him regret every word."

Frani flinched at the implication.

"Come in, Sheriff. You, too, Miss Landon, but if you write one word without my permission, I'll see to it you never work for another newspaper for as long as you live."

Frani swallowed the retort that would have reduced the sneering socialite to a pile of smoking ashes. If she wanted information, she had to play the game.

The interior of the gracious home was expensively airy. In the main room, a long, beige leather sectional sofa surrounded a large fireplace. Candace made a beeline for the wet bar against the opposite wall.

"Would either of you care for a drink?" Pointedly, her gaze lit upon Cam's Stetson. "We have beer, but it's imported."

"Bottled water is fine," he said.

"Same for me," Frani said.

Candace handed over the Perrier. She ignored a wine rack filled with bottles from Jessup Vintners, one of the finest and most lucrative wineries in northern California. Instead, Candace poured herself a straight shot of whiskey over ice. The movements of her manicured hands sparkled as the directional lighting hit the diamonds on her fingers and the ones that circled her wrist.

Although her black slacks and sweater looked like a casual après-ski outfit, Frani knew from the cut and fabric that Candace's clothing bore a top designer's label.

Talking with Candace Jessup would've been the sort of interview that Zach relished. His enthusiastic appreciation for the finer things in life made him comfortable with the rich and famous. Although Frani had accompanied him on a few of these assignments, she'd always remained quietly in the background, taking notes.

Now, she was center stage, and she felt a little out of her depth.

Though she never would have admitted to Cam that she was intimidated, he seemed to sense her hesitation. When he touched her elbow to direct her toward the sofa, he whispered, "You can do this."

Surprised, she glanced up gratefully. He believed in her. No one but Zach had ever encouraged Frani. Certainly not her family.

Cam winked and whispered again, "Go to it, Frani. Let's see you kick some high-class butt."

His confidence inspired her. Frani positioned herself nearest Candace Jessup and started right in. "Are you aware there are rumors that your sister, Pamela, has been located?"

"My sister died twenty-four years ago in Dry Creek, Texas," Candace said automatically. "She was cremated and her ashes are interred in the family mausoleum, outside the winery—where Daddy can keep an eye on her."

"A terrible mistake was made," Frani said. "Your sister is alive."

Not a muscle in Candace Jessup's impeccably made-up face moved. She seemed not at all surprised by the revelation that should have shocked her. "Why tell me? This matter should be taken up with the family attorneys."

She was colder than the ice in her whiskey. Frani wanted

to ask why Candace wasn't overjoyed by the possibility that her sister might be alive, but she avoided the question, sensing this woman was devoid of real emotion. "What share of the family assets will go to Pamela?"

"Since her death, of course, she's been written out of everything." She crossed one skinny leg over the other. "I suppose if she is really still alive, she'll have some hereditary claim. But, remember, she's still a felon." She shifted her gaze to Cam. "Bank robbery *is* still a crime, isn't it, Sheriff McQuaid?"

"That was a long time ago," Frani said, before Cam could respond. "How old were you at the time?"

"I'm three years younger than my sister. I was on the brink of my debutante season when she pulled her little stunt."

"You believe she engineered the kidnapping?"

"Daddy and I both believed it from the first."

"Was that why he wouldn't pay the ransom?" Cam asked.

"Yes. He suspected it was a hoax, a ludicrous attempt by Pamela to get attention. But he also thought it might set some sort of precedent, paying off criminals. We have a rather large extended family, and Daddy didn't want to start ransoming everyone."

But Pamela was his eldest child. How could any father be so callous? Frani was beginning to see where Candace got her coldness. "Your family was criticized at the time."

She rolled her eyes. "It was a dreadful scandal. Utterly humiliating. I've spent a fortune in therapy trying to come to terms with what my sister did to our family."

Beside her on the sofa, Cam shifted his weight and leaned forward. His dark eyes glittered with barely suppressed rage. Frani could imagine his thoughts. How, he must be wondering, could Candace liken her visits to a therapist to the hell Susan had gone through? Susan had been raped, kidnapped and brutally beaten.

Encouraging Candace to keep talking, Frani said, "What happened to your debutante season?"

"It was ruined, and it was all Pamela's fault. She was always self-centered, wild, determined to get her own way. If Daddy wouldn't give her the car, she'd steal his keys and go joyriding. She was expelled from two boarding schools, you know. No one could control her, not even her boyfriends."

An older woman, nearly as thin as Candace, with hair a subdued silver, walked into the room. "You're talking about Pammy, aren't you?"

Candace stood. "It's only more rumors, Mother. Another tabloid story, no doubt."

The older woman's face fell. "How I miss Pammy." Though she must have been in her sixties, there was an oddly childlike quality about her. Frani wondered about the strength of the tranquilizers the woman was obviously taking. "Pammy was always so pretty, so sweet..."

"Oh, stop it, Mother."

"It's true. Even Phillip said so. He always had feelings for her, you know?"

Frani exchanged a quick glance with Cam. "Phillip Gould?"

"That's right," the older woman said proudly. "The senator. I think he would have liked to marry her."

"Now, Mother, don't be ridiculous." Candace reached for the bottle and refilled her glass. "Phillip never had anything to do with Pamela."

"I'm Sheriff McQuaid, Mrs. Jessup. I'm pleased to meet you."

"You're a handsome one, aren't you?"

"Thank you, ma'am. Do you mind if I ask you a few questions?"

"Not at all."

"What can you tell me about Phillip Gould and Pamela?"

"He liked her a lot. I could always tell by the way he looked at her." She sighed. "And I had such hopes that Pammy and Phillip would get together. The Goulds are really a fine family."

"Mother, please..." Candace said.

"You can ask Phillip about Pammy when he arrives," Mrs. Jessup told Cam. "He's supposed to join us here today."

Before she could continue, Candace caught the older woman by the arm and tugged her none too gently into the hallway. "Mother, I think you should go take your nap." Over her shoulder, she said, "My mother hasn't been feeling well, have you, dear? And now if you'll just excuse her..."

When Candace returned to the room, she snapped, "This interview is over."

Cam planted himself in the middle of the chic, costly room like a stubborn ponderosa pine. "Where were you on Tuesday at approximately two in the afternoon?"

"You make it sound as if I need an alibi."

"Day before yesterday," Cam reiterated. "Where were you?"

"Not that I need to tell you, but I was on the slopes. My nephew fell and sprained an ankle, and I had to notify the ski patrol and help with the rescue. Is that a strong enough alibi, Sheriff?"

"During the time in question, you were with the ski patrol?"

"Yes," she hissed as she strode toward the door. "Now,

if you don't mind, I'm afraid I must insist you leave. Both of you."

She wrenched the door open and stood back as they walked out into the bright, cold mountain afternoon. "Oh, and Miss Landon. Don't forget what I said about quoting me. It would be a real shame to see the *Daily Herald* lose two of its best reporters in one week."

CAM COULDN'T REMEMBER ever disliking anyone as immediately and completely as he had Candace Jessup. On the drive back to the airport, he couldn't control his anger. "What kind of people would refuse to ransom their own daughter?"

Frani answered quietly, "The Jessups. You knew that, Cam. You read the file."

His anger wouldn't be calmed, and he fought an urge to drive too fast or to pull over and punch some rich tourist right in the jaw.

As they entered the Aspen airport, he concluded, "If Candace is an example of the rest of the family, Susan was well rid of them. I've never met such a mean-spirited person in my life."

Gently, Frani touched his arm. "Susan was lucky to find the McQuaids."

"I need to check in with my office before we take off," he said. "Seems pretty damn suspicious to me that the Jessups were so close to Cedar Bluffs when Zach was killed. I want to make sure Harold T. adds them to his list of suspects."

"If Candace's alibi checks out with the ski patrol," Frani said, "she's in the clear."

"That's a mighty big if," he muttered. "They could've hired a killer."

"Why?" Frani said.

"I hope to hell you aren't defending that woman. Because if you are, I've misjudged—"

"I found her every bit as disgusting as you did," Frani said. "But I'm trying to come up with an objective motive. Why would she want to murder Zach?"

"Sheer meanness. Jealousy. Revenge. You heard how she talked about her sister."

"But would she go after Zach?"

"I don't know," he said, exasperated. "I'd like nothing more than to hook Ms. Candace up to a lie detector, but with the battery of attorneys at her disposal, that will never happen."

"Too bad," Frani said. "It would give her something to discuss in her next therapy session."

Cam offered her a grim smile and then left her waiting while he found the nearest pay phone and punched in the number for the Chaparral County district attorney. His secretary put Cam right through.

"I'm glad you called," Harold said.

"I have some alibis for you to check out," Cam said. "Several people in the Jessup clan—including Candace Jessup—are staying in Aspen. They were in the state at the time of the murder."

Harold promised to check them out, before he said, "Cam, we found the murder weapon."

"Where?"

"About twenty yards from the gate, along the fence line. It had been buried in the snow."

This should have been good news, but Harold's voice sounded wary. "What else?"

"It matches the coroner's findings. A .38 revolver. Unmarked, unregistered. A throwaway. The kind of gun most cops own."

Most cops. Harold's implication was not lost on Cam. He was suggesting that even a former sheriff from Texas might find an untraceable weapon useful. *Most cops,* he'd said. In other words, even Jake McQuaid.

Chapter Eight

News photographs didn't do justice to the former golden boy from California. Senator Phillip Gould had aged expensively and well. His golf tan was a startling contrast to his extremely blue eyes, and his carefully colored hair held just the right amount of gray to lend sophistication. The precision-cut casualness fell perfectly across a relatively unlined forehead.

Frani recognized him immediately when he entered the Aspen airport with his small entourage of two youthful aides and a husky man in dark glasses who she figured was the Senator's personal bodyguard.

She'd met Gould once when she'd accompanied Zach to a political fundraiser in Chicago. At that time, even though she didn't like Gould's politics, she couldn't help being impressed by the Californian's boundless energy and charisma.

Now, she thought, it would take more than charm for her to ever forget the man was a rapist. If she'd had one shred of corroborating evidence, Frani would have been delighted to print the allegation. Unfortunately, the resulting publicity might be more painful for Susan than for Gould.

While his aides scurried to gather his luggage and attend to his every whim, Gould scanned the airport. His blue-eyed gaze passed over Frani and then returned and held. There was no conceivable reason for him to remember their one brief encounter, and yet he nodded, smiled and started toward her.

"We've met, haven't we?" he said, extending his hand. "I'm Phillip Gould."

Although she would have preferred spitting on his hand, she submitted to a handshake. "Francesca Landon," she said stiffly. "I worked with Zach Hollingsworth. We were introduced—"

"In Chicago," he said warmly. "At a fundraiser. Ah, yes. Now I remember."

His prodigious memory didn't surprise her. A politician's stock-in-trade was the ability to treat every acquaintance like an old friend. Gould's well-practiced phoniness made it difficult to read his thoughts, but Frani observed him intensely, hoping for glimpses of the man behind the mask.

He assumed an expression of condolence. "Terribly sorry for your loss. Zach was a brilliant journalist."

"Murder is always a tragedy," she said.

"We can only hope and pray the local authorities will rise to the challenge and find the perpetrator quickly."

Frani decided to take the bull by the horns. "Senator, would you care to comment on the discovery that Pamela Jessup is alive and well?"

If the revelation shocked him, he hid it well. "That rumor has been circulating for twenty years. Don't tell me you believe what you read in the tabloids, Miss Landon?"

"I have reason to believe it's true."

He studied her a moment and then exhaled a measured breath. "I can only say the Jessups have always been friends of my family. Fine people. I hope, for their sake, their daughter is alive and well."

"And you were close to Pamela at one time, weren't you?"

"'Close' is a bit of a stretch. As I said, I know her family. Ah, what a waste. As I remember, Pamela was a beautiful young woman. Unfortunately, her lack of self-discipline was her undoing."

"Were you ever tempted to tame that wildness?"

His brilliant blue eyes narrowed a fraction, and Frani knew her barbed question had struck a nerve.

"Well, Senator?"

"I dated her sister, Candace. But that was a long, long time ago. I never had any personal interest in Pamela. In fact, I hardly remember her. You know how time can fade memories."

Not for the victim of those memories, Frani thought bitterly. "Surely, you wouldn't forget an intimate relationship."

"Intimate?"

Ingenuously, she continued, "Gosh, Senator. You remembered me and we barely met. Surely, you'd remember a relationship with Pamela Jessup."

He seemed to stand a little straighter. "As I told you, Miss Landon, I wish her family all the best. If it's true that she's alive, I couldn't be more delighted that the poor, deluded woman might finally be reunited with her loving family and get the professional help she no doubt needs." His smile was condescending. "And now, if you'll excuse me, I don't care to comment any further at present."

"But, Senator, I have reason to believe that—"

"I said that's all, Ms. Landon. Your incessant badgering shows a lack of skill in the delicate art of interviewing. Zach didn't teach you very well, did he?"

"He taught me everything," she snapped back defensively.

"Well, then perhaps you know too much and understand too little."

You know too much. The comment echoed through Frani's mind. Was it an implied threat? "What do you know about Zach's murder?"

Before Gould could answer, Cam appeared out of nowhere to insinuate himself between them. The outrage he'd expressed after meeting with Candace had boiled down to a cold, sharp fury as he confronted the man who had sexually assaulted Susan. His fists clenched at his side. His jaw seemed to have turned to granite.

"Gould," he said. There was a wealth of barely restrained hatred in that single word. "Are you afraid to answer the lady's questions?"

The bodyguard moved in closer. "Back off, mister," the big man warned.

Cam didn't move an inch. Standing his ground, he was clearly a match for the bodyguard and ten more like him. Cam stared at Gould with such naked aggression that Frani feared he might assault the senator—an act that could only result in problems for Cam and for Susan.

To distract him, Frani touched his arm, feeling tensile steel beneath the split leather jacket. "Cam, please. Let's just go."

"Better listen to her, buddy," the bodyguard advised. He allowed his jacket to open, revealing a shoulder holster. "Just move along and no one will get hurt."

"If anyone gets hurt, if won't be me," Cam's voice was low, forcibly controlled.

The bodyguard had the good sense to look nervous. "Listen. This is your last warning."

Quick as the strike of a rattlesnake, Cam whipped the man around, disarmed him and pinned his arm behind his back. "I have just one thing to say to the senator. After I've spoken, I'll leave. If you understand, nod your head."

The bulky man nodded vigorously.

"Who the hell are you?" Gould demanded.

"Sheriff Cameron McQuaid. The woman you know as Pamela Jessup raised me."

Gould didn't flinch, but his eyelids blinked as if he were snapping a picture of Cam, recording his image indelibly. "All right, Sheriff. I guess I'll have to take your word for that astonishing bit of news. Now, what's the important message you have for me?"

"Stay away from Susan. Don't try to find her. Don't come near her or try to harass her in any way."

"Wouldn't dream of it," Gould said smoothly. "I apologize for my bodyguard's behavior, Sheriff. He's a new employee."

As soon as Cam released the big man, he stumbled back. Sheepishly, he asked, "Hey, what about my gun?"

Cam expertly snapped back the magazine and removed the clip before handing it over. "Get it out of here. Weapons aren't allowed in this airport."

Smoothly, he took Frani's arm and turned to escort her out of the building.

"Charming to see you again, Miss Landon," Gould said to their backs.

"Keep walking," Frani said desperately. "He's trying to bait you."

"I never forget a face," Gould added. "And I will certainly remember both of you."

She clung to Cam's arm, the arm that was tensing with anger. "Please, Cam. Don't listen to him."

"By the way," Gould offered as a parting shot. "Be sure to give Pamela my kindest regards."

Frani felt the explosion of unadulterated loathing inside

Cam as he slowly turned. Across the Aspen airport, Cam stared hard into the senator's face, silently communicating a threat.

Wisely, Gould removed his chiseled profile from striking distance and fled in the company of his stunned entourage.

"Let's go," Frani pleaded. "Now."

Outside, the Aspen sunlight glistened on the mountains surrounding the busy airfield where private planes swooped and glided like exotic mechanical birds against a background of pure blue sky. The tawdry scene in the airport seemed impossible against the backdrop of such astounding natural beauty.

Frani found herself almost jogging to keep up with Cam's long, angry strides. Wrapped tight in his own fury, his hand gripped her upper arm as tightly as a steel vise.

Frani dug in her heels. "Lighten up, Cam. You're hurting me."

"Sorry." Although he loosened his hold, his tension ratcheted up a notch. "I wanted to kill him, Frani."

"I understand."

"For what he did to Susan, he doesn't deserve to live."

She could have offered platitudes about how it was a long time ago and they had no proof. But she held her tongue, knowing nothing she could say would appease his rage.

Injustice was a fact of life. Frani understood that all too well. And eventually, this code-of-the-West lawman would have to realize it, too. What a strange turn of events, Frani thought as they made their way to the plane. Now *she* was the one wishing she could protect *him*.

HOURS LATER, after night had fallen over Cedar Bluffs, Cam still felt residual pangs of anger. He'd taken care of business: flown back home, gotten Frani safely tucked away at Addie Lindstrom's and returned to his ranch, where he retired to his office without talking to anyone.

The large wall clock with Roman numerals, a souvenir from an old schoolhouse that had been torn down, showed it was after nine o'clock. Cam was tired but still had work to do. He ought to check in with the ranch manager, ought to deal with the stack of phone messages on the desk, ought to put in another call to Harold T. Cisneros and find out how far the murder investigation had progressed. But only one piece of business captured his attention.

Centered in the middle of his scarred, ancient oak desk was a white envelope. Written in the neat, block letters used by Cam's secretary, Rachel Beck, was a single word: *Important.*

Cam sat behind the desk and slashed the envelope with his Bowie-knife letter opener. Rachel's penmanship was as legible as if she'd used a typewriter. The woman was an invaluable asset to the department as evidenced by her special trip to his home tonight to deliver this message. Cam admired that kind of loyalty and dedication, and he made a mental note to recommend an increase in Rachel's salary at the next council meeting.

In her note, Rachel mentioned the discovery of the murder weapon—a gun commonly used by police officers, men like Jake.

Also, she wanted Cam to know that one of the employees at the Circle Q had come forward, telling Joe that he'd overheard Jake cursing Zach Hollingsworth and telling Susan that someone was bound to be hurt if Zach broke his story.

A nurse at the hospital who'd tended Jake when he'd had his stroke had also made a statement. She said Jake had said he felt useless laid up, unable to protect Susan.

The witness had gone on to say she believed Jake seemed worried, as if he expected trouble.

Cam swore softly under his breath. It never ceased to amaze him how an innocent comment could be twisted out of context in the heat of an investigation.

As if those two pieces of testimony weren't bad enough, Rachel also wrote that an FBI agent had come by the office today. She said he'd identified himself as a friend of Cy's. But he also said to tell Cam he was getting pressure from higher-ups to move on the rumor of Pamela Jessup's tie to the Circle Q and Jake McQuaid.

Rachel concluded with a postscript. "You know how I feel about your family, Cam. If there's anything I can do, just call. We all miss you here at the department."

With a groan, Cam tilted back in his desk chair and kicked his boot heels up onto the desk. He couldn't stand the thought that Susan might be taken into custody, that she'd spend even one night in jail. If ever there was a victim of circumstances, Susan a.k.a. Pamela was one.

After meeting Candace Jessup and coming face-to-face with Phillip Gould, Cam felt more determined than ever to protect Susan from anything in her past that might threaten her present or future happiness. He'd rescued her once, when he was only eight years old. Now, he felt compelled to save her again, to protect the only mother he'd ever known.

Why had this happened to her? Susan was a good woman. Everything she touched bore the stamp of her decency. Even here, in his office, signs of her loving kindness were all around him. He hadn't bothered to do much decorating, just thrown up some bookshelves, lugged in a desk and a couple of file cabinets. It was Susan who'd hung the plaid wool curtains and found a couple of secondhand chairs she'd recovered in matching fabric. She'd framed the family photos for the walls she'd painted a sandy beige.

When Cam had asked her why she'd gone to all the trouble, she'd told him she felt it was her duty to make sure his house was a home until he found his own woman and started a family.

Though she never pushed him to get married, he knew Susan was hoping for a daughter-in-law and grandchildren. But somehow Cam had just never seemed to find that one woman. The right woman at the right time. Maybe that had something to do with his determination not to make the same mistakes his father had made, going through two wives before finally finding the one woman who seemed meant for him.

The door to his office swung open, and Cam blinked in total surprise as Jake stepped into his office. In a gruff tone, the old man said, "I thought I heard you come in."

"Dad! You darn near scared the life out of me! What are you doing here?"

"Some reporter tracked us to Glenwood. Before we knew it, there were ten more camped on the doorstep. We didn't feel right about doing that to our friends, so we decided to come here. Hope you don't mind, son."

"Mind? Of course not. I'm just glad you felt you could. But how did you manage to get out of Glenwood without storming a barricade of media?"

Stiffly, Jake lowered himself onto the chair opposite the desk. "We made a damn fine escape. Took off on horseback with Susan dressed like a man. Those reporters in their trucks didn't have a chance. There was no way they could follow us."

"You always were the foxy one." The idea of his aged father and Susan outsmarting a horde of media people pleased Cam. "Where's Susan? Is she all right?"

"She's fine. Sound asleep in the guest room." A satisfied grin stretched across his weathered face. "You should have seen her. She rode like the wind. That woman's got more spirit and grit than anyone I've ever known. They just don't make women like that anymore, do they, son?"

Cam wasn't so sure. Jake's description made him think of Frani. He frowned at the connection. Sure, there were similarities between the determined little redhead and Susan, but somehow he just couldn't picture Frani as a ranch wife. Wife! Was he losing his mind, putting the words "Frani" and "wife" in the same thought?

He looked at his father. "Tell me something, Dad. How did you know Susan was right for you? When you met her for the first time, did you…feel something? Was there some sort of signal or sign? How did you know it was right to let her stay?" He sighed. "For that matter, how does any man know when he's met the right woman?"

The old man's eyebrows raised and a curious expression crept over his features. "Are you asking for my advice, son?"

"I guess I am," Cam replied, although the request seemed suddenly as strange to him as it had to Jake.

For years, he and Jake had been standing on opposite sides of the fence, snarling at each other. The basis of the hostility had grown out of Jake's refusal to marry Susan and make an honest woman of her. The fact that the old man preached a code of honor and duty and then dishonored the woman he supposedly loved had seemed to Cam the highest form of hypocrisy.

"Well, slap a brand on my butt and call me beef," Jake said. "You're finally realizing your old dad has a few smarts, after all."

"I'm not saying you were right to keep Susan's past a secret. You should have told Cy, Matt and me that she was still legally married to somebody else instead of clamming up and—''

"I couldn't tell anyone," Jake interrupted. "Not even the three of you. By the time you boys were old enough to understand, you were all headed into law enforcement. It would have been your duty to arrest her. I couldn't put any of us in that position."

Cam wasn't willing to get into a discussion of duty. By rights, he and Cy should be turning Susan over to the feds now. "Just tell me, Jake. How'd you know Susan was the one?"

The old man pushed his gnarled fingers through his thinning, gray hair. "Well, that's kind of hard to explain," he drawled. "Susan just seemed...well, special." When he spoke of her, the years seemed to melt away from his craggy face. "She wasn't like anyone I'd ever met before. She was sweet and yet she could bring me down to size in a New York minute. I don't know how to explain it all, except to say she makes me happy."

"That's it? She makes you happy?"

"Not that she was ever the least bit afraid to disagree with me."

Again, Cam thought of Frani. If constant disagreement was the earmark of a good relationship, they were surely meant for each other. "Then you're saying conflict is the secret?"

"No. Of course not. Not all of it, anyway. But a little friction keeps things interesting, you know?" Jake said. "Life with Susan is everything I want it to be and, believe me, it's never been dull."

"But how did you know it was forever? That you'd still care for each other after all these years?"

"Didn't," Jake admitted. "I don't guess anyone ever knows anything for sure. But I knew how I felt about her and I thought I knew how she felt about me; for some strange reason she couldn't imagine life without me. And I knew I didn't want to live without her.''

"And I guess that's what they call love," Cam said. Would he ever feel that way about a woman? About Frani? "I envy you, Dad. Both of you."

"I know you always wanted me to do right by Susan," Jake said in a somber tone. "All I can say is that she's my wife in all the ways that count. I'd walk through hell for her. Do anything I could to protect her."

His statement echoed the testimony from the nurse. But had he? Had he walked through hell and murdered Zach Hollingsworth to protect his woman?

"They found the murder weapon," Cam said.

Jake's face brightened. "Good. That should get me off the hook."

"Not exactly. It was a thirty-eight. A throw-away."

"No serial number. No registration," Jake said. "The kind of weapon cops keep around, just in case."

"Did you ever have one, Dad? A throw-away?"

Jake nodded. "Sure. In Texas. But I got rid of it when I turned in my badge. I threw the damn thing as far as I could into the river on my way back to the ranch."

"Why?"

"I didn't like what it represented. The kind of law that has nothing to do with justice, or doing what's right. To me, that's the kind of law that forced a woman like Susan to become a fugitive. When I left Texas, I didn't just retire from being a sheriff, son. I turned my back on that kind of law."

"But you always said—"

"I taught you boys right from wrong. That's a code that runs deeper than the law, it's the kind of truth that can't be found in a handbook."

Cam sat staring at his father, realizing the depth of the old man's wisdom. It was a wisdom he'd tried to emulate in his own life. As the sheriff of a small county, Cam was charged with enforcing the law, with making sure folks did the right thing. Most times, right equaled legal. On a few occasions, however, he'd had to bend the rules to suit a special circumstance and work out a compromise. He'd never violated the code of his own conscience. He knew the law, respected it, in many ways, lived for it. The law could be black-and-white, but it left room for judgment calls. Until now, he didn't believe his judgment had ever failed him.

But there was no room for judgment calls when it came to murder, he reminded himself. And if anyone, even his own father, committed that heinous crime, he would have to face the consequences.

THE NEXT MORNING at the *Clarion* office, Frani planted herself at the desk, determined to take care of business. First on her agenda was drafting a response to the faxes from her managing editor. With a resigned sigh, she leaned over the keyboard and began to type.

Next, she decided it was time to check her answering machine in her apartment in Chicago. She punched in the series of numbers and codes until finally a mechanical voice informed her that she had twenty-seven messages. Groaning, Frani sat back with a pencil to take notes.

The first voice she heard was Zach's. "Sorry I missed you, kid. I'm on my way to Cedar Bluffs."

Her breath caught in her throat as she listened to the gruff tones, speaking to her from beyond death.

He continued, "I put in a call to Pete Potterfield at the Department of Corrections. I had a question about David

Eisman's parole. Potterfield will be calling you. I gave him your number since I'd be out of touch for a while.''

Eisman. The man who'd kidnapped Pamela Jessup and engineered the bank robbery. Why had Zach wanted to connect with the man, now?

"I'm off," Zach said. "Who knows, by the end of the day, I may have solved a twenty-four-year-old mystery. Keep a good thought for me, Frani.''

"Always, Zach." Her eyes stung with unshed tears. "I'll always have a good thought for you. Wherever you are.''

She hit the repeat button and listened to his voice again. Then, again. For a few moments, it seemed like he was with her once more, working on the investigation, shooting off questions, digging for answers. She missed him so much.

Six messages later, Pete Potterfield left his number.

His was the first message Frani returned. Unfortunately, he was away from his desk. The rest of her messages were a combination of condolences and questions regarding a memorial service. Nothing that couldn't wait.

Addie called to Frani from the top of the stairs. "Coffee's ready.''

Frani called Addie an angel of mercy and then waited as the older woman descended the stairs with the pot in her hand. She was dressed in her casual denims with ornate turquoise jewelry. Her long gray braid hung down her back. Although a naturally attractive woman, Addie's eyes looked sunken and shadowed this morning. The stress of recent happenings seemed to be taking a toll. Frani watched as the older woman carefully refilled her cup. Addie's movements lacked vigor. When she walked, her gait shortened, as if her hips ached. "Tired, Addie?''

"Oh, I'm all right. I had a good night's sleep last night, but I feel kind of stiff for some reason.''

"There's been a lot of excitement lately."

"Yes, and I wouldn't have missed a minute of it. But I'm an old woman, Frani. Much as I regret becoming a creature of habit, it's true. I guess I've grown accustomed to peace and quiet. I can't take the pace like I used to. You must admit, it's been wild around here."

Frani agreed. Cedar Bluffs had become the eye of a media storm, and the *Clarion* was one of the focus points as other news sources around the country contacted Addie in their quest for information. The phone rang constantly and the fax machine had been spewing messages like bullets from an M-16.

"I'm sorry," Frani said.

Briskly, Addie responded, "My dear, none of this is your fault."

"Yes, it is. If I could have just stayed in a motel like any other normal visitor, you would have been sleeping in your own bed. At least now, you won't be stuck baby-sitting me and you can go home and get some rest."

"I don't mind the company, Frani. I think we get along just fine," Addie said. Her bright blue eyes surveyed the chaotic office, and she shook her head in bemused disgust. "I think I'm just feeling overwhelmed. Just look at this mess! I thought I'd left all the chaos behind years ago when I retired from the *Denver Post*. I was a beat reporter, did I tell you that? I was assigned to work one of the busiest police precincts in town."

"But you never really retired," Frani observed.

"I guess in some ways a journalist never does," Addie said. "Once you get a taste of the newspaper business, you're always hungry for more."

She leaned heavily on her desktop. "Ah, Frani. It's a lot of work. Sometimes I do wish I could stop."

"But you won't."

"A community needs its own newspaper and if I give it up, who'll take over? Who'll cover all those day-to-day activities that mean so much to people? I don't know how much longer I can do it, but I'm afraid to stop. I feel I owe it to the community to keep the *Clarion* alive."

Frani froze at a sudden and unexpected thought. "Addie, if you don't mind my asking, is the *Clarion* making money?"

Addie smiled. "I don't mind the question at all. And the answer is yes, it supports itself and me—not in what you'd call grand style, but I live comfortably. I publish a weekly edition, but there's enough advertising to justify another run. It could easily go to a biweekly, with three sections instead of two."

"It does seem to be jam-packed with news and features. You put out a good paper, Addie. You should feel proud." Frani had read several back copies. The articles by Addie showed wonderful insight, plus she'd managed to string together several local people who wrote features, based on their special areas of expertise.

"Thanks for the vote of confidence, but this week, I'm not so sure what kind of edition it will be. I ought to be going to press the day after tomorrow, and I haven't even started putting together articles. Darn it! With all the media people in town, I wanted this to be my best issue."

She sat down on the chair facing Frani's. "To tell the truth, it was going to be my swan song." She looked down at her gnarled hands. "I was ready to put the *Clarion* on the market and suspend printing until it sold. Now, I'm afraid I'm not even going to get out that last edition."

An idea took root in Frani's mind and grew with the speed of light. "What if I help? We can build your last edition around the murder investigation."

"I couldn't let you do that, Frani. You've got your own deadlines to worry about."

"This is more important," Frani said. "Besides, what better place to tell the real story behind this whole mystery than in the hometown newspaper."

"What real story?"

"Susan's story," Frani said evenly. Then, in detail, she told Addie the truth about Jake McQuaid's woman. When she finished, she said, "I promised Cam I wouldn't break the story until I have all the facts."

Addie merely sat back in her chair with a sigh. Frani had expected more of a reaction. "You knew, didn't you?" Frani said.

Addie tilted her head. "I guess you could say I suspected something."

"But you never investigated."

"No. Even after the bank robbery and Pamela's disappearance, I thought the woman had been victimized. Later, when they reported she'd died, I forgot all about the story. By the time I met the McQuaids and started wondering, it was too late. I already loved the woman. I figured if Susan—or whoever she was—had secrets, it wasn't going to be me who uncovered them." Addie frowned. "That makes me a lousy journalist, doesn't it?"

Frani stood and patted the older woman's shoulder. "I won't make that judgment. But as far as I'm concerned, it just makes you a pretty special lady."

In the silence that ensued, Frani contemplated the similarities between herself and Addie. Zach would have been irritated by the way they let emotion lead them, but Frani found herself moved and touched by Addie's loyalty to the woman she called her friend.

"So what do we do about all the interlopers?" Frani

asked. "The rumors are flying and it's only a matter of time before someone discovers Susan's secrets."

Last night Frani had counted three trucks from three different networks. Each vehicle had an Insta-cam mounted on the roof. Addie had told her there were at least thirty journalists in town, including the two reporters from the *Herald* whom Frani was expected to defer to. Fat chance!

"It's just so unfair that you've been taken off the assignment. It's your story, Frani," Addie said. "You're the one who ought to break it."

"I intend to write the Pamela Jessup story," Frani said. "And I've already started on my remembrance of Zach. I'd like nothing more than to break them in the *Clarion.*"

"Don't tease an old lady. You're still working for the *Daily Herald.* Whatever you write belongs to them."

"Not anymore." Frani waved the letter she'd just written. "Not once my editor receives my resignation."

Addie shook her head. "Think long and hard about this, Frani. It's tough to land a job with a major metropolitan newspaper. Maybe you shouldn't walk away from the *Daily Herald* so quickly."

"To the editors at the *Herald,* I was always just Zach's assistant. Now that he's gone, I'm sure they'll find me irrelevant. I can just imagine the assignments they're going to give me now."

After working on high-level stories with Zach, she would never be satisfied covering flower shows and the latest meetings of suburban sanitation departments. Nor would she willingly submit to the demands of a managing editor who didn't respect her ability.

"I'm ready to quit. Question is, are you ready to take me on? I'd work for you on a temporary basis. For this one issue, if that's all you can offer."

Addie chuckled. "I was hoping it would be you who

made an offer, but I suppose we can talk about that later. For now, it sure would be fine to scoop all these other journalists, wouldn't it?''

''We can do it,'' Frani said. ''If we use all your contacts in town, we can scoop everyone.''

''Welcome aboard,'' Addie said. ''I think I'll make you the Executive Editor in Charge of Special Investigation.''

''Nice title,'' Frani said, ''but there's something I really need to make this story happen. I need to meet with Susan Hathaway.''

''Funny you should mention that,'' Addie said. ''I happen to have a hot lead on her whereabouts. According to the woman who does a gardening column for me, Susan and Jake are staying with Cam at his ranch.''

The mention of Cam caused an odd twisting sensation in the pit of Frani's stomach. This morning, when she awoke, she'd missed him. She'd been tempted to call his ranch just to hear his voice. ''Cam will never let me talk to Susan.''

''Well, then. It's lucky for us that Susan Hathaway has a mind of her own, isn't it? Believe me, Frani, Cam doesn't tell her what to do. And I've got a feeling he doesn't call the shots with you, either.''

''Addie, you're a treasure!''

In the course of her investigations with Zach, Frani had faced drug dealers, terrorists and murderers. She could certainly handle a little heat from Sheriff Cameron McQuaid.

Chapter Nine

Beyond the cattle guard and front fence, about two hundred yards from Cam's long pine ranch house, a television crew in a minivan, along with three TV reporters, had set up camp. As they stared in, Cam stared out through binoculars, cursing the intrusion upon his privacy.

From a rocking chair in the front room where she sat reading a book, Susan commented, "Wishing won't make them go away."

"What will?"

"We could hope for a blizzard."

But the sun shone clear in a cloudless sky. The snow that had fallen earlier in the week had almost all melted, leaving the earth barren and cold.

Cam turned away from the window and let his gaze fall fondly upon Susan. Steadfast and gentle, she was virtually unchanged from the person he'd known for most of his life. It was difficult to imagine her very different life-style as Pamela Jessup, heiress in a wealthy California winery family. Harder still to imagine her with a gun in her hand. "When you were young," he said. "Were there reporters around all the time?"

"Not as often as you might think. Usually just for social events," she said.

"Society page news?"

"That's right," she said, calm and matter-of-fact. "When I made my entrance as a debutante, it seemed like there were a million flashbulbs going off. I wore the most beautiful white dress, like a bride, and white roses in my hair."

"Sounds fancy. Do you miss that life-style, all the glamour?"

"Not in the least, but I often think about some of the people I knew and never appreciated when they were close. Like Byron Reeves. He was a good friend."

Cam sat in a wingback chair opposite her. He wouldn't upset Susan for the world, but he needed to pick away at her memories and find out more about her background. Buried somewhere in that past, he sensed must be the key that would unlock the identity of Zach's real killer. And get Jake off the hook.

"I met your sister yesterday," he said. "And your mother."

A surprised smile lit her face. "Oh, my goodness! I had no idea you had contacted them. Where? How? Did you fly to Napa Valley?"

"They're in Aspen on a skiing holiday."

"Only a few hours away." There was a wistful tone in her voice. "Did they look well?"

"Too damn skinny for my taste."

She laughed. "That's Candace, all right. Even when she was a little girl, she bragged about her tiny waist. What did you think of her?"

"Honestly?"

"Of course."

"Well, I'm sorry to say this, Susan. But your sister is a pampered, bitter, self-centered woman with a mean streak a mile wide. She mentioned two ex-husbands and a therapist.''

"Oh, dear." Concern deepened the fine wrinkles on Susan's careworn face. "I'd so hoped she might have changed and found the happiness that I have."

"As for your mother, she seemed...well, kind of child-like."

"Like a butterfly," Susan said.

Cam wouldn't have been nearly so generous.

She continued, "I always thought she was a lovely person, but somehow not quite real. Definitely not a disciplinarian. When I got into trouble, she'd smile and look the other way. At the time, I thought it was because she cared about me." She winced, the memories obviously painful.

"I'm sorry, Susan. This is hard for you."

"What about my father? Is he with them?"

Cam shook his head. "I didn't get the chance to find out."

"He probably stayed home to take care of business," Susan said. "That would be typical of him. He's made a lot of money, but he's still happiest when he's tending his grapes. Running a winery isn't all that much different from farming. We were always totally dependent on the soil, the temperature and the rainfall."

"I never thought of it that way," Cam said.

"When I was young, I loved to play outside among the grapevines, working with the pickers." She shrugged. "Maybe that's why I took to ranching."

"You've always had gardens," he said. "Even here in Colorado where the rocky soil will hardly take a seed, you manage to grow a bumper crop of vegetables."

"And flowers," she said. "You need food for sustenance, but the beauty of an open blossom helps you grow from within."

He crossed the room, leaned down and kissed the top of her head. "How did you get to be so wise?"

"I made a lot of mistakes." Her gaze fell to her lap where her fingers twisted together in a knot. "I guess I couldn't help learning from some of them."

Though he knew he should mention Phillip Gould and ask her to search for memories that might lead to Zach's murderer, Cam couldn't bring himself to push Susan. The woman had already given so much.

PUTTING THEIR HEADS together, Frani and Addie planned the next issue of the *Clarion,* the edition that would put the small-town press on the map in a big way.

"We need updated information on the investigation," Addie said.

"Agreed."

Solving Zach's murder was still Frani's first priority. The logic and the mounting evidence pointed toward Jake McQuaid, but a long shadow of doubt fell across her mind. Cam's theory might be correct: Zach was killed because he knew too much.

Nothing else accounted for the attempt on her own life. Someone had come after her because they thought she, too, had information. But just what was she supposed to know? Their meeting with Bud Coleman hadn't produced a single useful clue. Likewise with Candace and Gould.

If Frani was going to figure this out, she would have to draw on all her investigative skills. To Addie, she said, "Is there any way we can get something more than the worthless pap the D.A. is feeding the media? Any chance he'd give you a private interview?"

Addie considered for a moment. "It's doubtful. Harold T. is very much aware of protocol. He wouldn't favor one reporter over another, not even me."

"What about Joe Bradley?"

"Joe would be afraid of making a mistake." Addie sniffed. "The person who really runs the sheriff's office is Rachel Beck, the secretary. She's the one to interview. Unfortunately, they're keeping all the media—including me—out of the offices."

"Then we'll have to sneak in," Frani concluded.

"Undercover work? Oh, I don't think I'm up to that," Addie said. "But we can arrange something for you."

"Tell me how."

At one time or another, practically every person in Cedar Bluffs had either written an article for the *Clarion* or been mentioned in its pages. Addie's influence extended far and wide.

Working on the theory that everyone—even the people in the sheriff's office—has to eat lunch, Addie contacted her food columnist, the owner of the Sunrise Diner, who confirmed that someone from her restaurant would be sending a lunch order to the sheriff's office.

Within the hour, Frani was ready to play delivery person. She'd chosen a simple disguise, wearing Addie's khaki squall jacket over her forest-green crewneck sweater and jeans. Her distinctive russet hair was tucked up under a beige cowboy hat.

"Don't you look cute." Addie grinned. "You're a regular cowgirl."

"This must be an excellent disguise. I can't imagine punching a cow or whatever it is that ranchers do."

"It's a good life, Frani."

But a lonely one. Being out here on the high plains without access to cultural events and conveniences struck her as the height of monotony, one day flowing endlessly into the next.

Then she recalled the remarkable landscapes she'd experienced with Cam. He'd shown her the high, snow-capped peaks and the haunting beauty of the Great Basin Desert. The views had been endlessly exciting. Or had it been Cam's presence that had made the difference?

"So, Addie. Do you think I could fool Cam with this disguise?"

"And why would you want to do such a thing?"

"Sooner or later, I'm going to have to sneak onto his ranch so I can interview Susan."

Thoughtfully, Addie toyed with the heavy silver squash blossom on her necklace. "I don't like that twinkle in your eye. It's as if you're hoping he'll catch you."

"Maybe I am," Frani confessed.

Addie frowned. "Look, I'm going to tell you the same thing I told Cam. Don't do it. Don't get involved. A relationship between the two of you would never work."

"Why not?"

"Obviously, you're wrong for each other."

"Not necessarily."

She and Cam had shared good conversations. They'd laughed together and relaxed in comfortable silence. And they'd kissed. Wonderful kisses. Where did Addie get off telling her it would never work? "Just because we come from different places and have different occupations doesn't mean we couldn't find a middle ground."

"Really?"

"Cam's not fond of reporters, but he's a generous man and could learn not to hold it against me. And, even though I don't know what goes into running a ranch, I can respect a lawman. To tell you the truth, Addie, I'm beginning to fall in love with the West. It's so beautiful and—"

Frani noticed a playful spark in the older woman's blue eyes, and knew she'd been had. "Aren't you the clever

Cupid? Tell me I can't have something, knowing darn well I'd have to have it."

"Get going, Frani." Addie patted her shoulder. "And good luck."

At the sheriff's office, Frani breezed past a pack of reporters, including the two men from the *Daily Herald* who didn't recognize her. But why should they? All the time she'd worked there, she'd been hidden in Zach's shadow.

Once inside, Frani followed Addie's advice and sought out Rachel Beck, who was sitting behind a desk, phone clamped to her ear and paperwork scattered in front of her. Rachel glanced up when Frani placed the food container on the desk in front of her. "Who are you?"

"My name is Frani Landon, and I'm—"

"You're the reporter whose been spending time with Cam." Rachel hung up the phone. "How's he doing?"

"I haven't seen him since last night." She remembered Cam's barely controlled rage yesterday afternoon. "He's having a rough time."

"And it's going to get worse," Rachel said. She disconnected her phone call and gestured to the straight-backed wood chair beside her desk. "Sit."

Frani did as she was told. Though she hadn't been able to carry her shoulder bag with her tape recorder while she was pretending to be a delivery person, she had a spiral notebook in the back pocket of her jeans. She pulled it out. "Addie Lindstrom and I are trying to put together an article that tells what's really happening with the investigation. What can *you* tell me, Rachel?"

"Things don't look good for Jake McQuaid." Rachel flipped open the container and started in on her lunch. "There are two witnesses who overheard him talking about protecting Susan."

"So he had a motive," Frani said.

Rachel regarded her steadily as she chewed her tuna-fish sandwich and took a bite of pickle. "You worked with the victim, didn't you?"

"He was my mentor and my friend," Frani said. "I want to see his murderer arrested and convicted. But I'm not sure it's Jake McQuaid."

"Neither am I. But there's the weapon. The victim was killed with a .38 revolver and we found the gun. It's not registered, but it's the kind of gun most lawmen, like Jake McQuaid, keep around just in case. We call it a throw-away."

That meant Jake had both a motive and access to a similar murder weapon. Since he had admitted he was on the scene at the approximate time of the murder, he had also had opportunity. "But the evidence is largely circumstantial," Frani said.

"Short of a confession or an eyewitness, I don't think we'll get much more."

"What about the case against Susan Hathaway?" Frani asked. "You know she claims to be Pamela Jessup, a fugitive. Will she be taken into custody?"

Rachel glanced over her shoulder, making sure they weren't being overheard. "Off the record?"

"Sure," Frani said and closed her notebook.

In a low voice, Rachel confided, "If the FBI agent in charge wasn't a friend of the McQuaid family, she'd be locked up right now. He's holding off, claiming he needs time to gather all the information before he does a personal interview with Susan."

"Sounds like it's just a matter of time," Frani said.

"I'm afraid so. As soon as the FBI talks to Susan and she admits to being involved in a bank robbery, it's all over."

Poor Cam! Frani wished she could help him. He'd spent

his life upholding the law. Now both his father and the woman who'd raised him seemed to be looking at serious jail time. He'd be devastated by the very law that formed the backbone of his existence.

But Frani still had hope that her investigation would turn up another suspect. "Here's what puzzles me, Rachel. If Jake McQuaid's alleged motive was to protect Susan from exposure, why kill Zach? Surely, he'd know that a murder would cause even more publicity."

From behind her back, Frani heard another voice. "Interesting point, Ms. Landon."

She turned in her chair and confronted a gentleman in a three-piece suit. Beneath his thick black mustache, his lips formed a firm line. His equally bushy eyebrows held a slight scowl. Only yesterday, she'd seen his photograph in the Salt Lake City newspaper.

"You're the Chaparral district attorney, Harold T. Cisneros," she said, rising. "Pleased to meet you, sir."

He took her hand in a firm, politician's handshake. "How do you know me?"

When she explained about the newspaper article, he seemed pleased. "They quoted me in Salt Lake City? Well, how about that?"

"You're doing a good job of keeping this investigation under control," she said. "When the media descends on a town, things can get out of hand."

He cocked an eyebrow. "Sometimes reporters will even disguise themselves as delivery persons from the Sunrise Diner to sneak into the sheriff's office."

Though Cam had accurately described Harold T. Cisneros as an ambitious district attorney with political aspirations, Frani found him likable. "Would you care to answer my interesting question? Off the record, of course."

"Why would Jake McQuaid kill Zach Hollingsworth if

his motive was to protect Susan from exposure?'' he re-phrased her question. "The answer is simple. That wasn't his motive."

"Could you elaborate?"

"Jake wanted to protect Susan from something else—something in her past that no one else knows. I'm afraid your Mr. Hollingsworth might have uncovered new infor-mation that could hurt Susan more than merely revealing her past."

Zach knew too much.

Harold T. continued, "According to one of our wit-nesses, Jake said he would do anything to protect his woman. He said he'd kill anybody who tried to hurt her."

Which would explain why Frani herself was threatened at the *Clarion* offices. This last bit of information meshed with everything else she knew. For the first time, Frani truly thought it possible that Jake McQuaid had murdered Zach. And that he'd arranged for someone to come after her.

Jake had motive, means and opportunity. And yet Frani didn't want to believe it. She didn't want Cam's father to be the man who had murdered Zach.

When Harold T. stepped aside, she saw Cam behind him. Apparently he hadn't heard their conversation, because a reluctant smile tugged at the corner of his mouth. As he looked at her, his eyes held a warm welcome. *Oh, Cam. How could it be true? How could your father be a mur-derer?*

Zach's death demanded justice. She had respected his talent and was grateful for his tutelage. But beyond that, he'd been more than a father to Frani. She wanted Zach's murderer to pay.

But Jake? Arresting Jake McQuaid would hurt Cam so deeply. He looked tired, Frani thought. He was under siege from all quarters. And now, she was about to add her voice to the chorus of others demanding a solution to the crime, demanding the arrest of Cam's father.

"Frani, you shouldn't be here," he said. "I thought you were going to stay put with Addie."

"Sorry." Tension pinched her lips.

He arched one eyebrow questioningly as he studied her. Though Frani was doing her best to appear noncommittal, Cam clearly guessed at her inner turmoil, and he wasn't the sort of man who could simply turn and walk away.

He took her arm. "Well, whatever you're doing here, it's over. But as long as you're here, why don't I give you the cheap tour of the Chaparral County sheriff's office?"

With a parting glance at Rachel and Harold T., Frani went along with Cam.

On the lower floor were the jail cells. Like cages in a zoo, the iron bars separated eight rooms, each containing a simple cot, a sink and a toilet.

"No prisoners," Cam said.

"It's a quiet county."

"We have our share of crime. But winter is usually a slow time." He allowed the outer door to close behind them. They were alone. "What's going on, Frani?"

There wasn't any way to avoid the truth. "They have enough evidence to arrest your father."

"I know."

"Cam, I'm afraid he did it."

She searched his face, hoping he had some piece of evidence that would prove Jake's innocence. Frani needed to hate Zach's murderer. She needed to find satisfaction in seeing the killer brought to justice. "Tell me I'm wrong."

"I know in my heart that Jake McQuaid would never murder anyone."

Her gaze slid away from his face. She took a backward

step, bumping against the cold iron bars of the jail cell. "That's not good enough."

"It's all I've got."

"Let me talk to him," Frani said. "Let me talk to Jake, and I'll decide for myself."

"How are you going to do that? How will you know if he's telling the truth? Are you some kind of human polygraph?"

"I'll know," she said, more aggressively than she intended. "My instincts are good."

"You need to be more objective," he said, unknowingly echoing Zach. "It doesn't matter what you believe. Or what I know in my heart. Only facts are permitted in a courtroom. That's the law."

"The law is going to arrest your father."

When he opened the door to the cells, it creaked on the hinges, then clanged as it hit the iron bars of the first cell. The hollow sound seemed to echo deep within her.

"It's *my* problem," Cam said. "As for you, Frani..."

"Yes?"

"I suggest you saddle up and head back to Chicago where you belong. You've already got more story than anyone else."

But it wasn't only about the story. And, besides, she didn't belong in Chicago anymore. She'd just quit her job. Without Zach, there was nothing for her back there. Obviously, Cam was telling her there wasn't anything here for her either. His dismissal, his rebuff, hurt more than she wanted to admit.

Frani fitted the beige cowboy hat back on her head and glared up at him. "I'm staying right here until I have this crime solved to my thorough satisfaction. And besides, my story isn't finished. Now, either you can help me or you can stay out of my way."

By NIGHTFALL, Frani was even more determined to get her one-on-one interview with Susan. Any secret Zach might have known belonged to Susan. The only way to find the solution was to unlock her past. If Cam wouldn't help her, Frani would find her own way, thank you very much.

An hour later, Addie cut the headlights on her Jeep as she parked on the shoulder of a deserted dirt road that fronted Cam's property. "Are you sure this is a good idea, Frani?"

"It's worth a try." She peered out into the cold night. What could happen? "I'm in great shape. I jog every other day."

"These aren't exactly city sidewalks."

"I'm no hothouse flower, Addie," she said defensively. "I can do it."

Her plan was to sneak across the open range to Cam's ranch house. Once she got to the door and knocked, she was sure he'd let her in, even if it meant a face-to-face meeting with Susan. Although he'd told her to go back to Chicago, he must know she wasn't going. He also had to know there was unfinished business between them. Although at this point, neither of them was sure just how it would all end.

"You be careful," Addie said. "Out in these parts, we shoot trespassers."

"You're joking."

"Not a bit. Call if you need me. If I don't hear from you, I'll see you tomorrow morning at the *Clarion*. Eight o'clock sharp."

Frani slipped from the passenger-side door of the Jeep and crept up to the barbed-wire fence. She could see the lights of the ranch house glimmering in the distance. Though it didn't look far, Addie had guessed about two miles.

Big deal! Frani regularly jogged three. A stroll across the open fields ought to be a snap.

Her first clue that her trek might not be so easy was when she snagged her khaki jacket on the barbed wire, got herself tangled and fell as she squeezed through the fence.

The frozen earth was harder than concrete. Her hip ached where she'd landed on it. Glancing over her shoulder, she saw that Addie had already pulled away.

"What am I doing?" she muttered. This supposed plan smacked of sheer desperation. To be perfectly honest, her motive was more than finding the truth about Susan's past.

Frani hated the way she'd left things with Cam this afternoon. Yesterday, it seemed, they were developing a friendship, maybe something more. Today, they were snapping at each other like adversaries. Oh, God, how could she even be thinking about a relationship with him? A man whose father might have killed Zach.

Forget about Cam, she told herself. Any sort of understanding between them always seemed to dissolve before it had the chance to gel.

The cloudy night obscured her vision, making it difficult to pick her way across the uneven earth. More than once, she slipped.

Concentrating on the rolling hills that had looked perfectly even from the road, Frani didn't notice the small herd of cows until she almost ran into them. Of course, she'd seen cows before, in the distance on Midwestern farms. But these were mean-looking Western animals, raised for beef, not milk. These beasts were known for stampeding. A friendly Wisconsin dairy cow would never dream of the aggressive behavior she feared these critters were capable of.

Suddenly, there were four of them surrounding her, making obnoxious snorting noises as if they disapproved of her intrusion into their territory.

"Let's all stay calm, girls," she told them in a soothing, gentle voice. Visions of John Wayne movies flashed through her head. No wonder those cowboys stayed on horseback. They didn't want to get smooshed beneath thundering hooves.

On the other hand, the cows didn't appear to be very fast. Surely she could outrun them if she could get away from the herd.

Stepping carefully, Frani edged past the animals. By talking softly and moving slowly, she made her escape.

Then she discovered her next hazard—the steaming piles of what the cows had left behind. She hip-hopped on the uneven field, dodging fresh cow pies. The stench made her cough. And she was cold. The night air, though dry, was icy.

Abandoning any attempt to approach quietly and secretively, she walked like a convulsive scarecrow. This interview had better be worth all the trouble, she thought. At the very least, Susan should confess to stealing the Lindbergh baby.

Frani made it all the way to a stand of pine beyond the barn when she heard a harsh voice from behind her back. "Hold it right there!"

Frani whirled. An older man stared at her from behind the sights of a long hunting rifle. It was Jake McQuaid.

Chapter Ten

Standing in the chill Colorado night, Frani raised her arms over her head. Jake could kill her right now, bury her body somewhere on this vast spread and no one would ever know. If he'd shot Zach in cold blood to keep Susan's secrets, he could do the same to Frani. She should have been terrified. And yet, she wasn't so afraid that she couldn't ask the question that had been burning her brain since the day Zach died.

"Did you do it, Jake? Did you kill Zach?"

He muttered something. Through a gap in the clouds, a dull glow from muted stars shone on the long bore of his rifle.

"He was a good man," Frani said. A sense of resignation consumed her anger and her fear. "He didn't deserve to die."

She listened for the click of the hammer, the signal that she was about to be shot. This was a hell of a way to uncover the truth.

Jake lowered the rifle. "You're that reporter gal."

"Frani Landon."

"Sorry, miss. I didn't mean to scare you. I thought you were intent on rustling Cam's cattle."

"No, sir." She wouldn't know what to do with a cow if one followed her home.

"What the hell are you doing out here, gal?"

"Actually, I wanted to talk to Susan. And to you."

He sauntered up beside her. Unlike Cam, he stood only a few inches taller than Frani. His sideburns, peeking out from beneath his cowboy hat, were steel gray. In his eyes, she saw the resemblance to Cam. The irises were almost black.

"Well, miss, you have a mighty strange way of paying a social visit. But come on."

In the dark, she stumbled along beside him. Jake moved at a slow but surefooted pace. But Frani was less familiar with this rugged countryside. When she tripped over an unseen log and fell to her knees, he helped her to her feet. "Are you okay?"

"I'm fine." As fine as she could be after trekking through a field of cow patties and cows and having a rifle pointed in her face. He waited while she brushed the frozen specks of hard dirt off her palms. "Why were you out here, Mr. McQuaid?"

"I needed a walk. The idea of being in jail makes a man want to soak up as much of the outdoors as he can."

"Should you be arrested?"

"If I was sheriff, I'd probably arrest me. But I didn't kill anybody." As they neared the long, low pine ranch house, he picked up his pace. "I might have been tempted to commit murder if I'd thought your friend Zach was going to hurt Susan, but it was her idea calling him."

Frani almost toppled again as she stepped into a ditch. Recovering her poise, she said, "But you didn't think Zach would hurt Susan."

"I just told you she invited him." He'd reached the porch of the house. "She wanted the man to come."

"Do you know why?"

"Said she wanted the truth told right and nothing I could say would change her mind. Susan is a determined female." He pushed up the brim of his Stetson and studied her appraisingly. "Funny thing, Frani. You kind of remind me of her."

Frani followed him inside. Cam's house was a charming place, warm and cozy, with a fire dancing on the hearth. Heavy wood furniture rested on Navajo rugs.

In the rustic kitchen, Frani saw Susan, busy at the sink. Her longish blond hair, fading to gray, was fastened at her nape with a tortoiseshell barrette.

"Jake? Is that you?" Her voice was soft but carried an undertone of strength. "I was just making some hot chocolate."

"Put out another mug," he said. "We've got company."

When she turned, Frani studied the woman she'd seen briefly the night of Zach's murder, and recognized from photographs and reams of information. Twenty-four years later, Susan retained the natural beauty that came from great bone structure and a clear complexion. She wore no makeup, not even a dash of mascara on her light eyelashes. Her figure had filled out to an attractive fullness.

"I want to apologize," Frani said. "When I saw you at the gate, right after Zach had been murdered, I accused you without thinking."

"It's all right. Anyone could see how upset you were." Susan gestured toward the knotty pine surface of the kitchen table. "Will you have a cup of hot chocolate with us?"

"That's very kind of you." Frani circled the table and sat. "And I might need a ride back to town later. I didn't make any arrangements for a return ride."

"Cam's not home right now," Susan said. "He got

called out on some business. But I'm sure he'd want me to offer you the guest room for the night.''

"Thank you." Frani wasn't so certain that Cam would be pleased to see her. He'd made it clear that he didn't want her talking to Susan. Being here, Frani knew she was bound to face his anger. But what choice had he given her? Did he really expect her to sit quietly waiting for his permission to act?

"Susan, I'm putting together an article for Addie Lindstrom's next issue of the *Clarion*. It's about Pamela Jessup. Would you talk with me about your past?''

"You get right to the point, don't you?"

Susan whipped around the kitchen with a confident efficiency, preparing their drinks. She placed a mug in front of Frani, set another opposite her at the table and handed a third mug to Jake.

The smile she offered him was the companionable expression of seasoned love. "Would you excuse us, Jake? I want to have a private conversation with Frani.''

He lightly kissed her cheek. "Are you sure this is what you want to do?''

"She was Zach's assistant. I think this is what I need to do.''

As he left the room, she settled into the chair opposite Frani, picked up her mug and blew across the steaming, fragrant surface. "It's good that you're working with Addie. With her arthritis, I worry that she works too hard putting out the newspaper.''

"I'm not doing this out of pity," Frani said. "Addie is a good journalist and a terrific human being, but there's another issue here. I want to be able to write your story without limiting the length or censoring the reporting, and I can't do that any place but in the *Clarion*.''

"Thanks for your honesty. You seem like a woman with a cause," Susan said. "I like that."

"It's my byline. I want to tell it my way. That's what Zach would have wanted."

Susan recoiled, as if she'd been slapped, at the sound of his name. "I'm afraid his death is somehow related to my past. These old secrets have begun to fester. Zach Hollingsworth was murdered. My old friend, Byron Reeves, lost an appointment to the Supreme Court. I don't want anyone else to be hurt."

Frani placed her tape recorder on the table. "Do you mind? I want to be able to quote you accurately."

Susan nodded. "It's what I expected."

Sitting at the homey kitchen table with the pleasant glow from a hanging lamp, Frani realized that she had achieved her goal—an exclusive interview with the missing heiress. She had scooped the entire journalistic world. But where was the rush? Where was the heady feeling of victory? Why, all of the sudden, did that aspect of the Pamela Jessup story seem irrelevant? Zach would have said her heart was getting in the way. And for once, Frani wouldn't have argued.

"I'll start with the kidnapping," Susan said.

In great detail, she described how she had been grabbed and detained by David Eisman. Her terror was mitigated when Eisman began medicating her with drugs. "I don't even know what they were. I swallowed the pills he gave me so I could stay unconscious."

"There was some speculation," Frani said, "that the kidnapping was a scam. People theorized that you and Eisman were working together to extort money from your wealthy family."

"Completely false. As a matter of fact, when Eisman first took me captive, I thought he intended to kill me. I begged for my life. I told him I would do anything. Anything."

"What happened then?"

"I was tied up and blindfolded most of the time. Once I was locked in a closet for three days and nights."

In a calm, completely undramatic way, Susan detailed the physical abuses she had suffered. Only the steady administration of drugs made it possible for her to survive. "I came to depend upon Eisman, to look forward to his brief visits, to the oblivion of that drugged state. Finally, one day, he appeared to me without disguising his face. And he told me it was over. My family had refused to ransom me."

For a long moment, she paused. "Until then, I'd sustained myself with the hope that someday it would all end and I could go back to a normal life. When my family turned their backs on me, I truly wanted to die. Perhaps that wish is worse than death itself."

The truth in her words touched a chord in Frani's memory. She remembered the pain of her own rejection. Her father's indifference had not been limited to a single incident, like Susan's kidnapping, but the result was the same—an emptiness. Without love, without hope, life was bleak. Even though she'd lived all her life in the same comfortable middle-class house, Frani had always felt alone and homeless.

She reached across the table and touched Susan's hand. "I understand."

"I thought you might. There's a connection between us, isn't there? I can sense it."

"My father..." Frani began, but suddenly felt herself overcome by emotion.

"Go on, Frani. Tell me about it," Susan said gently.

Frani turned off the tape recorder. "My father couldn't love me. I wasn't his child."

She talked about her mother's affair, and the emotional distance Frani had experienced as a child. Although her mother had loved her, somehow her guilt had stopped her from showing it. She'd never given Frani the assurance she needed, the security of her own special place in the family.

In a role reversal that seemed perfectly natural, Susan became the interviewer. "Are you married, Frani? Have you found your true love?"

"Not yet."

"It'll happen," Susan assured her. "Just don't be afraid to open your heart. Don't let the pain of your past get in the way of your future. Someday, you'll find someone who loves you for who and what you are. And you'll wonder how you lived without him. Trust your emotions and take the chance."

How ironic! Zach had always advised her to stick to the facts, to the evidence that could be proven. Emotions were too fleeting and insubstantial. "I don't know, Susan."

"If it happened for me, it can happen for you." She patted the back of Frani's hand. "Isn't there some special young man in your life?"

A vision of Cam's face appeared in Frani's mind. His bemused grin and direct gaze tantalized her. Frani rubbed her lip, thinking about his kiss. "I guess I don't really know yet."

"You will," Susan predicted.

"Thank you, Susan," Frani said. "I don't know what made me break down like that. There's something so... warm and accepting about you. Now I know why your husband and sons feel the way they do about you."

Susan smiled and refilled their mugs as Frani directed her back to the interview. She turned the tape recorder on.

"After Eisman informed you that the ransom would not be paid, what happened?"

"I clung to him," Susan said. "I'd been abandoned by everyone else, and Eisman seemed to care about me."

"At that time, were you free to leave?"

"During the day, my physical restraints were removed. Possibly, I could have escaped. But I'd grown dependent on the drugs, and on Eisman. He was seductive, charming. In a way, I imagined I was in love with him."

Frani knew about the Stockholm syndrome—the tendency among hostages to become enamored of their captors. Their survival required pleasing the people who held power over them.

Susan continued, "After I made the colossal mistake of marrying Eisman, I realized how wrong I had been. Gradually, I weaned myself off the drugs. I began looking for a way out. Unfortunately, that was when Eisman came up with the idea of the bank robbery."

"With Bud Coleman?"

Susan offered a weary smile. "Cam told me that you visited Bud in the desert where he was living like a hermit. I couldn't believe it. Bud loved to socialize and was always ready with a joke. I'm afraid his is another life that has been destroyed by the past."

"Susan, you're not blaming yourself for all these things, are you?"

"It's my fault," she said. "Sometimes, I think it would have been better if Eisman had killed me."

"You didn't set these events in motion, Susan. You were the victim."

"I wanted to turn myself in. But Eisman, my husband then, began treating me like a hostage again. He kept me locked up, monitored my every move."

She detailed her eventual escape from the abandoned

warehouse where she'd been held when Eisman was apprehended by the police. "I want to be perfectly clear about this," Susan said. "I escaped on my own. Without help from Byron Reeves. He was utterly innocent of any wrongdoing."

She emphasized her point by pounding lightly on the tabletop with her fist. This was obviously the major point she had intended to make with Zach. Susan wanted to clear Byron Reeves's name.

Frani nodded. "I'll make that very clear in my article."

"Good." Susan sat back, as if she'd finished the story.

"What happened after that?" Frani asked.

"I fled to Texas and stayed there for several months until my bad luck caught up with me. Waiting for a bus, I happened to witness a murder. The killers beat me and left me for dead. That was when Cam and his brothers saved my life. And Jake took me in."

"What about the dead woman in Texas who was identified as you?"

"I don't know anything about it," she said.

Frani sensed a cover-up. "Could Jake have engineered the substitution?"

"He never told me, and I never asked."

"Do you have an opinion?" Gently, Frani reminded her, "You want to reveal the whole truth, don't you?"

"I spoke with my sister, Candace, today. She said the family had hired a private detective to locate me, and that he had traced me all the way to Dry Creek, Texas. Possibly, she had something to do with the misidentification. But I don't know."

"Wait a minute! Your sister said there was a private detective? Why?"

"It doesn't matter." Susan sat up a little straighter in her chair. "The story of my kidnapping ends with my escape after the bank robbery. Then the real story of my life begins with Jake McQuaid.''

For the moment, Frani left the questions raised by Susan's undercover stay in Texas. ''I'd like to go back to a time before the kidnapping. Tell me about Phillip Gould.''

''Turn off the tape recorder, Frani.''

She did as Susan had asked. ''Did he rape you, Susan?''

''Yes.'' A shudder went through her. ''I wish there were some way to prove it, but there isn't. At the time, I told my mother, but she wouldn't believe me. She thought Phillip was such a good match that I should ignore what happened, what she never believed happened, and marry him. I would rather have died.''

''Did you tell anyone else?''

''I hinted to Byron Reeves, but I was too ashamed to give him details. I was working up the courage to tell my father when I was kidnapped.''

Frani heard the front door opening.

Susan called out, ''We're in the kitchen, Cam.''

When he came through the door, Frani gasped, shocked at the change in Cam. His shoulders stooped wearily. His dark eyes were dull and bloodshot. The arrogant cowboy attitude was gone. Exhaustion weighed heavily upon him. She could only hope he was too tired to let loose the anger seeing her here was bound to unleash inside him.

CAM STRETCHED HIS ARMS up over his head and latched his fingertips onto the door frame, stretching his back and anchoring himself against the pull of even more frustration and worry. Every time he had the situation under control, another twist spun things awry.

In any other circumstances, the fact that Susan and Frani were seated together at the table would have been cause for outrage. Working in tandem, those two women could come up with a whole heap of trouble. The strange thing was, they looked so sweet and innocent, like a couple of angels.

"I can explain," Frani began.

"I'll just bet you can. I'll bet you have a whole line of fast talk all prepared, but don't bother. You're here. You're safe. That's all." He didn't bother telling her he'd been running all over town trying to find her, desperate, thinking something might have happened to her.

He looked to Susan. "Are you all right?"

"I'm fine, but you're not." Energetically, she rose to her feet. "Come on, Cam. You're going to sit down and put your feet up. Have you eaten?"

"I'm not hungry."

"Nonsense. I'll throw together a nice omelet."

Frani was right beside her. "Maybe a drink."

"Great idea." Susan pointed out the liquor cabinet. "Rum and Coke. That's probably all he's got in there, anyway."

Cam frowned at both of them. "I don't want an omelet *or* a drink."

But protests were futile. Against two of them, he didn't stand a chance. Cam allowed himself to be directed into the front room with Susan on one arm and Frani on the other. They grabbed his coat and hat, practically shoved him into the most comfortable chair in front of the fireplace and pushed him down.

When Susan darted back to the kitchen to fetch a snack, Frani positioned herself at his feet to help pull off his boots. Kneeling in front of him, she tapped his shin and ordered, "Give me your foot."

"That's enough," he said.

"You heard your mother," she said. "You should take off those boots and—"

"Stop it, Frani."

She gazed up at him with her emerald eyes. God, she was pretty—the most beautiful adversary he'd ever faced. And probably the most worthy.

Cam made no mistake about her position. She—and everybody else—believed Jake had committed the murder. They wanted an arrest.

Worst of all, Cam wasn't sure they were wrong. Jake had made no bones about how he would defend his woman. The discovery of the .38 had upped the ante. Though Cam had played every card to keep the old man out of jail, he was running out of ideas.

"What is it?" Frani asked. "Has there been a new development in the investigation?"

"If you were hanging out with the other journalists by the courthouse, you might hear the complete story from Harold T."

"But I'm here," she said. "So tell me."

He motioned for her to stand. "Get up."

But she shook her head, sending ripples through her russet hair. "Susan told me to get your boots off, and that's what I'm going to do."

"Is that how it is?" In spite of the threats that pressed in all around them, he couldn't help smiling. "You'll take orders from Susan. But not from me."

"Her instructions make sense. You need to rest, take it easy."

Having Frani kneel in front of him wasn't exactly an inducement to relaxation. "I only want to tell my story once. Why don't you help Susan in the kitchen? Get Jake in here, too."

"Okay, but don't get used to ordering me around."

"Wouldn't dream of it."

As she hustled off to fulfill his request, Cam allowed his

eyelids to droop closed. Frani and Susan were correct in assuming he needed rest. He desperately needed sleep tonight, but he doubted his mind would be still enough for real relaxation.

Watching them gather around the fireplace, he tried to figure out what to say. There wasn't a good way to break the news that Harold T., under pressure from state authorities, was on the verge of issuing a warrant for Jake's arrest. His father in jail? How could that be?

And what about Susan? Cam feared that a similar fate awaited her. "I called Cy," Cam said. "And he's on his way out here."

"Why?" Jake demanded. He stood with one arm leaning against the mantel, and a hand hooked in the pocket of his jeans. "We can take care of ourselves."

"I need the help," Cam said. If Jake was arrested, somebody was going to need to stay with Susan. "Cy can use his influence with the FBI."

Susan joined Jake at the fireplace. "Don't you boys go to any trouble on my account."

Didn't she understand? They weren't talking about an inconvenience. She could end up in a federal penitentiary for the bank robbery. And Jake? He would be accused of murder, an offense that was punishable by death in the state of Colorado. "Both of you sit down."

"I'd rather take this bad news standing up, if you don't mind," Jake said.

But Frani touched Susan's arm and led her to the sofa. "Let's give Cam a break," she said.

He was amazed by how easily she fit into this contentious, headstrong family. But why not? Those traits applied to Frani as well.

"Well, what is it?" Jake snapped.

"There's been another killing. A couple of cross-country

skiers found a body near Glenwood. Not too far from where you were staying yesterday.''

"I assume this person is connected to this case," Jake said. "How?"

"He had a shoulder wound that had been clumsily bandaged." Cam turned to Frani. "Most likely, he was the man who tried to break down the door of the *Clarion* offices."

"Oh my God, *I* didn't kill him, did I?"

"He didn't die from that bullet," Cam assured her. The man had been shot in the face, obliterating his features. "There's no identification on him as yet, but he had a newspaper article in his pocket. It was a recent column by Zach Hollingsworth, featuring an old photograph of Pamela Jessup."

Cam spelled out Harold T.'s theory. It was likely that the death had taken place while Jake and Susan were making their horseback escape from the reporters. The dead man must have been following them, looking for Susan. And—as everyone knew—Jake McQuaid would have stopped anyone who threatened Susan.

"Or," Frani said, "he might have been a killer. He might have been waiting in ambush."

Cam nodded. He'd put forward that possibility. "It doesn't matter. He's the one who died."

"That's the problem," Jake said. "Even if he had attacked us first, I'd be charged with manslaughter."

"But it's not true! None of this happened. You didn't do anything," Susan said. "We didn't see *anyone* on our ride from Glenwood."

"I know, Susan, but that's the law. A murder has to be investigated. Someone will be charged for that crime."

"Not you." Pale and trembling, she stood. "Not this time, Jake. You've protected me too long."

"What are you saying?"

"This has gone far enough. Too many people have been hurt. Two men have died."

Frani slipped a supportive arm around Susan's shoulder. Her voice dropped to a low, soothing level. "It's okay, Susan. You're not to blame."

"I did it," Susan announced. "I can't stay quiet any longer. I killed Zach Hollingsworth."

Chapter Eleven

Susan's startling declaration hit them all so strongly that no one dared to speak. Her chin lifted proudly as she repeated, "I did it."

Though Cam knew the confession was false, he would never insult Susan by calling her a liar. He respected her too deeply. For this desperate attempt to save the man she loved, he respected her even more.

When Cam glanced toward his father, he saw the diamond sparkle of a single tear in the old man's eye. Jake blinked it away and approached Susan. "I appreciate what you're trying to do, honey. But it's impossible. You and I were together in the house, waiting for Zach. I went out alone to check on the intercom and found him shot. You couldn't have killed him, unless you can be in two places at one time."

"Don't patronize me." Her tone of voice was an imperious echo of the troubled heiress, Pamela Jessup. Even after twenty-four years, she still could play the princess. "You've all forgotten that I had another life. I'm aware of how to use the wealth that was my birthright. And it is a considerable amount. Tell them, Frani. Tell them about the Jessup fortune."

"The family is worth millions," she said. "Not only is

the winery highly successful, but the surrounding lands are close enough to coveted Silicon Valley real estate to boost their assets sky-high.''

"If I wanted someone murdered," Susan said, "I could get hold of enough money to buy myself a professional killer. Don't you think my family would pay to keep my scandal from darkening their good name? Maybe I hired someone? Maybe someone like that man they found dead near Glenwood Springs.''

"Stop it," Jake said. "I won't let you take the blame because I'm a suspect. What kind of man do you think I am?''

"A good man." Her voice trembled. "You gave me the only happiness I've ever known. But it's over now, Jake. Can't you see that? I knew it was only a matter of time before my past caught up with me.''

"A phony confession won't help. We might be in trouble. But it's time we let the truth work in our favor for a change." He gently reached up and stroked her cheek. "You're not a murderer and we all know it.''

Wildly, she slapped his hand away. "You don't know what I was like before. I robbed a bank.''

"You were forced to participate," Jake said. "It wasn't your fault.''

"I held people at gunpoint," she said. "Innocent bystanders. I can never justify what I did. What makes you think I couldn't hire a killer?''

"Susan, honey, I—''

"No!" Again, she turned toward Frani. "Would you be so kind as to explain the bank robbery? I'm sure you've seen the videotape.''

"You had an automatic rifle," Frani said. "You waved it around. You pointed it at people.''

"You see." Susan glared at the two men. "You have no idea what I'm capable of doing."

Reluctantly, Cam stood. "I know your capabilities. You were able to take three ragamuffin boys and turn them into decent men. You gave a cranky old man a reason to keep living. Once upon a time, you might have been a head-strong, spoiled-brat heiress. But not anymore. You're Susan Hathaway."

"I hired a killer." She clung to her story. "I lured Zach out here, and I had him murdered."

Cam sighed. "Now I'm going to tell you why that isn't logical. In the first place, we're in Cedar Bluffs, not Los Angeles. For you to locate a hired killer would have taken some fancy finagling. Have you got phone records to verify your contacts with this killer?"

Susan's gaze flickered as she tried to come up with a decent fabrication. "I did it all from a public phone in Grand Junction."

"And where did you get the up-front money to pay this supposed assassin?"

"My credit card. I got an advance," she said haltingly. "I told him who I was. The Jessup heiress. And I promised him future payment, big money after the job was done."

"All right," Cam said wearily. "Then why did you have the murder committed on your doorstep? Your hired killer could have done the job anywhere."

As she glanced back and forth between father and son, her self-control dissolved. She sank onto the sofa and buried her face in her hands. Her shoulders heaved with silent sobs.

Immediately beside her, Jake rested his weathered hand on her arm. As soon as she felt his touch, Susan leaned against him. "Oh, Jake. I might as well have killed Zach

Hollingsworth. It's my fault he's dead. I can't let this go on. I can't have you arrested.''

"Nothing's going to happen, honey. If we just keep telling the truth, we'll be fine."

"You don't know." She lifted her tear-streaked face. "The truth isn't always a safeguard."

"She's right," Frani said.

"He's right," Cam contradicted her.

When Frani turned to face him, he explained, "We all want to find Zach's murderer. It doesn't help if we can't trust each other."

He was sending her a message. *Trust me, Frani.* They were both on the same side. They both wanted justice.

Susan appealed to them all. "It's only right for me to take the blame."

"Forget it, honey." Jake smoothed the strands of blond hair off her forehead. "We'll get through this."

"But Zach wouldn't have been here if it weren't for me."

"Susan," Frani said, "I was probably closer to Zach than anyone else, and I don't want to see the wrong person punished. He deserves justice. The truth."

"But the Jessups are rich," she said, dabbing away the dampness in the corner of her eye. "They'll hire the best lawyers for me, now. They won't risk the public scorn they endured by refusing to pay my ransom. I'm already in trouble for the bank robbery. There's no need for both Jake and me to go to jail."

"Hush, now." Jake stood up, pulling her with him. "Let's go to bed, get some sleep. In the morning, everything will look brighter."

Cam's eyebrows rose as he heard his usually grumpy father taking the optimistic route, sounding nurturing and soothing. Looking for silver linings in the rain clouds was more typical of Susan.

She smiled through her tears. "Oh, Jake. A brighter morning? That's supposed to be my line."

"Well, maybe it's time I made it mine, too."

Arm in arm they went toward the big guest bedroom at the rear of the house, and Cam watched them proudly. For years, he'd been angry at Jake for not marrying his woman. Cam hadn't realized the depth of their love, hadn't acknowledged his own good fortune. He had truly been blessed with a loving family.

Looking over at Frani, he shrugged. "Just another typical day at the ranch."

"They're wonderful," she said quietly. "I don't think I've ever seen two people so much in love."

She curled up on the sofa and hugged a throw pillow close to her breast. In her story, Frani wished she could convey the true depth of this surprising love between a cowboy lawman and a renegade heiress.

Susan was so utterly devoted to Jake that she would confess to murder to protect him. No doubt, she would have done jail time in the hope she could keep him safe. Hope. With love came renewed hope. Frani remembered how Susan had told her about the precious quality of hope. When life sank to its most dismal level, hope buoyed the spirits and gave one the strength to carry on. Susan gave Jake a completely unselfish love and hope.

And the devotion went both ways. Jake had given up his life as a Texas lawman and gone against his precious code to provide a life for his woman. When he told people he would do *anything* to protect Susan, he wasn't referring to murder but something far more difficult: commitment.

"Zach never could have written this story," she said.

Cam flopped down on the sofa beside her. "Why not?"

"He hated all the emotional stuff, but that's what this is about. Love, hope, commitment and caring."

"Doesn't sound like a news story," he said.

"Maybe that's why it should be. The newspapers and broadcast news spend too much time in detailing tawdry and horrific events. It *should* be news when two people fall deeply in love and make a commitment that lasts twenty-four years."

As she spoke, Frani wondered. Could such a love exist for her? It was hard to imagine. It was so different from anything she'd known, having grown up in a household where her parents stayed together without real love, where she felt abandoned despite the trappings of family. Her parents had stayed together out of obligation. She'd never in her life seen her mother gaze fondly into her father's eyes the way Susan looked at Jake.

Thinking of that gaze, Frani knew how she'd write her story. The tale of Pamela Jessup started with rape and treachery. She'd been kidnapped, drugged and forced to commit a bank robbery. On the run, beaten nearly to death, she'd found hope in an abiding love. The *Daily Herald* would never print it. Zach would never have approved. But it was a damn good story. And she would make sure it was published.

"Cam, do you have a computer?"

"In my office. Why?"

"I'm writing Susan's story for the *Clarion,* and I'm on deadline."

He groaned. "On deadline? Oh, hell."

Frani bounced to her feet. "What's that supposed to mean?"

"I recall your last deadline. You were too busy writing to identify the body of the man who was like a father to you."

"I'm a professional." Frani didn't have to defend her behavior to anyone, but his disapproval hurt. "This is how I do my job."

"Like a woman possessed?"

"Sometimes. How can you cast aspersions? Do you give any less to your profession? Besides, you hardly know me."

"I guess I don't."

Did she detect a slightly wistful tone in his voice? Did he want to know her better?

Frani gazed down at the darkly handsome cowboy who sprawled on the sofa before her. Though some of his tension had lifted, he still showed signs of worry and exhaustion. It had been a long, trying day for Cam. A dark stubble marked his chin. Beneath his weathered tan, his skin had paled.

As she studied him, she felt an overwhelming urge to take care of him, to make hot chocolate and help him pull off his stupid cowboy boots. "Can I get you anything?"

"I thought you had a deadline."

She did, but suddenly, he came first. Though she didn't know why, that priority seemed right to her. "I won't ask again."

"I'm okay. I just need to go to bed."

When he pushed himself off the sofa, they were standing close together. She could feel the warmth of his body. Her head tilted back and her lips parted, inviting him to come nearer. But instead she said, "Where's the computer?"

Across the foyer at the front of the house, he showed her into a large room with a very big, rugged-looking desk. Everything seemed oversized in this very masculine office. Frani was pleased to find that Cam's computer program was compatible with the *Clarion*, and he had a modem. "With any luck,'' she said, ''I can transfer the article to Addie first thing in the morning without even driving into town.''

''How about that?'' A lazy grin lifted the corner of his mouth. ''And how long were you planning on staying here?''

The word ''forever'' flitted across her mind, and she shook her head to erase it. ''Of course, I'll get out of your way as quickly as possible.''

''I didn't say I wanted you to leave.'' He came around the desk and leaned over her shoulder as she prepared a computer file for her story. ''I'd like you to stay, Frani. I'd like to show you around my ranch, maybe take you riding.''

''I don't think your cows like me.''

''What are you talking about?''

She gave him a brief version of her trek across the field, dodging cow patties and stumbling over every tuft of sage grass. ''I had a brief encounter with the herd. They looked mean.''

''Don't you have cattle in the Midwest?''

''Yes, but they don't make a habit of coming into the city. Not unless they're on the Bulls basketball team.''

She whirled in the desk chair so she was again facing him, near to him. This time, he bent down and lightly kissed her forehead. ''I like you, Frani. Even though you're a city gal to the core.''

Breathless, she hoped for another kiss. ''We've got nothing in common.''

''Except for the desire to find the truth.'' He straightened. ''Did you get Susan to open up about her past?''

Frani thought of the little tape recorder from her purse. ''A full cassette.''

''What did she say?''

''Nothing that sounded like a clue, Cam. It's pretty much

the way we've pieced it together from Zach's files and the information from Cy."

"I'm still interested," he said.

"How about this? When I'm finished, I'll let you read the article before I send it to Addie."

"It's a deal," he said. "Now, before you get started, let me show you where you'll be sleeping."

The small guest bedroom had a single bed and bright wallpaper with suns and rain clouds and umbrellas. "Cute," she said. "It doesn't seem to go with the rest of the house."

"The previous owner used it for a nursery. I've never gotten around to changing it."

"Maybe you'd want to keep it this way. For your own children."

With his big, callused hand, he traced the pattern of the perky wallpaper. "It doesn't look like I'll be needing it any time soon, but someday I hope to have my own kids."

Too easily, she imagined him as a proud father.

He stepped back into the hall. "My bedroom is right across the hall. Do you need anything else?"

A kiss for luck. A kiss for hope. A kiss that might lead to something more. "I don't think so."

As he went into the bedroom, she charged down the hall and started to work behind the giant-sized desk. Frani glanced at her wristwatch. It was almost eleven o'clock. She'd need to write fast.

FOUR HOURS LATER, Frani completed what she knew was the best piece of writing she'd ever done. Her article mixed good solid journalism with a warm, emotional tone. Re-reading her own words, Frani felt like cheering, patting herself on the back. If Zach had been here, she knew she would have had the pleasure of his approval.

She printed out a copy for Cam and centered it on the desk. If only he was still awake, she'd love to get his reaction. On the off chance that he might have been unable to sleep, she tiptoed down the hall and stood outside the door to his bedroom. She tapped lightly and whispered, "Cam?"

Frani thought she heard a sound from within, and she eased the door open. "Cam?"

She took two steps forward, bumping her toe against a chair.

The rumble of a male voice came from the center of the room. "What? Who is it?"

"Cam, are you awake?"

"I am now." The bedside lamp flicked on. "Is something wrong?"

Beneath the heavy comforter, he was bare-chested. His hair fell loosely across his forehead, and his nearly black eyes glowed with a sexy, hazy light.

Frani thrust out the pages. "Here. I'm finished."

Instead of chiding her for waking him, he extended his well-muscled arm and took the papers. He patted the edge of the bed. "Sit down while I read them."

Though she had the option of several chairs in the spacious master suite, Frani settled on the end of the bed so she could watch his reaction as he went through her article.

Near the beginning, he hesitated. "This is interesting. Susan said she thought Eisman was going to kill her at first."

Frani nodded. "I think there were a lot of people who wanted her dead. Her sister for one."

"Candace was only seventeen at the time," he said. "But I wouldn't rule her out."

"And Gould," Frani said.

"Do you mention the rape in here?"

"No, Susan told me about it off the record, so I didn't use it. But it was a horrible trauma. I think she was referring to that incident when she said telling the truth didn't work."

"She told people?"

"Her mother. Apparently, Mom didn't want to know. She thought Gould would be a good catch, whatever the cost to her daughter."

"Sickening," Cam said as he returned to her pages.

Though he was reading for clues, he was soon caught up in the story. Frani had fashioned an interesting picture of a desperate woman, drug-addicted and on the run from both the criminals and the law.

When he came to the concluding paragraphs about Jake and Susan, Cam realized that Pamela Jessup was decidedly the wrong woman for his father. They had virtually everything against them—a fugitive from justice and a lawman—and yet they had fallen deeply in love.

He finished the story and straightened the pages before he confronted the redheaded reporter perched at the end of his bed. "It's good."

"Really?" She beamed at him.

"You did a fine job. Made me think. Even choked me up. You're a talented writer."

"Oh, thank you." Impulsively, she bounced forward and gave him a little kiss. "When I was writing, it felt right. It felt like—"

Her gaze locked with his, and her words froze in her throat. She was the wrong woman in the wrong place at the wrong time. But he wanted her to be his woman. "Francesca," he whispered, "I want to make love to you. I can't make promises for tomorrow, but tonight—"

Solemnly, she said, "I understand."

He lightly stroked her russet hair. "If you were going to

stay in Cedar Bluffs, I would court you properly. I'd bring you roses and candy. We'd go out to dinner. Hell, we might even find someplace to go dancing. But there isn't time."

"It's okay, cowboy."

"I just can't let you slip away before we have a chance to do what feels so right."

"We're totally wrong for each other." She wriggled out of her forest-green pullover sweater.

But then so were Jake and Susan, as wrong as two people could be for each other, Cam thought.

When Frani peeled off the white turtleneck, he groaned. Her ivory skin shone luminous in the night. When she reached behind her back to unfasten her bra, he reached toward her. "Let me."

His hands were sure and steady as he worked the small catch and removed the bit of lacy material. Her breasts were high and firm. "Francesca, you're beautiful."

He stretched her out on the bed beside him and unbuttoned the waistband of her jeans. Eager anticipation coursed through him, and when he'd removed all her clothes, he leisurely appreciated every inch of her firm slender body with his eyes.

When he touched the taut peaks of her breasts, she trembled. Her shudders aroused him even more, and he tasted the honey of her lips.

She responded with abandon, stoking the flame of his passion beyond reason and far beyond control. Never in his life had Cam wanted a woman so badly. If she'd told him to stop right now, he would surely explode.

"Is this all right?"

"Yes." Her arms tightened around his neck, pulling him close. "I don't need roses. I only need you."

Chapter Twelve

The next morning, Frani wakened after only a few hours' sleep. Perfectly refreshed, she stretched and yawned and snuggled against the warm male body in the bed beside her, allowing their sweet passionate intimacy to surround her senses. She imagined the fragrance of honeysuckle and roses. Her ears heard a chorus of birdsong, though it was the dead of winter.

He'd called her Francesca when they'd made love, and he'd treated her with absolute respect, like a princess. Being with Cam was exactly the way lovemaking ought to be, the way she always dreamed it could be.

She looked down upon his sleeping face, memorizing his cheekbones and the thrust of his jaw. How would she ever bring herself to leave him?

If she stayed, he promised to court her with roses and candy and fond attention. *If she stayed?* What was she thinking? She couldn't stay in Cedar Bluffs, Colorado. She was a city gal. And she'd decided she hated cows.

Fact: She no longer had a job in Chicago.

Fact: She loved this vast, exciting western landscape, from the mountains to the desert.

Fact: Staying anywhere with Cam would be close to heaven.

His eyelids opened and he smiled at her. "Good morning, Francesca."

"I hope you're not going to call me that all the time. It's such a long name that our conversations could take hours."

"Only in bed." He pulled her close. "In bed, you're my woman, my Francesca."

Though she liked to think of herself as independent, Frani loved the idea of being this cowboy's woman. And she warmed to the idea of their future lovemaking. "But only in the bedroom," she warned. "I won't be anyone's possession."

"No, ma'am. It's the other way around. I'd do anything for you. Want me to slay a couple of dragons before we have breakfast? Or how about if I go beat up those cows who tried to push you around?"

"Is that what they mean by cowpuncher?"

He pulled her close against his chest. "What I mean is that you're special to me. I'd like for you to stay here for as long as you can."

That was the closest thing to a proposal she'd had in a very long time, and Frani tried to consider his words without reading too much into the invitation. "When you say 'here,' do you mean at the ranch?"

"I mean, here in my bed. In my arms. On my ranch. Close. I want to be close to you, Francesca."

The prospect both delighted and frightened her. Without considering the future or any other implications, she said, "I would like that."

"I know what else you'd like."

"What's that?"

"Let's get cleaned up. We can take a long shower."

"Together?"

In answer, he swept her off the bed and carried her into the adjoining bathroom.

AFTER WASHING every part of Frani's body and making love to her again, Cam wanted nothing more than to sleep away the day, wrapped in her arms. Unfortunately, a long day stretched before him. At eight o'clock when they emerged from the bedroom, they found Jake and Susan at the kitchen table.

Frani had decided to show the article to Susan before she sent it to Addie. "I'd rather not change it," she said. "But I'll respect your wishes, Susan. It's your story."

Though Cam's loyalties ultimately lay with his immediate family, he was prepared to defend Frani's article. He sipped coffee and watched with some nervousness as Susan read Frani's words with Jake reading over her shoulder.

As she finished the last line, Susan paused. When she looked up, her eyes were awash with tears. Impatiently, she dashed them away. "I haven't cried so much in a long time."

"Well?" Cam said. "What do you think?"

"It's perfect. Exactly the way I wanted my story told. It isn't all pretty. But it's the truth."

"Dad?" Cam looked toward the crusty old man who'd held his silence for years rather than betray his woman.

Jake stared hard at Frani. When he stepped up in front of her, Cam held his breath. He wouldn't be able to stand for it if the old fart insulted Frani or caused her the least bit of embarrassment.

Instead Jake wrapped his arms around Frani and gave her a big, strong, rib-cracking hug. When he released her, he was grinning from ear to ear. "Thanks, city gal. You did good."

She looked at Cam, and her eyes were sparkling like

emeralds. Pure happiness radiated from her. Her gaze circled the room, and she inhaled the scent of fresh coffee and hotcakes on the griddle. "This must be what it's like to have a family."

Her words touched him more than he could say, but Cam wasn't yet accustomed to openly showing his affection. Gruffly, he said, "You want me to help you send that article to Addie?"

"I can manage."

She hurried toward the office.

He turned and faced Susan and Jake. They weren't a family given to much discussion. Generally, the rules were so obvious they didn't need to be talked about.

Jake said, "Hang on to that one, Cameron."

And that was the final benediction, all that really needed to be said. They proceeded on with the morning as if this were any other day.

After breakfast, Cam took Frani outside and showed her around the ranch. Even though there was a mob of reporters standing outside the gate, he felt as though they were safe in their own little haven.

"I need to go into town," she said. "I promised I'd help Addie put this issue of the *Clarion* together."

"I'll take you. Matter of fact, I'd like to hang around and watch."

"Why?"

"I want to see what you do." He shrugged, not willing to admit how very much he wanted to be with her every minute. "This journalism stuff."

"Putting together the actual newspaper isn't all that fascinating," she said. "It's like a high school yearbook, only a lot more sophisticated because Addie has all the modern equipment."

"Do you *mind* if I watch?"

"Addie won't let you stand around. If you're in the office, she'll put you to work."

"Fine with me."

"And when we come back," she said, "I want you to show me how to ride a horse. It's not too hard, is it?"

"For you, anything will be easy. My Francesca."

He couldn't help kissing her. He found himself clinging to these precious, peaceful moments with Frani, fearing their idyll wouldn't last long.

Right before lunch, Cy arrived. Cam's older brother was a hardened FBI agent, just two weeks removed from cracking the case that had almost cost his fiancée's life. He stormed into the ranch house as if he were conducting a drug bust. His face twisted in a scowl. His manner was brusque.

Cam watched in amusement as his brother realized that instead of finding a tense household, full of fear and outrage, he'd stepped into a love nest. Jake and Susan snuggled together in front of the fireplace. Frani stood close to Cam, holding his hand, only breaking away when Cam introduced her and she shook hands with his brother.

She greeted Cy, "I've heard a lot about you. From Zach."

"I'm sorry for your loss," he said automatically.

Susan warmly embraced him. "Why didn't you bring Amy?"

"Well, I didn't know I was coming to a party." He nodded toward the office. "Cam, can I talk to you a minute in the office?"

Cam kissed Frani goodbye, followed Cy into the office and closed the door.

His brother spread his hands wide as if he were trying to grasp the whole situation. "What the hell is going on here?"

"I don't know if I can explain it." He leaned against the desk. "But I sure hope it lasts."

"Well, let me fill you in, little brother. My FBI buddy who's in charge of this investigation is going to need to get a full statement from Susan regarding her former criminal activities. She's lucky no one was hurt in that bank robbery and that the money was recovered. It's possible Susan can plead mitigating circumstances and get off with probation."

It was wonderful news. "Are you sure about that?"

"Hell, no. This is going to take some maneuvering." Cy shook his head. "Can you believe this? You and I are a couple of hard-nosed lawmen, and we're trying to figure out how to get Susan, a fugitive from justice, off the hook."

"I don't see a problem," Cam said. "We both know what's right, even when it doesn't fit the law. It's *not* right for Susan to go to jail."

His brother paced the floor in the office. "The news on Dad isn't so rosy. We're looking at a possible arrest. Your district attorney is under a lot of pressure, and there aren't any other suspects."

Yesterday, Cam had faced the dire possibility that Jake might be taken into custody. He'd done a lot of fast talking and called in favors to put off the inevitable.

"I think I convinced them to wait." A dark cloud, like an incoming storm front, blanketed his hours of perfect happiness. "He didn't do it, Cy."

"Are you sure?" Cy asked. "He'd do anything for Susan."

"Zach wasn't a threat. Frani wrote the article about Susan. She sent it to Addie Lindstrom and it's going to be published in the paper."

"Maybe it's not the whole story."

Cam knew where the problem might lie. In Texas.

Frani's article used Susan's reminiscences as a source, and Susan knew nothing about the dead woman who was falsely identified as Pamela Jessup, thereby ending the search. That mystery remained unsolved—and potentially explosive.

Jake might have been responsible for the fake ID, protecting Susan and breaking the law. But would he kill Zach to cover up what amounted to a minor crime? Or was there more to the story? "I wish we knew what story Zach was really looking for when he came here."

"What did it say in his notebook?"

Blankly, Cam stared at his brother. "What notebook?"

"Zach Hollingsworth was a reporter from the old school. He used a typewriter, not a computer. Instead of carrying a tape recorder, he had a notebook that he was always scribbling in."

"We never found a notebook. Not on his body. Not in his vehicle."

But suddenly, as he spoke, he remembered Frani's mentioning Zach's notes. With a sinking feeling, he realized exactly where Zach's missing notebook must be. The only place it could be.

WHEN THE TWO BROTHERS emerged from the office, Frani immediately knew something was wrong. Cam's expression had darkened. His eyes fired an angry message to her. "I want to talk to you alone, Frani," he said brusquely.

What was going on? She tried to brace herself, but her defenses were gone. Yesterday, she could have hidden behind a wall of bravado. Now, it was completely different. Last night, she'd given Cam more than her body, she'd given him her trust. Now she felt achingly vulnerable.

He slammed the door of the office behind her. When he

spoke, his voice held a dangerous note of suppressed fury. "What did you do with Zach's notebook?"

In the back of her mind, Frani had always known this confrontation would come. But she hadn't expected to care.

"We had an agreement, Frani. We were supposed to share information."

She couldn't lie to him, not even to save the fragile beginnings of what felt like love. "I took the notebook from Zach's body the night he was murdered."

"You were aware that it was evidence."

"It was his," she said. As she retaliated, the wall between them began to grow, one brick at a time. "I had a right to it. He would have wanted me to have it."

"You could have asked. After the investigation, the sheriff's office would be obliged to turn over his personal belongings."

"So, I'm supposed to follow strict police procedure? Is that right? You're willing to cut everyone else some slack, but *I'm* supposed to toe the line."

He moved across the office, only the huge desk was between them. "You took Zach's notebook because you wanted to solve his murder. You thought you could do a better job than the police and the FBI. You thought you could figure it out better than I could. You wanted the story."

"I'm not denying any of that."

He fumed.

"Besides, you could never have deciphered his shorthand."

"But *you* could. What did it say, Frani? What are you hiding?"

"He was planning to see Bud Coleman. Which we did. And he made a note to himself to interview Eisman. To meet with Candace. And to talk to Gould."

"Are you sure that's all?"

"That's all I found. Coleman. Eisman. Candace. Gould."

"What else haven't you told me?"

She saw no point in holding anything back. The damage was done. "On the morning he arrived here, he left a message on my answering machine in Chicago. He'd called Pete Potterfield at the Department of Corrections with some kind of question about Eisman's parole."

"What kind of question?"

"I don't know. I put in a call to Pete Potterfield and left Addie's phone number."

For a long moment, they stood staring at each other. Moments ago, Frani had been able to intuitively know everything Cam was thinking and feeling. She'd felt she'd seen the secrets of his heart. Now, he was merely a handsome stranger, cold and hard as the February weather.

From outside the window, Frani saw the sudden flashing of lights. She ran to the window. Two police vehicles had parked near the door. They'd come to arrest Jake. "Oh, God," she whispered. "This can't happen. It's wrong."

"I should have stopped it," Cam said. "I should have found the murderer."

And it was partly her fault that he hadn't. She'd kept information from him. "We can still do it, Cam. When I get the call back from Potterfield, we can investigate the—"

"Stop! It's over. *We* won't be investigating anything."

"But we must!" she said desperately. "If we stop now, we've lost everything. There's still a chance. We can piece it together, we can still find the murderer."

"I can't trust you." Bitterly, he said, "It's over, Francesca. But don't worry. You'll still get your story."

AT THE CLARION offices, there were two other people helping out with the always frantic process of compiling a newspaper. One woman was a typesetter. A young girl from the high school ran errands and fetched coffee.

Frani threw herself into her work. Side by side with Addie, she fleshed out the articles and selected appropriate photographs. *This is my life,* she thought determinedly. She was a journalist, a reporter. She wrote about life instead of experiencing it. How had she allowed herself to hope it could ever be any different? *Now I know why you were alone, Zach. Now I understand.*

Addie slid a couple of photographs of Cam toward her. "Which one?"

Frani should have been able to make a snap judgment, deciding which photograph should accompany the article. Instead, her fingers trembled as she touched the eight-by-ten glossies. His dark eyes seemed to stare at her from the pictures, accusing her of deception.

It was over between them. There would be no long afternoons in the sun, learning to ride a horse. No family breakfasts. No more whispered secrets in the night. The memory of their lovemaking came back to taunt her.

The McQuaid family had been shattered by Jake's arrest. They had all behaved with the utmost dignity when Joe Bradley and Harold Cisneros came inside the ranch house to take Jake away.

Susan had gently kissed her man goodbye.

Cam and Cy stood by, silent in their fury.

When Joe Bradley pulled out his handcuffs, Cam stepped forward. His voice was pure steel. "You won't need those."

Joe responded immediately. "Whatever you say, Sheriff."

And they'd led Jake out to the car.

Frani—suddenly relegated to the position of outsider—
had been driven to town by one of the cowboys who
worked at the ranch. And when she left, Cam refused to
meet her gaze.

"Frani!" Addie shouted across the offices. "There's a
telephone call for you. Pick up on line two."

"Thanks." She lifted the receiver to her ear, hoping to
hear Cam's voice. "Hello?"

"This is Pete Potterfield, Department of Corrections."

"Yes," she said. "I was following up on a question from
Zach Hollingsworth."

"Sorry to hear about his murder," Potterfield said.
"When's the funeral?"

"It'll be a memorial service. I'm not sure when, but I'll
let you know." She flipped open a notebook in front of
her. "Do you have the answer to Zach's question?"

"This isn't really my department, but I was able to do
some checking around."

"I appreciate it," she said. If there was one thing Zach
had taught her, it was to stay on good terms with sources.
"You must be well-connected in Washington, D.C."

"I do have my ways."

Frani was chomping at the bit. "About that question?"

"Right. Zach wanted to know about a prisoner in the
federal penitentiary outside Salt Lake. The name is David
Eisman. He's been up for parole four times. Each time, he
was denied."

"A troublemaker?" Frani guessed.

"Not according to my records. Eisman has been a model
of good behavior. No complaints from the warden."

"Then why was parole denied?"

"It seems a highly placed individual, outside the system,
advised the parole board that Eisman was still a threat to
himself and to others. And they chose to believe him."

Goose bumps chased up and down Frani's arms. She knew this was important. This was the key. "This highly placed individual," she said. "Was it Senator Phillip Gould?"

"That's correct, ma'am."

Frani ended the call as quickly as possible. Grabbing her shoulder bag and jacket, she charged toward the door. "Addie, I've got to go."

"It's okay. I think we have everything under control."

"Hold off on printing as long as possible. I might have a page-one scoop."

"Another one?"

Frani raised both hands with fingers crossed. "Wish me luck."

In her rental car, she raced back to the ranch. The other reporters were gone. They'd followed Jake to the sheriff's office. She could only hope that Cam was still there and that he'd speak to her.

She charged up to the door, prepared to beat it down if he wouldn't answer. She drew back her fist.

Cam opened wide. "What are you doing here? I thought you had a newspaper to print."

She absorbed his bitterness without comment. "I have the answer," she said breathlessly.

"Explain," he said tersely.

"Gould and Eisman are connected. That's what Zach was working on. We have to go to the federal penitentiary in Salt Lake and talk to Eisman."

He eyed her with a cold consideration that broke her heart. Then finally, "I'll get my hat."

Chapter Thirteen

When they disembarked at the small private airport outside Salt Lake City, Cam watched Frani as she hopped down from the Piper Cub. It had been a long three hours in the cockpit—enough time for his anger to cool and a diffidence to set in between them. He wasn't feeling inclined to apologize and he was pretty sure Frani wasn't either.

But that didn't stop his wanting her, a longing inside him that refused to be ignored. One look in her direction and he felt himself aching to touch her.

The confidence in her walk combined with the enticing swing of her hips made her an appealing little package, even when she was fully clothed in her jeans, jacket and those idiotic steel-toed boots. What in hell had he done, falling for such a woman? The kind of woman who would never make anything easy?

When she whirled around and waved impatiently to him, Cam sighed. What could he do but follow? Remembering how her hands had felt on his skin last night, he could almost feel the heat of their mutual passion.

But neither could he forget she'd deceived him. He'd trusted her and she'd held back information that might have speeded the murder investigation and saved Jake the humiliation of being taken into custody.

Wrong woman. Wrong place. Wrong time. Could it get any more complicated? How could he have allowed her to get under his skin, so close that he'd let himself forget who and what she was?

Right from the start, when she'd lied to him on the road and bolted before he could catch her, he should have known she'd be nothing but trouble. Constantly scheming. Always intent on achieving her own goals. She was as driven as anyone he'd ever met. Determined, single-minded and stubborn. The most pig-headed woman he'd ever known. And, yet, she'd wriggled her way into his heart, and—damn it all—he'd gone and fallen in love with her.

Behind all that blind determination and bravado was a sweetly vulnerable woman who filled a void in his heart, a place he hadn't even known was empty. Something about her made him want to take care of her, to hold her unhappy past at bay and fill her with the same unbounded joy he'd found in her arms.

When she stamped her foot, he quickened his pace to catch up to her.

"Honestly, Cam," she complained. "Could you move any slower?"

"Eisman's in prison. He's not going anywhere."

But he fell into step beside her, watching, bemused, as she took charge and arranged for a rental car in curt, quick commands. Now that she had a tangible goal, she moved like a house afire, a redheaded flash. How could he help but admire her, a woman who charged into the fray seemingly undaunted by the odds? And the odds were considerable. Especially for Jake and Susan. And if the killer couldn't be found, for Frani, as well.

While they waited for the car, he said, "There's something I should tell you. It's about the man they found dead near Glenwood."

"An identification?" she guessed.

"Coming up with his name wasn't too hard. His finger-prints were on file and cross-referenced. He had a criminal record as long as my arm. For a while, he was held in the same facility as Eisman."

"Another connection," she said. "Cam, it's all falling into place. If we can tie that man to Gould, we'll have the whole picture."

The same thought had occurred to him. Gould was in Aspen at the time of the second murder—close enough to have committed the crime himself, and certainly close enough to arrange it.

"Thank you, Cam," she said with a perfectly lovely smile. "If I didn't know better, I'd say we're partners again."

"Don't push it, Frani."

"Me, push?" she said innocently, her green eyes spar-kling. "Look, everything's going to turn out all right. Trust me, if you can. My instincts are on overdrive and I sense we're coming very close."

She was asking him to trust, to hope, and he had to admit he felt their luck had shifted. But he still didn't know how he was going to get past her betrayal. She'd pushed him into this uncertain partnership, and then held back. Trust was a two-way street. He wouldn't settle for less.

After a short drive, they arrived at the ultramodern fa-cility. A nice piece of architecture, but it was still a jail. Cam shuddered to think of his father or Susan being locked away in a place like this. They were people of the land who needed wide open spaces to survive. In some ways, espe-cially for his father, imprisonment would be worse than a death sentence.

"It won't happen," Frani said, reading his thoughts. "Jake is telling the truth. He won't go to jail."

"I was thinking," he said, "about what happened in Texas. When that other woman was identified as Pamela Jessup. Do you think Jake had anything to do with that?"

"If he did, Susan wasn't aware of it." She shrugged. "I know she wouldn't have approved."

"He knew the right people in that part of the country to pull off a switch in identity. He could have taken advantage of a Jane Doe corpse to give Pamela Jessup a final out."

Frani's beautiful green eyes seemed untroubled by suspicion. "Jake doesn't strike me as the sort of man who could manage a conspiracy. Keeping Susan's secrets was different. All he had to do was clamp his stubborn mouth shut."

"Could be." He hoped she was on the right track. He didn't want to spring Jake from one bad situation only to have another arise. "He *was* a sheriff, after all."

"Jake would have done everything in his power to find out the woman's identity," she said firmly. "He would have had too much integrity to inflict that kind of suffering on a family wondering what had happened to their loved one."

It was mighty lucky that David Eisman was being held in the Salt Lake prison. Utah and Colorado law enforcement worked closely together, and Cam had connections with the warden. He'd been able to arrange an interview with Eisman on short notice.

After they were searched and Frani's shoulder bag confiscated until they'd finished the interview with Eisman, they were shown into a square sterile room. The only furnishings were a table and four chairs. The only window was the one in the metal door.

With her fiery hair and bright eyes, Frani contrasted strongly with the cold, dead prison surroundings. Vivacious energy shot sparks around her.

"This doesn't scare you," Cam observed.

"Maybe a little," she admitted before drawing a deep breath. "All right, Cam, you're the expert on criminals. Any advice as to how I should proceed with the interview?"

Heartened that she'd asked for his help, Cam said, "Keep cool. He'll no doubt try to rattle you. And another thing, don't mention Gould. Let me introduce the subject when the time comes."

"Okay." She stuffed her hands inside the pockets of her jacket, but not before he noticed them shaking.

"Are you going to be all right?"

"I'm fine. I just want to get on with it. Do you realize we might actually discover the true identity of Zach's murderer?"

"And that's what you've wanted all along."

"In the beginning..."

"And now?"

Her expression held a subtle promise. "We'll talk about that later."

Eisman, accompanied by the jingling of wrist and ankle shackles, was shown into the room by a uniformed guard.

"I'll be waiting just outside the door," the guard told them. "You've got twenty minutes." Before he left, he added, "In the meantime, if you need anything, just signal. This room isn't wired for sound, but I'll be watching the whole time through the window."

The security seemed excessive to Cam. The ashen-faced man sitting across from Frani didn't appear to be much of a threat. His skinny body seemed to disappear inside his prison-issue orange jumpsuit. His skin hung in loose folds from sallow cheeks. He had the flat, dead eyes of someone who's been locked up for most of a lifetime.

Studying Eisman's face, it struck Cam suddenly that David Eisman was still Susan's husband. It was a fact not easily comprehended. Cam couldn't fathom what Susan had ever seen in this shell of a man. She'd called him charming, but that was a generation ago. Today he seemed only pathetic.

Eisman focused on Frani. "You the reporter?"

She nodded. "Frani Landon."

"All right. What's this all about? No one's been interested in interviewing me for twenty years."

"Well, I'm interested now," she said.

"Are you?" He smirked.

"Yes," Frani said evenly. "I want to ask you a few questions about the bank robbery and the kidnapping."

"You're a fine-looking woman, Miss Frani, and I'd rather stay here with you than go back to my cell. Ask away, sweetheart. But don't hold your breath for answers. Nothing personal, but I don't much care for the press."

Completely cool, she said, "Before we get started, I'm curious about why you've never been paroled."

Eisman flopped his hands on the table with a clank of chains. "Yeah, well that makes two of us."

"What if I told you I think I know why your bid keeps getting turned down?"

Eisman tried to maintain his air of detachment, but Cam could see that Frani had his attention. The lady was good. She handled this hardened criminal with the skill of an experienced interrogator.

"Think so? Then why don't you tell me?"

"Why did you kidnap Pamela Jessup?" Frani demanded.

"What about my parole?" he pressed.

Cam had done some digging and discovered that according to the parole recommendations, Eisman should have been released two years ago. Every day must seem like an eternity to the man.

"Later," Frani said. "First I want answers. Why Pamela Jessup?"

Eisman slouched back in his chair. "She was pretty. Like you."

Slowly, he ran his tongue around his lips. In case Frani missed his obvious message, he did it again. "Lean a little closer, sweetheart, and I'll show you how I treat a pretty woman."

It was all Cam could do to keep from reaching across the table and choking the slime out of Eisman. Only a pointed glance from Frani kept him in his chair. It said, *I can handle this.* And Cam believed her. This was her lead, her interview, and he had to let her find her own way. He had to trust her.

Without showing the least bit of fear or discomfiture, she said, "Answer my question, Eisman. Why did you choose Pamela Jessup as your kidnap victim?"

Cam could see Eisman toying with an answer, but he sensed the con wasn't finished playing games.

"You know, it's been a long, long time since I've seen a pretty woman like you. Why don't you take off your jacket and get comfortable?"

Cam had had enough. "Cut the crap, Eisman."

"Answer the question, damn it!" Frani demanded.

"Ooh, a temper." He leered at her. "You must be a real redhead."

"Listen, I don't—"

"Tell me, sweet thing. Is your hair red all over?"

"That's it," Cam said. He stood up and pulled Frani with him. "We're wasting our time." He motioned to the guard and the door opened.

"Wait a minute," Eisman said quickly. "I thought you wanted to talk."

"Too late," Cam said and started for the door, his hand

firmly clasped around Frani's arm. "Far as I'm concerned, you can rot in here for the rest of your life."

"Okay, okay. I got the message, man." Eisman tried a smile. "Come on, sit down. I want to hear what you have to say."

The guard shifted his gaze to Cam.

"Then you'll treat her like a lady," Cam said. "Or we're gone, and you'll never know why you've been denied parole."

Eisman shrugged. "Can't blame a guy for trying. Okay. Let's get on with this."

With a nod from Cam, the guard left them alone again.

"And just so you won't think I'm holding my breath, I know why I haven't been sprung," Eisman said bitterly.

"Oh, and why is that?" Cam asked.

"Because they have it in for me."

"That's a joke, Eisman. You're nothing," Cam said. "Nobody cares about a lousy bank robber who couldn't even manage to get away with the cash."

Eisman sneered. "You can blame those damn fools I was hooked up with for that. Bunch of lousy amateurs."

"Like Bud Coleman."

Eisman frowned.

"Did you know your pal, Bud, has been out for years? We paid him a visit. Got a real nice little place out in the desert. Wide open, great view," Cam taunted.

"Bud's a fool," Eisman said savagely.

"Yeah? Then how come he's out enjoying the sunshine and you're still locked up?" Cam allowed his gaze to encompass the room and rest upon Eisman's manacles. "Kinda makes you wonder who the real fool is, doesn't it?"

Eisman stiffened. The veins in his scrawny throat stood out, but he said nothing as Cam leaned back in his chair.

"Let's start over," Frani said. "Why Pamela Jessup?"

"Why not? She was rich, wasn't she? I thought I could get money from her family."

"But how did you select her? Had you seen her? Did you do any research before you grabbed her?"

"Yeah," he said with a hint of pride. "Sure. I heard she was kind of wild, and I thought it would make it easy to get to her."

Between his fingers, he held two links of the chains which he nervously pulled back and forth in an endless seesaw.

"Hell, I liked her," Eisman said. "Even married her."

"Even drugged her," Frani added.

"Did Bud tell you that?"

"You *did* drug her."

"She wanted it," he said. "Couldn't get enough."

Nausea crawled from Cam's gut to his throat, but he betrayed no sign of his feelings. To show his disgust would give Eisman the illusion of power.

"About the bank robbery," Cam said, "where'd you get the money for the guns and the getaway car?"

Eisman shrugged. "I don't remember."

"Sure you do. Who planned the job? Who set you up, Eisman?"

"Nobody sets me up!" Eisman declared. "I planned the whole thing."

"With what? Who financed the job? Paid for the guns?"

"Me." Eisman was sticking with his story. And it was a fabrication. Every instinct told Cam the con was lying.

Eisman fidgeted on the hard wood chair, like a man who had just remembered he had someplace else to be. "Now, it's my turn to ask questions. What do you know about my parole?"

"Not yet," Cam said, glancing at his watch. They'd already wasted half their allotted time and they still had nothing.

He turned to Frani. "Go on."

"Mr. Eisman," she said, "I'm wondering if you've ever heard of Zach Hollingsworth."

"The reporter who got killed," he said. "I read about it in the newspaper. Is that why you're here? Something to do with Hollingsworth?"

"We're investigating his murder," Frani said.

"Well, you're barking up the wrong tree, sweetheart." He darted a nervous glance toward Cam. "I don't know anything about the guy. And as you can see, I have an ironclad alibi."

While Frani tossed out questions regarding Zach's prior investigation into Byron Reeves, Eisman seemed to relax. It was as if he knew he was in the clear. It became clear to Cam that Eisman knew nothing about Zach's death. His responses were calm, relaxed.

"Here's a name for you," Cam said. "Phillip Gould."

Eisman's jaw twitched slightly. His fingers stilled on the chains, but his tone remained steady and unchanged. "Never heard of him."

"Phillip Gould knew Pamela Jessup," Cam said.

"So? It's not like we ran in the same social circles." Eisman's smile was cagey.

"But you know the man, isn't that right? The senator from California?"

The tension in the room elevated by several degrees. Eisman's shoulders hunched. His Adam's apple rolled up and down as he swallowed. "I don't know what the hell this has to do with me."

"Simple," Cam said. He purposely lowered his voice so Eisman had to listen hard. "You've been up for parole four times in the last two years. The warden says you're a good boy. He'd vote to release you, the same way they released Bud Coleman. But someone higher up has been using his influence to keep you under wraps, to have parole denied every time.''

With Eisman hanging on his words, Cam whispered. ''I'm betting it's Gould. And if you think about it, I think you know why.''

''I don't know what you're talking about. I don't believe anything you've said.''

But Cam sensed doubt and pressed harder. ''He's using you, Eisman, playing you for the fool he thinks you are.''

''No!'' Eisman's lip quivered. He was sweating hard, and Cam knew he was on the verge of an explosion.

''It was Gould,'' Cam said. ''He's been at the bottom of this from the start. He hired you to kidnap Pamela, he set you up for the robbery, he's the reason you're here now and—''

''Hell, no!'' Eisman blurted out. ''He didn't want her kid—'' He stopped, and in the silence that followed, he seemed to shrink from the realization that he'd made a fatal mistake.

''What?'' Frani asked. ''What did Gould want?''

''He wanted her dead,'' Eisman replied in a low voice. Frani tried but failed to stifle a gasp.

''He paid me ten thousand bucks to kill her. He wanted her to disappear, understand? Permanently.'' His voice seemed to gain strength as his long-kept secrets poured out. ''But I didn't do it. I figured I could score big ransoming her, and besides, she was just so pretty...'' His voice trailed off, before he added. ''But they didn't pay. Damn cheapskates.''

''When Gould found out she was alive, what then?''

''He suggested the bank robbery,'' Eisman admitted. ''He arranged for the guns and the car. He didn't care if I lived or died, but he wanted to make sure Pamela was discredited forever." He expelled a wretched gasp. "I wasn't thinking straight, doing too many uppers. Thought I could conquer the world, give Pam back the life she'd lost. I thought I was going to be rich."

"But you got caught instead," Cam said.

"That's right. And I thought I could give up Gould and get out of jail free. But Gould sent one of his men to see me. I thought I was dead, but the guy wasn't there to kill me. He'd come with a message from Gould, said if I'd keep my mouth shut, I'd finally get the big payoff. A million dollars at the end of my sentence. Nobody figured it would go on this long," he said bitterly. "Especially me. Look at Coleman, with good behavior, out in under twenty. What did I have to lose? I was going to jail anyway."

"A million dollars," Cam said. "That's a big payoff. Too bad you'll never see it."

"He'll pay!" Eisman beat his shackles on the table. "He has to pay me! I kept my end of the bargain."

"Until now," Frani reminded him. "Gould is a powerful man, powerful enough to block your parole, and powerful enough to keep on blocking it until you die an old man, still behind bars."

Cam could see Frani's logic had shaken Eisman.

"Give it up," he said. "Tell the feds what you told us and you'll be out of here by the end of the week." It was a promise Cam was prepared to make good.

Eisman blinked as if he'd been sucker punched. He was stunned.

Cam pressed his point. "You can be a free man, Eisman, just like Coleman."

"And do what? Die broke of old age on the outside? Why should I?"

"Your testimony against Gould will save an innocent man," Frani said.

"Nice story, but you're talking to the wrong guy. I don't give a damn about anyone but myself. Get that? No one. I tried it once and it failed. I cared about Pam, and she ran out on me."

Cam gripped the edge of the chair to keep from shutting Eisman's mouth permanently.

"This conversation's over," Eisman said as he scraped back the chair. "In fact, it never took place."

Disbelieving, Cam said, "You're prepared to go on protecting Gould?"

The sweat beads turned to streams on Eisman's forehead. "Like I said, I take care of myself. Listen, lawman, do you know what happens to snitches in a place like this?" He shuddered violently as if there were bugs crawling on him. "I repeat, this conversation is over."

He rose from his chair and shuffled toward the door where he hammered at the window, signaling the guard.

Without Eisman's testimony, Cam knew it would be next to impossible to implicate Gould. There were allegations. There was the truth, but a court of law demanded evidence. Evidence strong enough to convict a killer, in this case a powerful man with seemingly endless resources and all the luck on his side.

IN THE RENTAL CAR driving back to the airport, Frani was bubbling over with excitement. In her mind, the visit with Eisman had been a complete success. "We did it, Cam," she declared. "We've got our man. Gould paid Eisman to kill Susan. He wanted her dead before she could embarrass him with an official accusation of rape."

"Twenty-odd years ago, that kind of allegation would

have destroyed him politically," Cam said. "He was just starting out."

"I can't wait to see him behind bars," she said. "He financed a bank robbery, suborned perjury from Eisman. From there, it's only a matter of time before we link him to Zach's murder. Zach was on the trail. He would have made the connection between Gould and Eisman eventually and Gould knew it. He might be powerful enough now to survive an old rape charge from a woman whose own credibility would be severely questioned, but murder is another story."

She spared a thought for Zach Hollingsworth, her mentor and friend. His training had made it possible for her to pull this all together. She could just imagine how delighted he'd have been to watch her bring down the powerful, corrupt, despicable senator from California.

"There's just one problem," Cam said. "Eisman is still clinging to the possibility of a payoff. And he's scared. Even if he believes Gould has sold him out, he still won't testify."

"It doesn't matter." She reached into her pocket and pulled out her little tape recorder. "I got every word."

The shock registered on Cam's face. "How did you smuggle a tape recorder into a maximum-security facility?"

"I knew they were going to keep my purse, so I hid it behind my belt buckle. When we were in the room with Eisman, I slipped it into the pocket of my jacket."

"You're a genius, Frani Landon, despite your nasty habit of skirting the law." She welcomed his smile. "Did anyone ever tell you you think like a felon?"

She laughed. "I'm just a reporter," she said. "Just doing my job."

Zach would have been so proud. In the past few days, she had truly earned her wings. She'd had the guts to quit the *Daily Herald* after filing her very first front-page byline. The *Clarion* edition would be fantastic. And she was on the verge of solving a murder.

All at once, the exuberance seemed to seep out of her. For some reason, none of it seemed to matter any more. But why? Logically, she examined the evidence.

Fact: She'd proved herself as a reporter.

Fact: She'd proved herself worthy of Zach's trust.

Fact: She'd lost Cam.

Despite all the professional success, as a woman in a relationship with Cam, she'd proved a miserable failure.

They'd come so close. Their lovemaking had been nothing short of spectacular. The feelings she had for him consumed her. He was the kind of man she could love and respect forever. She adored his family, had even started feeling a part of the clan.

But if he couldn't forgive her, if he couldn't find a way to bend, they'd both be broken. The tentative bond of love that she'd felt pulling them together would be severed.

Was there still a chance? she wondered. Or was she kidding herself, thinking he was feeling the loss as deeply as she did? She thought about what Susan had said about hope, how love and hope go hand in hand. Did she dare hope she and Cam could have a future together? If she made the first move, she risked having her heart and her pride shattered at the same time. If she didn't, she risked losing the one man who made her believe love was not just for other people.

They were back in the Piper Cub, soaring through clear Colorado skies past spectacular Rocky Mountain vistas when she finally found the nerve to broach the subject that was weighing on her heart.

Into the headset, she said, "I've heard that making-up sex is really terrific."

"Making-up sex?"

"You know, after an argument is resolved." Her heart pounded so furiously that she thought he would hear it. "What do you say?"

He hesitated for only a moment, but it was the sixty longest seconds of her life.

When he reached for her hand, her heart turned over. "Sounds interesting."

For the first time since she'd met him, she couldn't come up with a single snappy retort.

"Making-up sex," he murmured. "I don't know..."

Frani drew in a sharp breath. Was he telling her he wasn't ready to take the risk? "I don't either, but I think it's worth a try," she said breathlessly, her heart in her throat.

When he turned to face her, his eyes simmered with the passion she felt flooding her own veins.

"What do you say, cowboy?"

He unlatched his seat belt and answered her with a kiss that told her their partnership had a better than even chance of surviving.

Chapter Fourteen

By the time they arrived at the Cedar Bluffs airport, Frani was so happy she could have flown by stretching her arms and soaring the last few miles.

Cam wanted her.

Not only wanted to make love to her again, but he couldn't stop talking about the ranch and how he wanted to teach her to ride, how he couldn't wait for her to see the wildflowers in spring, painting the hillsides.

As she climbed out of the cockpit and fell into step beside him, she said, "That sounds like an extended stay."

"As long as you want to be there." He thought a minute. "Hey, do you suppose that's what Jake said to Susan?"

Her heart froze with the unspoken implication. "Could be."

"My brothers and I never approved of Jake and Susan living in sin."

"Oh, Cam. That's so old-fashioned."

"I know right from wrong, Frani. A man's got to have a moral compass to find his way and mine's never failed me yet."

She rolled her eyes. "And a woman's got to have a pot holder to take the brownies out of the oven."

He chuckled. "Are you making fun of my homespun wisdom?"

She merely laughed. "What do you think, cowboy?"

"Tonight," he said. "You and I are going to do some straight talking about our relationship. Then we'll give that making-up sex a try."

Would wonders never cease! Here was a man of the Old West, a cowboy for goodness' sake, and he was volunteering to talk about relationships. When she'd dated supposedly sophisticated Chicago men in three-piece suits, none of them had ever made that offer without turning slightly puce. "You're a brave man, Cam McQuaid."

In the airport, she found a pay phone and called the *Clarion*. It rang three times, then the answering machine picked up. "Hi, Addie. It's me, Frani. Are you there?"

She was answered by silence and imagined her voice bouncing around in the offices. Frani checked her wristwatch.

"Addie? It's about nine-thirty. If you're there, pick up..."

But still no answer. She might be downstairs, Frani decided, doing some adjustments to the presses. They would all be working overtime tomorrow, cranking out the best edition in Chaparral County history.

"Addie, I just wanted to let you know I'd be stopping by. I have a sizzling hot story on the Eisman angle, and I want to work it into the issue. If you get this message in the morning, call me at Cam's before you start printing. Bye."

Their plan was for Cam to take Eisman's tape and go directly to the sheriff's office where he'd begin the procedure of arranging for the next step in apprehending Senator Phillip Gould. While he was busy destroying Gould's career and hopefully setting California's golden boy up for serious jail time, Frani would check in at the *Clarion* offices.

Even if Addie was already in bed, Frani could check out the finished layout of the paper that would be printed tomorrow. She intended to try to work the Eisman angle into an existing article or put together a sidebar that wouldn't land Addie in a libel suit.

When Cam pulled up outside the *Clarion* office, her hand was on the door handle, ready to depart.

"Hold it," Cam said.

"What's wrong?"

He pulled her toward him and kissed her hard, sending a jolt of excitement through her entire body. "Just so you won't get any ideas about working all night," he teased as he drew his mouth away from hers. His smile was perfectly handsome.

"Not a chance," she said softly.

As he pulled away from the curb, Frani found herself humming a country-and-western song about a woman who stands by her man. As she turned the key in the lock and pushed open the door, she was immediately assaulted by the stink of turpentine and printing solvent.

Inside, she reached for the light switch, closed the door behind her and gasped at the sight of the man sitting behind Addie's desk.

The man with the .38 revolver pointed at her heart was smiling.

"SO THOUGHTFUL of you to call ahead," the senator said.

Frani's mind raced to take in this bizarre turn of events, but no matter how fast her thoughts spun, they couldn't keep pace with her suddenly erratic heart rate. Her mind fixed on only one thought: escape!

There had to be a way out of this. She hadn't yet refastened the dead bolt on the door. All she had to do was to whip around, twist the handle and yank it open.

Her hand tensed on the knob. Then she saw Addie slumped beside the fax machine. Thick red blood seeped through her gray hair. With a cry, Frani crossed to the unconscious woman and dropped down on one knee beside her.

Addie was still breathing, but her pulse was thready. "Oh my God! Addie! Quick, we have to get her to a doctor."

Gould strolled up beside her. "Not possible," he said flatly. "Neither of you will be leaving here tonight. Not alive, anyway. By this time tomorrow, you'll both be as dead as that story about Pamela Jessup."

"Whatever you do to me, it's too late," she informed him, coming to her feet. "We've got you dead to rights."

"Save your breath, Miss Landon. I read your story and there's nothing that implicates me. No matter what you think you know, I've covered all my bases. Now all I have to do is make sure your next story never sees the light of day."

"But why Addie? Why hurt her?"

"She wouldn't cooperate, stupid old woman. What I offered her to kill your story would have bought a dozen rags like this one." He shrugged. "She gave me no choice. The next solution was destruction. So many volatile chemicals used in the printing process, you know. All too easy for a wood-frame building like this to go up in flames."

He was smug, certain he could get away with his deadly plan. But Frani had other ideas, ideas that included bringing him to justice and living out a long, happy life with the man she loved. She wasn't going to die, not without one hell of a fight.

tonight," Cam said. "There's a police escort waiting at the end of my drive. Joe and my other deputies are expecting you."

As Frani and Cam stood watching Jake and Susan drive away, an uneasy silence descended between them. Frani held her breath, waiting for him to make the first move.

She didn't have to wait long. As soon as he closed the door he turned to her.

"We need to talk," he said. He took her hand and pulled her with him into the living room.

"I know," she said simply. She'd been waiting for this, anxious and scared spitless at the same time. After all the harrowing events of the day, it was time for their own moment of truth. Time to find out if the sense of belonging she'd craved since her childhood could be found here, in the West, with people she'd come to love and respect.

Time to discover once and for all if the love Susan had predicted Frani would soon find was waiting for her, as close as Sheriff Cameron McQuaid's two strong arms.

"In the plane coming back from Salt Lake, we talked about giving our relationship another try," Cam said. "Is that what you want, Frani? Are you sure?"

Sure? She'd never felt more certain about anything than she felt about the love that pounded like a second pulse inside her for Cam. But still Frani hesitated. She needed to hear him say he trusted her. That he'd forgiven her for concealing Zach's notebook, for slowing the investigation, for holding back and not giving him her all.

"I didn't leave the last time you tried to send me away," she said with as much strength as she could muster. "And I haven't packed my bags yet. Surely that must tell you something. Now, you tell me something, Cam. We can't go on until you do."

"*Quid pro quo,*" he said, frowning. "Is that how this is going to work?"

Frani's heart froze. "For the time being, yes, I guess so."

"All right. Fair enough." He took a step toward her, so close it was all she could do to keep from touching him.

"Tonight, I almost crossed a line," he said. "I've never wanted so badly to turn my back on who I was and everything I've always stood for. And maybe I would have. But by some miracle, you were there. You made me remember what was important, the real meaning of the code I've trusted all my life. You saw the worst side of me, lady, but you didn't turn away. Instead, you reached past the darkness and touched my heart. You're a part of me, now. The best part."

The force of his declaration left her breathless.

"My life was in your hands tonight, and you gave it back to me, Francesca. Trust you?" He pulled her into his arms and nestled his face in her hair. "Hell, lady, it isn't even a question anymore."

"Oh, Cam…"

"And since you're asking, I'll tell you what I want. I want—I need one very long night with you in my bed, with no light except the glow from a western moon shining across your satin skin. I want to breathe the perfume of your hair until I'm drunk." He feathered kisses across her face. "I want to touch you until I know every inch of your body by heart."

"I want you too, Cam," she murmured.

"I want a whole lifetime of nights with you, Frani," he said. "Each one better than the last. And your days, too. I want them all. I love you. I want you to be my wife." Then his lips covered hers and he kissed her with a tenderness that brought tears to her eyes.

"Will you do it, Frani? Will you agree to love, honor and ob—"

She drew back quickly, feigning anger. "If you value your life, cowboy, you won't even think of finishing that sentence."

He held her at arm's length, reared back and laughed. The sound of his joy wrapped ribbons of sheer delight around her heart.

When his gaze met hers again all traces of humor had vanished and his expression could not have been more serious. "Will you do it, Frani? Will you marry me and make me the happiest man alive?"

Frani slid her arms up his chest, over his brave lawman's heart and locked her hands behind his neck. His warmth became hers, their hearts beat as one. "You've got yourself a deal, cowboy," she said and then kissed him. "From now until forever." Partners, lovers and friends.

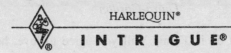

If you enjoyed what you just read,
then we've got an offer you can't resist!

Take 2 bestselling
love stories FREE!

Plus get a FREE surprise gift!

Clip this page and mail it to Harlequin Reader Service®

IN U.S.A.	IN CANADA
3010 Walden Ave.	P.O. Box 609
P.O. Box 1867	Fort Erie, Ontario
Buffalo, N.Y. 14240-1867	L2A 5X3

YES! Please send me 2 free Harlequin Intrigue® novels and my free surprise gift. Then send me 4 brand-new novels every month, which I will receive months before they're available in stores. In the U.S.A., bill me at the bargain price of $3.34 plus 25¢ delivery per book and applicable sales tax, if any*. In Canada, bill me at the bargain price of $3.71 plus 25¢ delivery per book and applicable taxes**. That's the complete price and a savings of over 10% off the cover prices—what a great deal! I understand that accepting the 2 free books and gift places me under no obligation ever to buy any books. I can always return a shipment and cancel at any time. Even if I never buy another book from Harlequin, the 2 free books and gift are mine to keep forever. So why not take us up on our invitation. You'll be glad you did!

181 HEN CNEZ
381 HEN CNE3

Name   (PLEASE PRINT)

Address   Apt.#

City   State/Prov.   Zip/Postal Code

* Terms and prices subject to change without notice. Sales tax applicable in N.Y.
** Canadian residents will be charged applicable provincial taxes and GST.
   All orders subject to approval. Offer limited to one per household.
   ® are registered trademarks of Harlequin Enterprises Limited.

INT99

Amnesia...
an unknown danger...
a burning desire.
With

HARLEQUIN®

———————————————————

I N T R I G U E®

you're just

A MEMORY AWAY

from passion, danger...
and love!

Look for all the books in this exciting new miniseries:

Missing: One temporary wife
#507 THE MAN SHE MARRIED
by Dani Sinclair in March 1999

Mission: Find a lost identity
#511 LOVER, STRANGER
by Amanda Stevens in April 1999

Seeking: An amnesiac's daughter
#515 A WOMAN OF MYSTERY
by Charlotte Douglas in May 1999

A MEMORY AWAY—where remembering
the truth becomes a matter of life,
death...and love!

Available wherever Harlequin books are sold.

HARLEQUIN®
Makes any time special ™

HARLEQUIN CELEBRATES

FIVE DECADES OF ROMANCE

*In March 1999, Harlequin
Historicals introduce you to the sexy,
heroic men of medieval England and
the Wild West as we celebrate
Harlequin's 50th anniversary.*

JOE'S WIFE
by Cheryl St.John

**MY LORD
PROTECTOR**
by Deborah Hale

**THE BRIDE OF
WINDERMERE**
by Margo Maguire

SILVER HEARTS
by Jackie Manning

*Look for these fabulous Historical
romances at your favorite retail store!*